Catherine Wilson

WHITE   IS   THE   COLOR   OF   DEATH

WHITE
IS THE
COLOR
OF
DEATH

A Mystery by

J.N. Catanach

A Foul Play Press Book
The Countryman Press
Woodstock, Vermont

Book design by Leslie Fry
Typesetting by The F.W. Roberts Company
Printed in the United States of America by Arcata Graphics

Library of Congress Cataloging-in-Publication Data
Catanach, J. N.
White is the color of death : a mystery / by J.N. Catanach. —
1st. ed.
p.   cm.
"A Foul Play Press book."
ISBN 0-88150-104-2
I. Title.
PS.3553.A8193W4   1988
813'.54—dc19   87-33031
CIP

A Foul Play Press Book
The Countryman Press
Woodstock, Vermont
05091

For my boiler

"If you sit long enough in a warm bath, a thought comes to you"

Hegesippe Simon

WHITE IS THE COLOR OF DEATH

The pilot twisted round, yelling above the din of the engines: "Hold tight! Going to have to duck her down." He made a swooping gesture with his hand.

Charles Quint relayed the warning to his fellow passengers, then looked down through the window. He watched the shadow of the ten-seater plane racing in from the sea up the beach and over the red roofs and azure swimming pool of what could only be the Langkawi Inn. It struck him that there was no one on the beach. Then the image disappeared in the shadow of a forested ridge that rose up to meet them. They cleared the top— narrowly—and a valley bright green with rice paddies unrolled below. At its far end, where it flattened to meet the sea, he saw, with relief, a landing strip; at the same moment the plane dipped and lurched. A man behind him screamed, and it crossed his mind that, after all, they might not make it.

But they did, bumping over the brown earth past swaying palm trees. "The winds,"—the pilot, now visibly relaxed, leaned towards Quint—"very gusty this time of year over the islands. Unpredictable." A burly Bengali with a trace of Oxford in his accent. "Sometimes, can't even take her up."

The twin-engine Islander taxied across the grass to

1

where a knot of people clustered near a small cream-colored bus. The passengers—tourists plus a smartly uniformed Malay policeman—scrambled from the plane with the euphoria of newly released convicts.

The presence of the law was soon explained by the pilot: "Law-abiding," he winked. "No police post on the island." While passengers retrieved their baggage and struggled towards the bus which bore the logo of the Inn, the policeman walked to a nearby shed. He emerged with four men who staggered under the weight of a long, coffin-like box. Quint paused to watch as the pilot and the policeman took charge of loading it. He could see no way, short of leaving the doors open, that it was going to fit. An attempt to remove seats was scotched by passengers waiting to depart who shouted urgently about connections.

"I am Vellu." The Indian-soft voice at Quint's elbow belonged to a small man the color of black grapes with a greying mustache and a benevolent stare.

"Ah, I'm Quint." They shook hands. The agent had said he'd be a Tamil.

"The car is this way," Vellu announced. They walked towards it.

"Are we to assume, Vellu, that a body is in that box?"

"Indeed, sir."

"A long one."

"Verily."

"But dead."

"Irretrievably, sir. Yes."

"A friend, perhaps? Someone you knew?"

"Oh no, sir. An American."

A backward look showed the pilot now siding with the

2

passengers, leaving only the policeman and an official with a clipboard to fend for the coffin. Quint felt sorry for whoever was in it. The hotel bus pulled away. "A tourist? Staying at the Inn?"

"No, sir."

The afternoon sun was far too hot for bodies, alive or dead, to lie around in. As if contemplating lending a hand, Quint took a few steps back. All of a sudden, the men put down their load and seemed to attack it, prying open the lid. He edged closer and saw a bright blue, shiny plastic bag. The bag was hauled to a sitting position. After a brief tussle, two of the men managed a firm grip, stuffing it unceremoniously into the hold with the baggage. Problem solved.

"An American, you say?"

Vellu led the way to a brown Mercedes, sleek and squat like himself, vintage. "It was very messy, so I heard." He smiled apologetically.

Quint beheld his bag already on the seat: a black leather grip such as country doctors might have toted in pre-revolutionary Russia. Indeed, with his neatly trimmed spade of a beard and sober dress, he himself might have passed for one—had the time and the place been right. He climbed in next to Vellu. "You received the message, I take it? From the agent?"

"Oh yes, Mr. Quint. Line was not down, for once. Very clear."

"Well, that's something." Quint's faith in his travel agent had been known to waver. The matter of the rented car in Bosnia; those two days in Bombay Airport; and, on this trip, the nude Germans at Phuket, from whom he fled. "And here, on the beaches, no naked Germans?"

Vellu sighed—commiseratively, Quint thought.

"But Americans? Any live ones?"

"Not that I have heard," Vellu reassured. "A number of English. Swiss, I think. French."

"French?" Quint smelled trouble. He was in no mood to do battle with half the tribes of Europe. In twenty-four hours he had described in the air almost three sides of a triangle: from the Thai island of Phuket a few miles to the north, to Bangkok, to the Malaysian island of Penang, and now the forty-minute flight here to Langkawi, also part of Malaysia. 'Ninety-nine legendary islands,' the brochure said, 'standing in splendid solitude at the point where the Indian Ocean melts into the Malacca Straits.' It was the 'splendid solitude' he sought. The last few weeks of the school term had been particularly gruesome. " . . . *her barbarous sons/Came like a deluge on the south, and spread/Beneath Gibraltar to the Libyan sands.*"

"Milton," commented Vellu.

"Indeed." Quint removed his straw hat; not as much in deference to Milton as because the car was baking hot. "So the American wasn't sight-seeing?"

"An anthropologist, they say." Vellu gave the word a quizzical flip. "Staying in Malay *kampong* not far from Inn where you will be putting up, is it not so?"

"Ah yes, an anthropologist." Quint wasn't intimately acquainted with the species. "How did it happen?"

"Slaughtered, like animal." Vellu shook his head. "Highly regrettable. But not to worry overmuch. Here on Langkawi, peace-loving people. No policeman on whole island." A point of local pride, it seemed.

Though paved, the road was narrow, its verges lush

with growth. Endless palms—Quint noted several species he'd never seen before—and paddies, and here and
there, set among the trees, wooden houses on stilts, some
with ornately carved eaves. Occasionally a water buffalo
looked up from munching or snoozing but their passage
mostly went unremarked. The brown Mercedes seemed
as much in sync with the drudge of daily life on this island
as any lumbering beast. Even the monkeys in the trees ignored it. "Peace-loving," Quint remarked, after a pause.
"I see what you mean."

Vellu beamed. He had beautiful teeth.

"Just the occasional human sacrifice?"

"No, no, no, Mr. Quint," came the shrill protest.
"Langkawi people never do such a thing."

"An unfortunate accident? A crocodile, or perhaps a
shark?"

Behind the wheel of the car, Vellu squirmed uneasily.
"You are making very bad joke, I think, Mr. Quint. I am
thinking you already know more than you are saying."

It occurred to Quint that he should end this absurd
exchange forthwith and settle down to enjoy the scenery.
But curiosity, his besetting sin, got the upper hand. "And
no one came to claim the body? No next of kin?"

"Next of kin. Next of kin." Vellu clucked his tongue
disapprovingly. "You die at own risk, is it not so? You are
like *Orang Laut*, the Sea Gypsies." He added dryly:
"Doubtless also writing book."

Quint turned to the Indian, arching thick eyebrows.
Should he take this accusative *you* personally, he wondered. Of course he was writing a book: he was a professor. What on earth was Vellu getting at?

Whatever he thought, Vellu did not elaborate. Instead—somewhat ironically—he asked, "And you yourself, Mr. Quint, what shall you be?"

"Well put, Vellu. What indeed?" The man certainly had a way with words. "How about a tourist, plain and simple? An agent—if you like—of international contamination."

Vellu frowned. "International agent of contamination." They drove for a while in silence. "Apologies, Mr. Quint; but timing, last minute reservation—people may be suspecting. Yesterday, one goes. Pphtt!" He released an invisible bird from his hand. "Today, you come." The bird alighted again. He added, with an exaggerated wink, "Not I, myself, naturally."

"I'm afraid I'm not an anthropologist, if that's what you're saying, Vellu; and I'm not really even an American."

Vellu smiled knowingly. "As you are wishing."

What, Quint wondered, had his travel agent claimed, perhaps to squeeze him onto an already full flight? "Charles Quint is a tourist," he reiterated. "Neither more nor less." They drove on.

Vellu maintained his air of amused scepticism. "I hope it's not impertinent to ask, since it's none of my business, Mr. Quint: why did you want to see the body?"

"I assure you, it's none of my business either. Let's just say I have an innate, perhaps morbid, interest in such matters, and leave it at that."

"Ah, embalmer! I shall pass the word to the wind. A touring embalmer. This will bring respect."

"As you wish." Quint had not so far in his middle-aged life conceived of himself in these terms. For the moment he was visiting professor of government at an obscure college in Fort Wayne, Indiana; itself an obscure town in the American mid west. "I suppose for my age I am pretty well preserved," he conceded.

"No, no, no." Vellu's hands fluttered at the wheel. He had not meant to give offense. He squeezed the car past an old truck which seemed to have broken down and been forgotten. Then, very gravely as if pronouncing judgment, he said, "Mr. Quint, do not leave Langkawi Inn by yourself. It is not safe for you. But not to worry. I will arrange everything. I, Vellu, give you my word."

"Not safe?"

"Best of times. Worst of times. Charles Dickens. Now, for one week, maybe two, is worst of times. Then," his face brightened, "best of times."

"But I'm only booked for a week."

"Not to worry. I, Vellu, will arrange. You will see. Nothing will happen."

"What," Quint probed warily, "happened to the American?"

Vellu's sigh was eloquent. Resignation filled the Mercedes. He inverted a black hand, fingers splayed, a very elegant black hand. "You know mangrove? You know how mangrove roots are growing like birdcage—so? American was found by fisherman in early hours of morning tangled up in mangrove. Died on way to clinic. Boat was found, washed up. Boatman," he shrugged, "vanished."

"He was drowned?"

Vellu touched a point near his neck. "You know *parang*—jungle knife everyone is using? Shoulder half severed, they say. Bleeding to death is obvious

7

conclusion, you see. But this is good boy. Not run amok. Too obvious, you see."

"Thank you, Vellu. I shall avoid mangrove swamps and shun obvious conclusions."

Perhaps Vellu detected a crispness in this response, for he said—and it was a warning—"There are strangers about. At night, Mr. Quint. That is what the wind is saying."

They had reached town: a double row of shops, eating places and houses in varying states of dilapidation. Quint noted a bank, and a couple of newer concrete buildings. People moved slowly or not at all, hugging the shade. One or two other cars disturbed the dust and they passed an old Chinese pedaling a trishaw stacked with crated fowl. Beyond the town stretched the shore, green, flat, and peaceful, merging imperceptibly with the bay, palms rising gracefully like posing fashion models: a painting. A tiny mosque with one gold onion dome and one white one looked like a child's toy. A backdrop of rocks and smaller islands jutted dark against the pale-green placid sea, with here and there an anchored boat adding a splash of red.

Quint looked at the sky; no hint now of turbulence, or was it up there still, invisible? Without clouds, how could one tell? The road, bleached and dry, followed the curve of the bay, rising gradually to a low headland beyond which protruded the town jetty. Here travelers waited under a broad-leafed tree of great girth beside a stall advertising Fanta Orange Drink, and a lopsided bus revved its engine. The road veered sharply, rounded another point, and bore down upon the red-painted metal gates and multi-hued flower beds of the Inn.

She had given him, the woman at the desk assured, their very best room. And at their very best price, Quint suspected. The place was laid out like outspread arms, on two floors, facing the sea, with the restaurant and lounge area in the middle where the head should be. The feel was airy, modern, comfortable without being plush— curvaceous concrete interspersed with polished wood. A family hotel, she'd emphasized. In Quint's travel lexicon, this meant screaming in the halls. He was downstairs, right arm, end room, sea view.

How simple, Quint mused as he sat that evening alone on his little balcony contemplating the early stars, for someone to vault the low parapet. A flash of steel in the moonlight. His hand touched his neck and its coolness made him start.

Voices from above: two of his fellow passengers from the plane; he'd put them down as Australians, the sort of white men without much luggage that haunt the airports of the East. They'd sat at the back, one fat, the other thin, yawned continually, and snored. Tweedledum and Tweedledee. Something of the overgrown schoolboy in each that vaguely disturbed him. Cockneys, Quint now decided, not Australians.

"Yeah, but he should 'ave leveled wiv us. I mean to say . . . "

"Yer mean to say what, yer dope? All expenses paid? Go on wiv yer." This was the fleshy one: Tweedledum. He'd been topped up to overflowing as they boarded at Penang, cowardly drunk, begging for reassurance in front of the kids. The scream just before the landing would have been his. ("Mummy, why did that man scream?" a small girl had asked.)

"So spill the gen, O knowledgeable one. Out wiv it."
The thin one.

"Lift the old elbow, a bit of brown ass like the old days,
remember? Enjoy. In other words, Carry on London.
Ouch! Bloody bugger." Quint heard the sharp scrape of a
chair. "Fuckin' eaten alive!" A man's high-pitched laughter. A door banging. Soon the hum of another air-
conditioner dimmed the shrill night sounds.

Out in the bay a light flickered. Quint breathed deeply,
in and out. His gaze searched the heavens. There she
was, Canopus, queen of the southern sky. Some things
never seem to change. He turned to go in. It had been a
tiring day. God is a travel agent.

CHAPTER TWO

A helicopter throbbed low along the beach and disappeared in the direction of the town. A little while later, Quint heard it coming back. He was sitting on the terrace eating papaya—a long, red, refreshing slice—and waiting for his toast: the toaster, they said, was back-logged. He made a mental note to come earlier to breakfast.

A small boy in goggles ran by and Quint recognized a traveling companion of the day before; one of a family of five, English by the sound of it, with him on the plane. "Hey, Daddy, quick. Look!" The child's father obediently raised his head and smiled slightly in the English way. Among the other guests, the helicopter seemed to stir little interest. A routine visit, Quint surmised, noting the army camouflage—jungle greens and browns—and, in an opening in the side, the little brown gunner crouched behind his weapon.

The waiter, when he returned, seemed to share the general disinterest—what helicopter? his neutral gaze implied in response to Quint's question. Quint resolved to get hold of a Malay dictionary; his request for spiced milk, an item not on the menu, had been perfectly understood.

He sipped the milk and buttered the toast, resenting the intrusion of this war machine, resisting the thought that his future was in some way linked to it. This prescience, more than the noise itself, jarred his languid mood. He felt as he imagined some basking field mouse might, alerted by the shadow of a bird of prey. Yet the breeze continued to ruffle the hibiscus and stroke the palm fronds through which glimmered the sea; the brown waiters moved quietly on sandaled feet; the guests chattered; and the occasional splash and cry floated up normally from the pool. But under it all, or over it, hovered this presence, unnatural and unnamed. And—besides himself—only a nine-year-old boy had paid attention. Or so it seemed.

"I am Hilton, your captain." Quint looked up to see a man in a brown tunic and slacks like those of the waiters standing beside him. A little badge on his chest proclaimed him a dining room captain. Cupping a questioning ear, Quint pointed towards the faint rumble now behind them and out of sight. "No problem." The man beamed. "I speak American." He draped himself over the back of a chair, eager to communicate, dismissing Quint's query with a wave of the menu, treating him instead to a monologue on the ninety-nine islands of Langkawi: their remoteness, dullness, and lack of even such civilized amenities as a cinema. He was unused to such a backwater, he declared, his previous post having been a luxury hotel on the mainland. How—he appealed to Quint—could he blame his wife for hieing off to the high life, robbing him of the last pleasure without which existence palled and which, even now, doubtless some stranger was enjoying? Carried away by his eloquence, he began listing the things he, Hilton, personally would do to that stranger if, by chance, Allah delivered him into his hands, such as gouging out his eyes, cutting off his manhood, not to mention . . .

The stench of stale beer these brave words unleashed suggested to Quint pleasures that Allah might not smile on. He pointed again at the now silent sky. "I merely wondered . . . "

A conniving grin creased the captain's face. Appraising eyes focussed on Quint. "No problem. I will arrange everything. At the Malacca Hilton, the Americans came to me. They call me, Mr. No Problem."

"I'm not exactly an American."

"No problem." Raising both palms in a valediction, Hilton the captain backed happily away. Why bother, Quint thought; I am on holiday. He stretched out his legs and leaned back in his chair the better to observe, from under the brim of his straw hat, his fellow breakfasters.

With the appearance of the wife and mother the English family was now complete. She seemed a good deal younger than her husband, early thirties, perhaps, or had weathered well in the way of English women Quint knew. Doubtless the dampness of the climate. Memories of school days in that mossy isle still made him shiver. She looked sensible, attractive, with a tan that, since it was December, she could hardly have acquired at home. The husband, by contrast, was pale under his floppy hat: the English tan, they called it. His face, thin-lipped, angular, seemed always anxious. As for their children— two girls and the boy—Quint's attitude was simply that they were there. The first fifteen years of life must be forgiven. Though had not he himself been a reigning princeling almost to his eighth birthday? Arguably his sole credential in his current post.

At a center table, five men were going at each other in French while a woman, ash blonde, followed it all with intelligent, sceptical eyes. Should she open her mouth, Quint suspected, the words coming out would singe the hearers' ears.

In the corner towards the pool a number of Indian families had spread themselves over three or four tables. Quint wondered if they'd come from the motherland, or belonged, like Vellu, to Malaysia's large Tamil community, descendants, for the most part, of indentured workers imported by the British to work their rubber plantations a hundred years ago.

A young man seated alone at another table caught his attention because, in all the bustle, he was so still. Pink as a piglet, a lock of lank brown hair obscuring one eye, his chin cupped in his hand, he stared into an hibiscus bush as if at the oracle at Delphi. As Quint watched, a little drama unfolded. Two women, one small, dark, tough, wrinkled, the other tall, young, with swishing auburn hair and dark eyes, brushed past. The eyes of the tall one flashed this way and that but found no free table. Quint was about to offer his, when the pink young man rose and gestured an invitation. The woman smiled, pleased, and grasped her much older friend's hand, but as they advanced a terse command issued from the back of the room that caused both women to turn: "Over here!" The older woman started obediently towards the summoning voice, but the other wavered as if contemplating defiance. Then, with a wry, resigned smile at the young man whose pink had deepened to puce, she followed her friend.

14

Quint now saw the source of the command, a stiff, stocky man with the complexion of ripe figs. Given a swagger stick and a row of medals on his starched tropical suit, he'd have done credit to any club of ex-colonial administrators. This fig-faced martinet had commandeered a table at which he protectively seated his womenfolk. If the younger one was indeed the daughter, Quint marveled at so shapely a splinter falling from so crass a block. Rising, cup in hand, he moved towards the pink young man. "Good, bad or indifferent?"

The man looked up, embarrassed.

Quint bowed. "May I?" He sat down. "Forgive me, but your gaze was so intense, I thought perhaps, in that bush, you had seen the future."

"Well, maybe."

"As bright, I trust, as these petals."

"None too bright, as a matter of fact. By the way, I'm Peter Forbes." He held out a hand as soft and pink as his face.

"Charles Quint."

"Don't think I've seen you around."

"Perhaps there was little room in your eyes." Quint's own twinkled mischievously; the other blushed. "But you are right. I came only yesterday. And you?"

"Two days ago." Peter Forbes uncrossed his legs and swivelled to face Quint. "Actually, I feel a bit of a fraud for being here at all."

"Aha. The infernal conscience. You are not, by chance, English?"

The other laughed. "What about you? American?"

Quint shook his head. "Though I just came from

there." The helicopter seemed to be returning. Before reaching the Inn it veered out to sea. They watched it go. "Apparently our guardian angel."

" 'We protect you so you can play.' "

"Play . . . ?"

Peter Forbes smiled apologetically. "Just a campaign jingle going around in my head."

"A *campaign* jingle? Aha, a soldier. Then perhaps you can tell me what that war-machine is playing at?"

"Afraid I soldier away in advertising; equally destructive, you might say. I'm trying to come up with a sales pitch for a contraceptive called Guardian Angel." He glanced again at the black dot of the helicopter, screwing up his eyes. "Perhaps it's advertising to the locals the might of the ruling elite, lest they fall out of line. I do just happen to know about fourth hand that it's a U.S. gunship with Thai markings."

"I'm impressed."

The pink again reddened. "Well, actually, it was Leila . . . Oh, you won't have met her . . . "

"Of the auburn tresses and flashing eyes?" Quint nodded. "I think I've seen her."

"She got it from her old man who's some sort of arms dealer on the Gulf; keeps the sheiks' loos stacked with old weapons catalogues, that sort of thing."

Quint smiled. "Not a very kind assessment. But not the most endearing chap either, I should imagine."

"I'll say." Peter ran a hand distractedly through his hair. "Wait till you meet him."

Quint had no intention of doing so. "I have a car coming at ten. Care for a spin around the island?"

"Thanks. Did that yesterday." Peter looked glum.

"Dragooned today into a picnic. Our peerless leader is dead set on group activity. Won't take 'well, er' for an answer. All rather vexing."

"So you're with a group?" Quint glanced around.

"Oh, he's not here. Ate hours ago and jogged off down the beach. That sort. Health nut. He runs on the beach, his wife at the mouth. Not unconnected. Marathon Mouth, I call her. Scares every winged thing for miles."

"A family outing?"

"Old friends of my dad's."

"And your father? Not here?"

"Been dead for years. I suspect I'm sort of a stand-in for him, as a matter of fact. Weird. The whole thing stinks, if you ask me." He shrugged, stood up, and strode off towards the beach.

"So sorry to hold you up, Mr. Quint." Vellu arrived at the Inn a few minutes after ten. When they were in the car and moving, he whispered, "I am hearing some more news—concerning your late American."

"*My* American, Vellu?" They were retracing the route of the day before, past the jetty and through the town. "I protest. I disown the man. I present him to you."

Vellu was undeterred. "That boatman; you will recall he disappeared. He has been found."

"So it's all cleared up then?" Quint suggested hopefully.

Vellu shook his head and drew a long hand across his throat, making a clicking noise.

"Also dead?"

"Neatly severed by *parang*. Again *parang*. They found

him washed up on nearby island, thanks to circling scavenger birds. Helicopter spotted him. Picked him up this morning." He stopped to lean from the window and harangue some youths lounging outside a shop, then drove on, burbling indignantly. "They expect payment, they must work. C.O.D. is it not? Today, everything is free, they think."

"That helicopter, it was searching for him?"

"Not for him actually *per se,* I understand." Vellu was noncommittal. "For someone. But they found boatman. It is very annoying, actually."

"I'm not sure I follow."

"Before, everyone happy. Everything comes to zero. The one cancels the other out. Now," Vellu shrugged enigmatically, "there is talk of crocodiles. But crocodiles with *parangs*? Besides, for long time no crocodiles are coming to Langkawi. So, as we say in bookkeeping, it does not add up. You see, Mr. Quint, I am also accountant."

"Indeed? And who *were* they looking for?" Quint's curiosity stirred.

Vellu sighed. "The authorities have it in their heads," he began reluctantly, "that a highly wanted insurgent leader is hiding in these islands; very troublesome man as far as they are concerned, having high price on his head. They are calling him guerrilla, warlord, dope-runner, bandit, separatist, communist, multi-millionaire even. They are saying his private army patrols Thai coast from here north to Burma and stirs up trouble in name of freedom, justice, dignity of man, and so on and so forth." He waved an impatient hand.

"What makes them think he's here?"

18

"Who am I, Mr. Quint, to question authorities in their infinite wisdom?"

"You have no notion whatsoever?"

"Notion, Mr. Quint. Notion." Vellu became agitated. "You talk to me of notion. I, Vellu, who have survived British Empire, have survived Japanese occupation, have survived Chinese communist terrorism, have survived— touch wood—" he tapped the dash, "independence under Malays. I have not done this by having notion, Mr. Quint; certainly not by repeating it to every Tom, Dick and Harry."

Quint waited, giving him time to cool off. "This man they're after, does he have a name?"

"They call him Ah Sook."

"Ah Sook. Chinese?"

Vellu lifted a hand from the wheel in token of assent. "They say he was trained by British during so-called State of Emergency. In counter-insurgency."

"And became an insurgent?" The Emergency, he gathered, was the pre-independence, communist-inspired jungle war.

"British are supreme educators."

"So, while searching for a live Chinese guerrilla, they find a dead Malay boatman."

"In nutshell, Mr. Quint."

Quint stroked his beard. Against his better judgment, he was becoming intrigued. Wherever his vacations took him, the allure of mystery seemed to present itself, almost as if his agent planned it. "He didn't talk before he died?"

"Boatman?"

"I was thinking more of the American."

They had left the town behind them. Vellu shifted down to take a hill. "May I ask: is this official question?"

"Official?" Quint was puzzled. "I'm not an official." Vellu cleared his throat in an unconvinced sort of way. Quint persisted. "I presume he spoke Malay, if he was living in a *kampong.*"

"I also presume. Anthropologist must speak local language, is it not?"

"And did he? Did you hear him talk Malay?"

Vellu fell silent. Then he said: "Mr. Quint, in years to come, when you and I are gone, my great-grandson will relate legend of white man who came from far to live simple life in Malay *kampong.* By then, no doubt, this man will have fallen in love with brown-eyed, needless to say beautiful Malay maiden with stern, unyielding father. One night he sails off to deserted island with heart's desire disguised as boatman. After night of rapture under the stars, father catches up, wreaking cruel vengeance. Tourists, like your great-grandson, will pay good money to be lied to by my great-grandson who will point out sand, needless to say still blood-red from lovers' wounds. In other words, Mr. Quint, is it truth that matters—or what is thought to be truth?"

He bumped off the road onto a track, pulled up and announced, in a smooth, guide's voice, "Mahsuri's Tomb. Visit to this spot is recommended for embalmers and lovers of folklore. Langkawi is sometimes being called Island of Legends because of legend of Mahsuri, Malay princess unjustly accused of adultery who proved innocence when white blood streamed from her body at execution. Blood seeped into earth, accounting for unusually snow-white nature of Langkawi's shores . . . "

They progressed from legend to legend by undulating, shaded roads, walking to less accessible spots along paths thick with wildflowers and butterflies. Once a string of rented Vespas roared past shattering the peace; but as the last one disappeared, they were again engulfed in bucolic serenity. They sat for lunch on the cool, grassy carpet of a rubber plantation in which Vellu, when pressed, admitted to holding an interest. The smooth, chalk-grey branches of the trees curved overhead like the carved naves of European cathedrals Quint had known and loved, plunging him into a reflective mood. The food—brought mysteriously in sealed containers by a small Tamil boy—was rich and savory. He watched two women in bright sarongs move in and out among the trees emptying liquid latex into buckets, and dozed a bit. Fort Wayne, with its dirty wintry boulevards and interminable faculty squabbles, seemed very far away; and even the helicopter gunship and the dead American belonged to some other existence.

Driving back they came upon the Inn bus nuzzling a bank like some fodder-hungry animal. The left front wheel was off. The Mercedes passed, then reversed. A gentle accident, Quint saw, apropos of the country generally. No one appeared hurt. Among the milling passengers he knew several faces—surely the picnic party Peter Forbes had mentioned. The English family, Peter himself, Fig-face and his two women, even, surprisingly, Tweedles Dum and Dee, his cockney upstairs neighbors. An odd assortment. Quint got out, offering help.

21

W eighed down under an extra five hundred pounds, the Mercedes covered the last three miles to the Inn at a crawl, and at each metallic scrape Vellu uttered a sigh. Sighing seemed a favorite outlet. Quint sat between him and a quivering little old apricot of a woman in a fuzzy orange turban who kept him pinned down under a verbal barrage. Marathon Mouth, no doubt about it. In the back seat, Fig-face's two women maintained silence. Craddock was their name: Mrs. and Miss Leila, though a less fitting tag for mother or daughter Quint could scarcely imagine. Mrs. Craddock spoke only Turkish, apparently, while the daughter was as fluid and full of grace as the name was stolid, yet seemingly restrained by her wary companion. Mrs. Cardew-Smythe, the English mother—here the name was tailor-made—and her younger daughter filled the remaining space. Vellu halted the car smoothly at the Inn entrance.

"I don't know what we'd have done if you hadn't stopped I'm sure, Mr. . . . ," Marathon Mouth burbled.

"Quint. Charles Quint."

"What an unusual name. And rescued us. Gone and got ourselves cooked, I wouldn't wonder. I shall have to have a lie-down before dinner. Oh, you will join us, won't you, Mr. Quint? Half seven. Really, the least we could do.

Such adventures . . . " She trotted off into the lobby.
The others trailed damply behind, muttering their
thanks. Vellu, protesting weakly, left to pick up the men.

The evening proved eventful, and puzzling. Dinner was
rescued from total tedium by the captain's lavishing on it
his tipsy attention, in the process making an eternal
enemy of the hostess, whose real name turned out to be
Lady Gwendoline Jake. Lady in her husband's right. In
the middle of the terrace three tables had been pushed
together to accommodate the entire picnic party less the
Turkish Mrs. Craddock who was indisposed. "Oh, dearie
me, thirteen at table after all," cried Lady Jake—"Call
me Gwendy, everybody does"—clearly dismayed. Quint's
inclusion had apparently been designed to avoid this.

She dithered interminably over the seating till at last
her husband—the knight—jerked out a chair and sat
down, bidding everyone do likewise. So this was the
peerless leader, Peter Forbes' 'health nut': small, gruff,
well-knit, a man used to getting his own way. "What is
this then, Gwendy-luv, Buckingham bloody Palace?"

This launched her ladyship into a description of a royal
garden party she had graced at which the Queen had
stepped back into a rosebed and laddered a stocking—a
small price to pay, Quint thought, to escape extended
conversation with Lady Jake. Next to her the thin cockney with the giggle (whose name was not Tweedledee but
just as suitably, Sneed) tittered and bobbed his head
attentively. Cardew-Smythe, seated on her other side,
mustered a dutiful smile. He seemed to Quint to be in a
state of suppressed pain.

Quint found himself between Peter Forbes and Leila
Craddock and hence very much in the way. Across from

him the Cardew-Smythe children conspired together as the captain confused the drinks orders, so that the older girl was well into Lady Jake's gin fizz before anyone noticed. Beyond the ties of nationality, Quint could see no logical bond linking these people. Perhaps nationality was enough. The French coterie seemed happily self-absorbed; the Indians banded clannishly together; and a party of young Chinese, who seemed now to have replaced them, were doing the same. So why not the British? Yet Quint was hard put to recall sitting down with a more mismatched group. He looked around the table. What had brought them together? What constrained them? A negative force, he felt. Not as strong as hate. Apathy? Was that it? A profound apathy.

Individually, they seemed unexceptional. Leila, with whom he developed swift rapport, was intelligent, a graduate of a well-known London university, full of plans for improving the lot of women in the Muslim world; the antithesis of her apoplectic father who sat on her right and—whenever her conversation with Quint became animated—distracted her with a nudge or a comment or clumsily involved her in small talk with Sir Frankie Jake, seated at the far end from his wife, or with Mrs. Cardew-Smythe opposite. The jealous parent, Quint thought, reluctant to share his daughter with other men.

Leila, outwardly compliant, always turned back and took up the thread. "Then you are all alone here, Mr. Quint. You did not know anyone from—" she paused, momentarily at a loss for words, "—from before?"

"Before?" Quint raised an eyebrow.

"In another life, perhaps?" She laughed.

He looked around the table. He had known many people in another life—including English people—but certainly no one present. Slowly, he shook his head. There had been a casualness about the question, yet nothing she said was really casual. He felt that in some way she was probing.

"Leila,"—it was Craddock—"be a good girl and tell Sir Frankie here what it was you learned at that damn college I sent you to that nearly broke me, and I don't mean the twaddle about women's lib."

"Women's rights." Leila scowled.

Craddock slapped down his beer—his seventh of the evening—and appealed to Jake with a helpless look. "What did I tell you?"

Quint heard a rumble from his left, where Peter Forbes, hunched over, toyed with his food. It sounded like, "The children's teeth are set on edge." A new jingle? Toothpaste? The other leading brand? Quint's glance wandered speculatively to Sir Frankie's mouth which was open showing long, yellow molars. The Cardew-Smythe children, desserts eaten, charged off towards their room.

At the table, where recently squirmed the flower of Anglo-Saxon childhood, a gap now existed. On one side sat Mrs. Cardew-Smythe, her face bathed in Buddha-like benevolence, immune to her surroundings; on the other the loud-mouthed cockney, Tweedledum, peeped from a ruddy, Falstaffian countenance, eyes fixed, Quint felt, on him. This man's name was Miller. Sneed, his sidekick, thin, patchy mustache looking as though it had been planted but hadn't all come up, nodded and tittered as Marathon Mouth pressed forward her litany of complaint, comparison and contumely through coffee, cordials and stifled yawns, until a message for Quint, delivered by a waiter, became the general excuse to rise.

Vellu was waiting in a dark corner of the spacious lobby and made for the door, beckoning, as soon as Quint appeared. On the far side of the drive the Mercedes loomed up in the darkness and Quint saw in the back a man sitting. A Malay. "He has come," Vellu announced mysteriously. "You may question him."

In vain Quint searched his memory. "Who is this?"

Vellu's eyes opened wide and very white. "The fisherman."

"But—I thought you said he was dead."

"No, no, no, Mr. Quint,"—Vellu's impatience broke through—"that was *boatman*. This man is man who is finding American in mangrove." He splayed the fingers of one hand. They got in. The figure in the back did not stir. "Ask him about last words."

Obediently, Quint turned in his seat, wishing he knew even one word of Malay. A word of greeting. "The American, he was still alive when you found him?"

Vellu translated. "Still alive," he confirmed.

"Did he say anything, anything at all?"

Vellu translated. The man clutched his head in his hands, rocking to and fro. He was small and skinny, wearing a torn shirt and a sarong and from his betel-stained lips issued short, pathetic, high-pitched moans.

"Is he ill?"

"He is showing how American behaved." Now the man was whispering to himself. Quint listened intently. The same sound, over and over again.

"What's he saying?"

27

Vellu held up a hand. Suddenly the man's head slumped sideways. His breathing seemed to stop. "He is now dead," Vellu announced. *"Dayang bunting, dayang bunting, dayang bunting.* It means pregnant maiden, pregnant maiden, pregnant maiden."

Quint looked at the Indian. "Why?"

"There is lake on one island here by that name," Vellu suggested. "The Lake of the Pregnant Maiden. Maybe he is referring to that lake."

"Could it mean anything else?"

Vellu shook his head. "Ask him what else was said."

The answer came: "That is all."

"What does he think the American was trying to tell him?" Quint asked. A vigorous exchange ensued between Vellu and the Malay, during which Quint, looking around, saw a figure he recognized standing very still in the lobby window of the Inn.

"He does not know what the American was trying to tell him. He thinks, perhaps, he was speaking to his god. He has heard that white man worships pregnant maiden. I am telling him, nonsense."

"Had he seen this American before?"

The fisherman nodded. "He says, many times."

"And did the American have enemies in the *kampong?*"

"He says, no. American was well-liked."

"Did he speak Malay?"

"He says, yes."

"Well?"

"For white man, well."

A shape loomed at the window of the car. All three men looked up. "Oh, Peter," Quint said, "You startled me."

"Sorry." Peter Forbes bent to see inside, pushing back

his hair with his hand. "Actually I was wondering what the chances were of a ride downtown." The rather plaintive appeal embraced both Quint and Vellu. He seemed the slightest bit unsteady.

"Most sorry, sir." Vellu became the obsequious Indian. "As you are seeing, I myself am booked solid just now."

"It's past ten," Quint observed.

Vellu chimed in: "The gentleman is correct. Everything is shut tight by this time. No possibilities whatsoever."

"Oh come off it, you're bloody lying."

Quint left some *ringgits*—Malaysian dollars—on the seat for Vellu to give the fisherman. He didn't quite know why. Sad as it was, the American's death was hardly his business. "Come on, old man." He took Peter's arm and walked him down the drive. The Mercedes rolled off in the town direction, gathering speed. Soon its lights disappeared around the curve.

Though headlights were hardly necessary. The moon threw stark shadows, and gilded every shrub and tree. They passed beyond the hum of the air-conditioning plant and wandered towards the tennis court which was down below the pool. "I want to get drunk," Peter grumbled, "and the bar here's too depressing. Besides, Craddock's there." He unhooked his arm from Quint's and stuck his hand in his pockets like a petulant child.

"Ah, Craddock. Your Great Wall of China."

Peter stopped and kicked out violently at a shrub. "What's the matter with me? I'm grown up, reasonably sane, answerable to no one, yet the way I carry on I might as well be on a chain gang in a gulag." He laughed bitterly. "Dammit, my mum's not even here. Every night I say

29

to myself: tomorrow, I'll be different. We'll get a taxi; we'll find our own beach; we'll spend the day together. And in the morning, guess what? I sign up for the chain gang, subject myself to Marathon Mouth—torture that defies refinement, even by the Chinese. Tonight I was ready to throw dishes."

"But, being a good son of England, you didn't. Greeks throw dishes; Russians too, I believe, when drunk. You should try it. Surprise yourself."

"Run amok, eh, like a Malay?"

"Not quite that drastic. You don't have to kill anyone."

As they walked, Quint couldn't get the fisherman out of his mind. Why had Vellu brought him? What was he trying to tell him? What, if anything, should he, Quint, do? On the whole, he was annoyed at Vellu. But it was his own fault, he supposed, really. He asked too many questions. One day, he would learn.

Peter's voice intruded: "I say, you couldn't lend a hand? With Leila? Thing is, I can't seem to get past the guards."

"Does she want you to?"

"Oh yes."

"How do you know?"

"It's in her eyes."

Quint laughed. "Then she'll find a way. Aucassin and Nicolette, remember?"

Up at the Inn the nightly film show was winding down. From where they stood they could see the back of the screen flickering with jungle imagery; of all things, a revival of Tarzan, swinging through the trees, triumphant. A smattering of applause. "What did you mean, tonight, about the children's teeth?"

"You don't miss much."

"Sour grapes?"

"Should we pay for the sins of our fathers?"

"Usually there's no choice."

"Well, in this case, there is. I, for one, intend to stop payment. And I don't see why Leila shouldn't, too."

"Do you mind if we sit?" They were by the pool. Quint dragged two plastic chairs together. "Tell me, if it's not too painful."

"Painful?" Peter bridled. "Why do you say that? I wasn't even born. For Dad . . . Well, Dad was Dad. Not the world's most jolly good fellow, but OK by me. Had a shoe shop in Woking. Repairs. Never left the place to speak of. Something on his mind, he always said. Mum wouldn't let him confess. Afraid it was a woman, I suppose—from his army days. So he ended up telling me. Then he died. Must have known he was going to." Peter stretched out full length on his chair.

"And was it—a woman?"

"No." Peter addressed the moon. "Some bloke he'd killed. Out here in Malaya in the Emergency. I said, 'Look, Dad, you were in the bloody army. That's what you were bloody paid for. Killing was your job.' He looked at me, kind of smiled, and shook his head. As if I could never understand. And that was that."

They lay on their backs, looking at the stars, till a footfall on the stone steps leading from the beach below made Quint sit up. Someone was climbing slowly towards them, bent over, preoccupied. Quint coughed.

"Mr.—er—Quint?" It was Cardew-Smythe.

"Beautiful evening."

"Yes, quite." Cardew-Smythe peered nervously a-

31

round, then, as if feeling a need to explain himself: "The children suddenly remembered they left a flipper down there, so poor old daddy is dispatched to retrieve it." He kept going. "Goodnight. Goodnight, Peter."

"Goodnight."

A little time went by before Peter said, "Makes you bloody wonder. My father was his batman, which, in the British Army, in case you didn't know, is a kind of glorified male nanny. My dad was a regular, and Cardew-Smythe was a nineteen-year-old second lieutenant on National Service. Still wet behind the ears, but, according to Dad, a hell of a nice bloke. Now look at him: a tired old nursemaid, picking up after the kids. Makes you wonder."

"I supposed it's coincidence, your meeting out here now."

"Coincidence?" Peter sat up. "I thought you realized. That's *why* we're all here. It's old man Jake's idea of a joke, only no one's laughing. Jake's jokes make blokes choke. Ha, ha. He was the sergeant of the outfit."

"Ah, indeed. And the others at dinner?"

"All in the same outfit."

"But the battle stories, the reminiscing? Come, come, I've been a soldier."

Peter got up. "Zilch. I tried. I thought at least Cardew-Smythe might have a memory or two of Dad, who all but changed his nappies for him for a year. Hell, it *was* thirty years ago. But no. The man's as closed as a cockleshell. I am an embarrassment to him. Or that's what he makes me feel like with his tight-assed 'goodnight, Peter,' 'good morning, Peter.' And, as for that snooty bitch he married;

well, if she wanted a batman, that's what she got. I guess he learned the ropes from poor old Dad."

"Time I turned in." Quint, too, stood up. On the terrace, they shook hands. *"Courage et confiance.* You'll find a way." Passing the bar, he noticed that Craddock was still there, alone.

A little later Quint stood on his balcony breathing the night air before sleep. Why, he asked himself, would a dying American anthropologist repeat the words pregnant maiden over and over, and in Malay? And why was he, Quint, worrying about it when he was supposed to be enjoying a hard-earned vacation?

Shadowy figures were filtering up from the beach: the newly arrived Chinese. Perhaps they'd been reciting poetry to each other in the moonlight. If so, he envied them.

CHAPTER FOUR

Ian Cardew-Smythe harrumphed as only Englishmen of a certain class can. Quint raised both eyebrows at once, a rare occurrence. He had merely asked—literally a passing remark—as he greeted the family at breakfast, whether the lost flipper had been found.

"We haven't lost a flipper," the boy with the goggles piped up. "We haven't snorkled at all. We can't see anything." All three children looked accusingly at their father.

Cardew-Smythe rubbed his chin. "I really think I must go and shave." He pushed back his chair. "Before it goes off again." He strode away.

Quint's stab at an early breakfast had been thwarted by a power cut. It wasn't the power cut that surprised him, however. He had learned to take nothing for granted—not life, not death, certainly not electricity. What did surprise him was the panic that lit momentarily in the Englishman's eyes. He turned to the children. "You like it here?"

Three freckled faces considered the question. "No," allowed the youngest. "The beach is all muddy." So much for the white blood of the princess, thought Quint.

"No good for snorkling," added the boy, grimly.

"And the pool's slimy and full of Indians," the other

girl huffed. She added reproachfully, "At Penang at least it had a cocktail bar in the middle."

Quint sighed. Three pairs of eyes glared at him. Was *anyone* having a good time, he wondered. Then he heard a familiar sound. The helicopter—right on time. He returned to his own table to await his toast, but it wasn't toast that came. It was Ian Cardew-Smythe. He strolled over, fingering his now smooth chin as if to say, 'Look, I have done what I said I would.' "Sit down," Quint invited.

"I really mustn't." But the Englishman did, after a quick glance to where his wife had now joined the children. For a moment the two men looked out across the sparkling bay to the wooded islands. "Grand, isn't it?" A large boat was making good speed across their line of vision, its decks alive with people. "Morning ferry from the mainland," Cardew-Smythe went on. "We're thinking of going back that way. Only two and a half hours and pretty smooth sailing. Train's a bit grueling though— right down the length of the peninsula. All day, all night. Fun for the children, if not for poor Phoebe, I fear."

"You're from Singapore?" Quint knew it already from dinner talk.

"For the time being. I've a two-year contract with eight months to go. Renewable."

"And do you plan to renew?" Cardew-Smythe didn't answer. His thoughts seemed elsewhere. They watched the boat till it rounded the point, heading for the town jetty.

Suddenly he leaned over. "I say, I really must apologize for that shameless lie I told last night. You rather caught me with my pants down just now. Out of the mouths of babes, and so on. Actually," he glanced over his shoulder, "I do have an explanation, though a rather lame one. You might almost say, irrational."

"As truth often can be," Quint reassured.

"Would you mind . . . ?" Cardew-Smythe's left fist, lying on the table, unclenched towards the beach.

"Not at all." Quint stood up and led the way to the steps. It wasn't till their feet were firmly planted on the sand some three minutes later that his companion spoke.

"Hard on the children." Cardew-Smythe surveyed the mud and the clumps of rotting seaweed. "I rather sold them on the snorkling possibilities of this place, but the winds this time of year do seem to churn things up. Goes to show you can't rely on the literature. Poor Phoebe despairs over what she calls my gullible self: it sounds good, therefore it is. No, it wasn't the flipper; it was the film they showed last night. I just had to get away, be alone. Last straw, I suppose."

"The children—didn't they like the film?" Quint was aware of an unpleasant smell, like raw sewage. Perhaps it was just the seaweed. "But wasn't it *Tarzan?*"

They had begun to walk. "*Tarzan of the Apes.* You see we showed those films in the New Villages, Saturday night after Saturday night." Cardew-Smythe looked helplessly at Quint. "I'm talking about Malaya thirty years ago. History." He gave an apologetic little laugh.

"Ah, history. My special fascination."

"Rather a backwater, this particular bit." He added, with surprising vehemence: "For those not fool enough to be caught up in it."

" 'In the backwater hatches the flood-tide', to quote a little-known savant of my country, Hegesippe Simon."

Cardew-Smythe grunted. "Don't think I know him. But

it certainly swept me off my feet. Damn near drowned me." They followed the curve of the beach which ended where a rocky promontory tumbled into the sea. "I was nineteen, a second lieutenant on National Service. A year at home, a year overseas was the drill. They had a war on here—Emergency, with a big E, they called it; but that was really just a euphemism. So they shipped us out to defend the frontiers of Empire, and, incidentally, the rubber. The jungle was crawling with CT's—communist terrorists, that is. Our job was to hunt them down and kill them. Some of us rather overdid it."

It seemed to Quint that Cardew-Smythe suddenly lost interest in what he was saying, like a child who picks up something, say a sea anemone, and drops it seconds later in disgust. He nudged gently: "The last straw, you said."

Cardew-Smythe picked up a shell, examined it, and tossed it into the waves breaking gently some way off. "It's all frightfully sordid. And entirely my own fault. The fact is, I shouldn't have brought the family here. Of course, I rationalized as usual: free holiday, a break for Phoebe from the infernal stewpot of Singapore, adventure for the children. But it was really something *I* wanted: punishment, I suppose; self-flagellation; goodness knows what a psychiatrist would say. Which was probably why I dragged them out to Singapore in the first place. Though it's a tad late to see all this now. They're stuck with me. Sorry, I wonder why one is impelled to pour out one's past transgressions . . . "

A man was splashing down the beach towards them from round the point. Quint saw that it was Sir Frankie Jake, running steadily, doing all right for a man who must be pushing seventy. They watched in silence. As he came abreast, he held up a skinny arm, but neither his expression of grim concentration, nor the rhythm of his stride, changed: a slight, wiry body glistening with sweat. They waved back and watched his diminishing form jog on along the sand.

Cardew-Smythe said, "You won't believe this, but once upon a time that man had to salute me." He sounded awed, not boastful. "He was my sergeant. Now he's a millionaire, knighted this year in the birthday honors. Fit, fulfilled, a veritable dynamo. The best of post-war Britain. And look at me: a mere schoolmaster, doubting, tired, scarcely able to support a family. Yet we were through it all together. Funny, how differently it takes different people . . . "

"You're here at his invitation, I gather?"

"So you know. Not just me; the whole patrol—what's left of it. At his expense, too. Can you imagine?"

"You were—all of you here—one patrol?"

"Bar young Forbes, naturally. His father, though. He was my batman. Dead now, but doubtless Peter told you." A sidelong glance at Quint. "Royal Wessex Yeomanry, 3rd Battalion, D Company, Four Platoon, Patrol Section Easy."

"Easy?"

"Able, Baker, Charlie, Dog, Easy, Fox. They've changed it all now, I understand. Craddock was a lance-corporal, Miller and Sneed, the somewhat raucous cockney pair, were privates. There was another chap, also a private, who hasn't turned up yet. Bit of a queer fish. Seven, all told. Out of ten. Survived."

The tide was going out. They had rounded the point, hopping from sandbar to sandbar, managing to stay dry. "Survived *what,* may I ask?"

"Oh, stupid of me: the ambush. Oh, I say, look at that!"

A little cove stretched before them, its far end choked with dense green foliage which seemed to march on wooden legs through grey mud into the water. Sir Frankie's feet, cutting clear tracks in the muddy sand, appeared to have led him straight into it.

"I do believe . . . That's not a mangrove swamp?" Quint hadn't been this close to one before.

"Mangroves, all right. See how the roots drop from the lower branches, like giant lobster pots? Isabella Bird, in her commendable book on these parts, took great exception to them: 'Aquatic birds haunt their slimy shades'— if memory serves. How's that for hyperbole?"

"I'm afraid Sir Frankie will have scared off any birds."

"I'm glad he emerged unscathed, actually. They're supposed to be great breeding grounds for crocodiles and what have you—mangrove swamps."

They followed the footprints. Quint said, "I suppose it's not unnatural—at the apogee of one's career—to want to invite old comrades in arms to celebrate; soak up a little reflected sunshine, so to speak. And from what I've observed, hardly out of character."

"Except we aren't 'old comrades' by any stretch of the imagination. In fact, the incident must have been—in all our lives—the absolute low point. Something to obliterate, not celebrate."

"But you couldn't forget. I daresay that goes for the others, too." Quint saw Cardew-Smythe's jaw tighten so that his neck veins stood out. "Did you know they would all be here, by the way?"

"Good heavens, no. And if it wasn't for Phoebe and the children, I'd leave. It's an intolerable situation."

"I take it you haven't kept in touch over the years then—except with Sir Frankie."

"Not even with him. Of course his name's been in the papers now and then—the knighthood and so on—but this came quite out of the blue."

Up close they saw that the tracks didn't enter the swamp after all, but ran up the beach beside it and plunged into jungly undergrowth beyond the sand line. Here they were harder to follow. The ground was compact and matted with vegetation, but after a few yards Quint spotted a sandy hollow which showed signs of use. "Perhaps he rested. At his age one can hardly blame him."

Cardew-Smythe was eyeing something at the edge of the sand. Quint joined him. "Used to stick those over our rifle barrels to keep them clean in the jungle. If this was Singapore there'd be a $40 fine for littering."

"I underestimated," Quint murmured. " 'We protect you so you can play.' "

"What was that?"

"Just something Peter said."

"Young Forbes?" It was a chance for Cardew-Smythe to change the subject. "Particularly tough on him, I'm afraid, being dragged through all this." He glanced at his watch. "Good Lord, look at the time." With the tip of a very white tennis shoe he thrust the offending object into the sand. "*In natura lapsa.* He said as much."

"You mean he . . . ?"

But Cardew-Smythe had turned away. "Better be heading back."

They had climbed the steps from the beach and were passing the swimming pool when Cardew-Smythe spotted his wife stretched full length in the sun. He strode over to her. "I say, Phoeb, where are the children?"

Not moving, she replied, "Somewhere around."

"I don't think it's frightfully wise to let them wander off." He sounded peeved, perhaps by her vagueness. "The bus leaves in ten minutes. Where could they have got to?" He peered about.

"Danny said something about giant lizard tracks." This casually delivered comment produced what Quint guessed was the desired effect, for Cardew-Smythe charged off towards the terrace. A time-honored game: you can't shock me as much as I'm going to shock you. A favorite with couples down the centuries. Phoebe Cardew-Smythe gazed sleepily up at Quint. "It's not as though he hadn't done his jungle orientation course. Dear Ian—" she sat up—"I think in some previous incarnation he must have been a sheepdog. He does so love rounding things up. He missed his vocation. He should have been a tour guide in Venice."

"Why Venice?"

"The humanizing effect. We went there on our honeymoon. Absolute bliss. I parked myself by some edifice or other and painted. Ian dashed to and fro with the guidebook. At supper, over Chianti, we swapped yarns. We've never quite managed such synchronized bliss since."

"Having children, naturally . . . "

"Another of Ian's ideas."

Quint pretended he hadn't heard. He was afraid of this woman, who brought to mind an aunt who had shot bears in Transylvania. "So where are you all off to today?"

Phoebe Cardew-Smythe groaned. "Absolutely no idea. That's Ian's department." She groped around in a canvas beachbag and held out a book. "It's in there somewhere. Oh why, oh why, on holiday, can't one simply lie in one place all day and do nothing?"

From the book—*Malay in Three Weeks*—protruded a Xeroxed sheet which proved to be the week's sightseeing schedule. Quint read the day's entry aloud: " 'Ten sharp board bus for Seven Falls. Debus and wander 2.4 kilometres on jungle paths brimming with butterflies while bright birds hue and cry overhead . . . ' " Vellu himself couldn't have bested such prose.

Phoebe laughed. "If anything hues and cries it'll be Lady Jake. One more garden party with the Royals . . . I mean, honestly."

"Yes, I suppose royalty can get boring."

"I've nothing against it personally. Something for the Gwendy Jakes of this world to go on about. Which is all very well, provided one doesn't have to listen."

Quint went back to the schedule: " ' . . . and monkeys cavort for your pleasure. Plunge into the cool waters of the pool of your choice which gleams calm in the wooded cleft like dumb waiters, one atop the other . . . ' "

"Like *what?*"

"Dumb waiters." He shrugged, skipping down the page. "Aha!" Something caught his eye: " 'The Lake of the Pregnant Maiden.' "

"Oh, how too macabre. That can't be a real place."

"Yes indeed. They've saved it to your last day."

"Well, with a name like that, I'll simply have to paint it." She struggled to her feet, avoiding Quint's preferred assistance. "Better make an effort, though the bus has yet to be on time. The Malays seem to have no notion of punctuality, and it infuriates Ian. He simply won't accept it. Chinese are much more his cup of tea. He can't wait to get back to Singapore. My philosophy, on the other hand, is not to anticipate. Let it happen. If one doesn't know what's *supposed* to happen, one can't get all hot and bothered when it doesn't."

Quint's philosophy too, up to a point. "But surely you like it here?"

"It's nice to be somewhere Somerset Maugham wasn't, for a change."

Quint flipped through *Malay in Three Weeks* looking for 'helicopter'. Five words, it seemed, constituted a helicopter. He closed the book and handed it back.

By the time Quint reached the lobby for the rendezvous he had arranged with Vellu, the bus had left. A woman was standing quietly among the tubs of greenery that flanked the entrance. At least he assumed it was a woman: a figure swathed in the white veil some Moslems adopt, no features showing. Over at the desk an argument was under way. A man was yelling letters of the alphabet: "B-R-I-S-C-O-E. Briscoe. Does anybody here parlez-vous English?"

The woman clerk on duty spoke perfectly good English. She murmured soothingly, insisting, Quint gathered, that the Inn was booked solid.

"Look here, I'm the personal guest of Sir Frankie Jake," the man expostulated, emphasizing the 'Sir'. "Does that mean anything to you at all?"

The woman partially melted. "We are expecting someone named *Padinki.*"

"Padinki? You got Padinki?" The man grabbed whatever paper she was consulting. "Make that Briscoe,
ducks, there's a dear. Mr. *and* Mrs. I want the best suite
in the place, too. And if anyone asks for Padinki, you
never heard of him. OK?"

"We cannot accept gratuities, sir," Quint heard the
woman say.

As he stepped out of the Inn, Vellu greeted him like a
long-lost brother. "Oh, my dear sir, I am pleased to see
you, so pleased. I thought we might never meet in this incarnation again, though some other time maybe as fishes
in the sea or birds in the air." When they were in the car
and moving, he said, "Terrible, horrible thing has
happened. That man from last night, who sat there, in
that seat . . . "

"Dead?"

Vellu's eyes bulged. "You are knowing already? Ah, but
I should have known."

"Purely a guess."

"The helicopter—they found him this morning. Like
vultures, they find only dead people." When Quint said
nothing for a while, Vellu looked at him. "Mr. Quint?"

"Yes, I'm listening. How did it happen?"

"Same. Exact same."

"Do you mean a neat chop to the neck as to the boatman, or a messy, wounding swing as to the American?"

Vellu indicated his neck. "A warning to others, this is
what is being said, is what the wind is saying. I tell you
frankly, Mr. Quint, this is very brave man. I, even I, Vellu,
am wondering: where will it end?"

45

Yes, Quint acknowledged, a brave man. "Where are we going, Vellu, today?"

"Today, by motorboat if you please. The Cave of the Banshee."

"With all due respect to the Banshee, I think not. Another day, perhaps. Today, Vellu, we go to Seven Falls, where bright birds hue and cry overhead and monkeys cavort for our pleasure. We have work to do."

"*We,* Mr. Quint?" Alarm sounded in Vellu's voice and flared in his eyes. "Oh, my God."

CHAPTER FIVE

A little general store, thatched with *attap,* marked the point where the jungle track left the road. Vellu bought two sodas, a packet of coffee-creams and a bunch of tiny yellow bananas, and committed them, and Charles Quint, to the care of a small brown boy in a brown velvet *songkok* who seemed to live nearby. He would return in the Mercedes at four sharp, he explained.

The path breasted little ridges, forded trickling streams and skirted compounds where naked children rushed off giggling at their approach and thin dogs barked. They passed fields where bands of bowed women in colorful sarongs wielded hoes, calling to each other, pretending not to notice Quint. Anything less jungle-like he couldn't imagine. Ahead sloped the upper reaches of a broad, blue mountain—the one they had flown over—which, as they walked, sank from sight behind its forested foothills. The lower slopes had been cleared of timber, and great dusty root-knots bleached in the fierce sun at weird angles. Along the streambeds blue butterflies fluttered desultorily. The boy marched ahead, setting a fast pace, now and then looking back to check on his charge. The frown on his thin, intelligent face showed the seriousness with which he took his mission, and made him appear to Quint ageless.

When, after forty minutes, they did reach jungle, it was like entering an air-conditioned room. With one step, Quint felt the power of the sun cut off with a snap as green leaves and tall grey trunks enfolded him. His shirt, wet through with perspiration, felt deliciously cold to his body. Almost at once the path began to climb steeply, and, to Quint, the clink of the two bottles carried by the boy just ahead—but out of reach—became torture; like crawling towards a mirage. He knew the Malay words for pregnant maiden, but he did not know stop, I'm tired, I'm thirsty. His dependence was laughable.

The sound of running water helped revive Quint's flagging spirits. Soon he was crossing a stream, jumping from rock to rock with the boy on the far side smiling encouragement. It was the first time Quint had seen him smile. He paused, listening, hoping to hear voices, welcoming the sun on his shoulders. The path plunged into thick bamboo, emerging again at the streambed, where it stayed. As he groped his way from boulder to boulder, a roar grew in Quint's ears. Then another sound impinged: shouting and screaming humanity.

He saw the waterfall first, dropping white and narrow fifty feet into its pool, ringed by strange, slab-like rocks, defying perspective, bringing to mind an Uccello painting. The sound was coming from the pool, from some half-dozen kids tossing a ball. Up an expanse of rock which sloped off to the right into the trees, the boy scrambled. Quint balked. He looked about. His arrival seemed largely unnoticed. The smell of cooking reminded him that he was hungry. Three or four Malay families were camped out on the sloping rock, around smouldering fires. On the far side of the rock, near the falls, he finally saw the group from the Inn. They had staked out a few square yards of territory. It was for this enclave that the boy was making. Bending down, moving on all fours like an ape, Quint followed.

The party seemed, at first glance, complete—notwithstanding the rebellious rumblings of the day before. They had spread themselves on purple Inn towels in attitudes of sun worship, except for the Jakes who were unpacking a hamper, and Ian Cardew-Smythe who, from under his floppy hat, was watching the pool. Quint's Malay boy set down his precious load and waited, resolutely ignoring Lady Jake who yelled and flapped her hands at him as if at an importuning squirrel in St. James's Park. Her mouth opened and shut like a carp's, and though the words were lost on Quint in the enveloping din, the intention was clear. He gestured reassuringly at her, and handed the boy a *ringgit*. "Go. I'm all right now." He pointed downstream. The boy said something and Quint looked about, half-hoping to see *Malay in Three Weeks*. How did one say thank you? It was then he realized that Phoebe Cardew-Smythe was missing. When he looked back, the boy had vanished. Was he down there splashing in the pool? Without the velvet hat it was hard to tell.

Quint's throat badly needed wetting, and the Jakes' hamper—he rightly divined—contained a bottle opener. Gwendy deplored the fact that they didn't have an extra lunch, but said she was sure people would chip in, which made Quint feel like a refugee waiting for a handout— which, conceivably, was her intention. Tomorrow, if he cared to join them, she effused, she'd be sure to order sufficient. Oh, no trouble at all, would it be, Sweet? Sweet, a.k.a. Sir Frankie, was distributing lunch packs. "What was that, Gwendy-luv?"

"I told Mr. Quint we'd be pleased to have his company tomorrow. I'll order an extra lunch."

Sir Frankie, Quint saw at once, was against it. "Yes, indeed, Mr. . . . er . . . now let me see." He consulted his watch. "Tomorrow . . . "

To save the world from one more lie, Quint held up a hand. "Off on a boat tomorrow," he shouted.

"Leaving us so soon, Mr. . . . ?" Jake was clearly relieved.

"No. An excursion. I'm here till Sunday."

"Oh, so are we!" Gwendy Jake clapped her hands. "We must see lots and lots of you. I was only saying just now to Sir Frankie, what's the good of foreign travel if we don't befriend foreigners?" She glanced at the picnicking Malays. "Intelligent ones, I mean. There was such a nice American came round to the hotel when we arrived, but then Americans don't really count, do they? And anyway, this one has simply vanished."

"Indeed? An American?" Quint's interest was aroused.

"I say, Quint," Cardew-Smythe had come up quietly, "would you mind awfully keeping a weather eye on the children?" He held up a lunch box. "I'd better hunt up Phoebe."

"Let me go," Quint took the box. "Children aren't my strong point. She is painting, perhaps?"

"Up there, somewhere," he waved a hand at the falls. "How very kind of you."

Gwendy Jake scowled. "Poor man," she said, as soon as Cardew-Smythe's back was turned, "not a proper mother, that wife of his. Letting her three bathe with the natives; no telling what they'll catch. Schistosomiasis, blackwater fever . . . " People without children always know what people with children are doing wrong, Quint had noticed. "If I were you, I'd eat that lunch myself. Serve her right, running off. Why not let one of the younger ones go after her?" Her gaze lit upon Leila, sprawled nearby. "Nice girl, that. Leila!"

Leila Craddock, in a scanty swimsuit, her towel draped around her shoulders, sauntered over. Her hair hung wet and smooth to her waist. "Of course," she responded to her marching orders, "but I shall have to take Mr. Quint with me—to scare off the snakes. Daddy says you die in thirty seconds if you aren't careful. And he can share my lunch."

Quint downed the last half of his fizzy drink, wincing at its sweetness. He followed Leila up the rocky slope, conscious of at least one pair of eyes on them: sitting apart, knees drawn up to his chin, Peter Forbes looked a picture of dejection. Quint wondered how long before they would be followed, and by whom. They picked their way through the feasting Malays, stepping over babies and pans of food, smiling, apologizing. A hint of a path twisted away among the trees, and soon sight and sound of the party on the rock were blotted out.

The path climbed steeply along the edge of a ravine at the bottom of which, hidden by greenery, cascaded the falls. Leila seemed sure of the way, and, at first, Quint was content to follow, sometimes literally hauling himself from tree to tree by thick, drooping creepers, Tarzan-style. The sound of the falls became fainter and fainter till it faded altogether; then the path, too, petered out.

"Lost?" Quint panted, catching up. Leila had lit a cigarette and was leaning against a tree, waiting.

"Enough."

"Enough?"

"Lost enough so we won't be interrupted."

"Doing what, is it permitted to ask?"

"Eating." She tossed him her lunch.

"Shouldn't we complete our mission first?"

"I'm sure she's in no hurry to be disturbed."

A rocky ledge jutted from the brown carpet of the
forest's uneven floor. It seemed a safe place to sit. Leila
popped open two beers and passed one to Quint.
"Cheers."

Cold beyond hope. "Where did you get this?"

"The boys—Miller and Sneed. I call them 'the boys'
because they're schoolboys, aren't they, still? Sometimes
they're a scream. Sir Frankie disapproves of drink, so
they have to smuggle it."

"Sir Frankie has other vices, perhaps, to compensate."

She looked at him with interest. "If he became a Moslem, like my father, he could take more wives. Legally, I
mean. They say he's one of the richest men in England."

"I trust he hasn't suggested a role of that kind to you?"
Quint sounded properly detached.

"He didn't get very far. Of course, if Daddy found out,
he'd kill him. That's why I'm afraid for Peter."

"For Peter?"

"Poor, moonstruck Peter. The problem is, I'm engaged," she went on. "And I haven't told him." It was taking on the aspect of one of Vellu's legends.

"Well, I suppose *I* could mention it."

"No, no," she responded quickly.

Quint looked up to where patterns of blue sky shone through the trees. "Though in his eyes it mightn't be a problem, since your fiancé apparently isn't here."

"It is a problem, believe me, Mr. Quint. I am afraid. Please help me."

Quint's expression did not change, though from the sudden urgency in his companion's voice he knew she was getting to the point. "I like to know my enemy before I champion a cause. Perhaps you think me old-fashioned?"

She smiled. "God knows what you think me, luring you out here like this. And, to be honest, I don't really care. You see, I don't have much choice. I'm desperate." She said it quite simply, stating a fact.

"Do you know what I thought when I first saw you? I thought, Aha! Titian's *Gypsy Madonna:* resigned, yet lit by some inner conviction. Now I see I was wrong. You are his *St. Margaret,* scrambling distraught over rocks and serpents at the bottom of a cliff, clutching a crucifix."

"A crucifix!" She laughed. "No, not a crucifix. But escaping, yes. I have five days, Mr. Quint. Five days in which to get away."

"From your parents?"

"Parents? Jailers."

"What brought you here in the first place—to this island?"

"Ages ago my father was in the British army. From the way he talks, you'd think he'd been a general. They call him that at home: The General. That's how he knows Sir Frankie Jake . . . "

"But you, why did *you* come?"

"I didn't; I was brought. He knew, if he didn't, he might not see me again."

"And was he right?"

"Oh yes, he was right."

"And Sir Frankie, were he and your father close friends?"

"Not that I know of. At least *I'd* never heard of him, not that that means much."

Quint brought his palms together in a mosquito-squashing clap. "I will do what I can," he promised. "I have observed your father's vigilance on your behalf."

"Where we live, it's a brave woman who doesn't wear the veil."

"And he's absorbed some of that? Too long out of England, perhaps?"

"He hates England. He hasn't lived there for years."

"Since army days?"

"I think so."

"And—excuse me—your fiancé: how does he enter the picture?"

"It's he I'm running from. Mr. Quint, do you know, if I return, what will happen to me? I will be locked in a room with barred windows. Once a week I will be taken out and raped. That will be my life."

"Not a love match."

She looked at him coldly.

Quint drained his beer. "Very well. Tomorrow I shall hire a boat. We shall explore. If you don't object, I shall ask Peter."

She smiled. "You'll both be on Daddy's hit list."

They found Phoebe Cardew-Smythe at the third falls. She was in her element. She had quite forgotten lunch. "Oh, already?" She put the proffered box in her lap and squinted critically at the pad in front of her. She'd managed, Quint saw, to convey something of the leafy, grotto effect of the small rock pool, light filtering through the trees. In her picture a young man with wild hair squatted in the foreground, wearing little more than an unsheathed blade stuck through a band at the waist. Quint looked around. The man, if he'd been there at all, was gone.

"I'm afraid I gave your father short shrift just now," Phoebe said to Leila, dabbing at the painting. "But there are seven falls, aren't there? I told him to go and find his own. The boy was marvelous. He had a rather large knife which I think finally did the trick." She looked up. "Oh, he's gone. I meant to give him something. Don't know how I'd have managed to scramble up here on my own. I gathered Mr. Craddock was looking for you. He had that sallow youth in tow. Peter something."

"Daddy—and Peter Forbes?" Leila frowned. "Together?"

When the three of them rejoined the main group, Quint was aware of changes in the way people looked at him. Craddock, who'd heretofore scarcely acknowledged his existence, seeped hostility like an open sewer. So did the Turk, his wife. Miller and Sneed, beery and benign, encompassed him in a sort of conspiratorially approving leer. Peter strained hard at nonchalance. Cardew-Smythe dithered over the children, one of whom had gashed her knee, now swathed in a bloody handkerchief. Lady Jake, eyes darting mischievously, most likely was savoring the juicy tales she would tell, while Sir Frankie . . . Sir Frankie was his enigmatic self.

On the wearying walk back to the road, Quint heard a voice close behind him: "Thanks, pal. Thanks a lot." It was Peter.

"On the contrary,"—though the path was narrow Quint drew him alongside,—"it worked like a charm. Alliances, my friend, alliances. You and the bull Craddock now share an enemy: myself. Good heavens, man, you're speaking to each other. You should have seen Leila's face when she heard that. The next best thing to being friends is sharing enemies."

"I must say, he's not quite the ogre I imagined," Peter stammered.

"We'll see about that tomorrow."

"Tomorrow?"

"When we play truant. You and Miss Craddock—alas, accompanied by yours truly. Chaperon, from the French word for 'hood.' I will protect you so you can play."

Peter looked at him unbelievingly for a second, then clapped him heartily on the back.

"By the way," Quint added innocently. "I don't suppose you ran across an American anthropologist at the Inn? Before I arrived, it would have been."

Peter, equally innocently, stared back. "Why? Have you lost one?"

CHAPTER SIX

"I do not like it," Vellu observed for the third time. In the face of Quint's self-absorbed silence, he added: "Such goings on." Then, as if to underline his point, he beeped furiously at a water buffalo that was hogging the road. They were heading back to the Inn. The bus was some way behind. "That person who came this morning from Perlis, with woman; queer fish. You noticed, perhaps, Mr. Quint?"

"Perlis?"

"Mainland. Came on ferry from mainland: the man, and the woman in *purdah*."

"Two persons from Perlis, one in *purdah*," Quint repeated. "Well, well." *Queer fish,* he thought absentmindedly, hadn't Cardew-Smythe used those very words? "So they came over on the morning ferry? Took their time getting up from the jetty."

"Precisely, Mr. Quint. You are not unobservant. Which is why you must be very careful. To be noticed noticing, it is unfortunate."

Quint abandoned the conundrum he had been wrestling with and switched his full attention to the man beside him. "And how are the destinies of these persons entwined with ours?"

"Very well put. Very poetic. You see, it is like this, Mr.

Quint. On way to Inn, this man stopped at bank to change money. Thai *baht* to Malaysian *ringgit*." He added, apologetically, "Nephew's wife's sister is teller."

"Can you blame him? The exchange rate at the Inn is highway robbery."

"Exchange rate is not point, Mr. Quint. Point is, this man is coming from *Thailand* . . . " He paused, letting the sentence dangle suggestively.

"So did I."

"Ah, but by plane, via Penang." He held up an admonitory finger. "This person did not arrive by plane." He looked at Quint as a teacher looks at a slow child—coaxingly.

Quint made an effort. "I know. You have just said: he came on the morning ferry."

"Sometimes, Mr. Quint—please forgive me—I wonder if you are greenhorn or very cagey type, indeed. For your own sake, I hope the latter."

"One way or the other, you must bear with me, Vellu. What exactly are you trying to say?"

"As you are perhaps well aware, Thailand is the base of aforementioned insurgent leader, Ah Sook. As is also well-known, Americans are helping Thai government stamp out opium trade. Why, I say to myself, should there not be white men also helping insurgents who ply trade? But," he ended piously, "it is no concern of mine."

Quint shrugged. "Nor mine."

They passed a colorful Hindu temple set back among palms. Then Vellu tried again: "Much money, he is cashing."

"An unpleasant character, I grant you."

"Also, I must tell you frankly, Mr. Quint, I have heard something quite perplexing about the American: no name, no identity, no one enquires after body."

Quint was impressed. "Your spies are everywhere, Vellu."

"Marriages." He gestured helplessly. "It so happens I have cousin in Penang whose daughter is betrothed to clerk in police morgue."

"Refresh my memory." Quint massaged his beard. "When exactly did our anthropologist arrive on the island?"

"Three weeks, one month ago."

"Well before this British group."

"They are here only day or two."

"Lady Jake mentioned this morning that on the day she arrived an American came to the Inn. They talked, or more likely she did, and the American hasn't been seen since. Which is understandable, except how many Americans are there on the island? He visits the Inn, then he dies; that poor fisherman, he goes there and he dies. Coincidence?"

Vellu took both hands off the wheel and his voice rose in a wail, "And I, Vellu, I, too, will die!" The car careened across the road as if bent on fulfilling the prophesy. No damage was done, except to Quint's nerves, but the shock sobered Vellu. "I am not like you, Mr. Quint: here today, tomorrow going away. Family is here, home is here, whole livelihood is here. Where can I go?"

"You are afraid, Vellu." Quint looked probingly at him. "Why?"

"I am afraid, Mr. Quint, like the ant is afraid when the

river floods its banks and the path through the jungle shifts and runs by my anthill and rumble of every footstep threatens to obliterate me."

"What has caused this flood?"

"In the north, as you know, on Thai-Burma border, war rages against opium. They are bombing the forest hideouts and the factories. New groundwork must be laid, or so it is said. Why not here in the south, along this wild coast, where rebels lie in wait preparing for days of power denied them many years ago by British soldiers?"

"And Ah Sook—this is why he has come?"

Vellu's eyes opened wide. "Why else? Many hiding places, many caves in these islands, Mr. Quint. In old days, whole fleets of *perahus* vanished like magic before the guns of British men-of-war." He flapped an accusing hand at Quint, "Or why would American anthropologist come looking for so-called Sea Gypsies, which, as is well known, died out many years ago except for tourist purposes. Why is going by canoe to various places, writing, writing in a book?"

"A book? A book?" Quint brightened. "And what became of that book?"

"Now you are asking," Vellu scolded, as if he had been expecting this question. "Nothing is left. No trace."

"Had he a radio? Or transmitter?"

"Believe me. Nothing to arouse suspicion."

"Then you're guessing?"

"Mr. Quint, elephant does not walk around with label. But it is still elephant."

Quint had a hunch this was meant for him personally. "That helicopter; when did it first appear? Before the American died, or after?"

Vellu considered. "One day before."

The road from Seven Falls met the road from the airstrip at a T-junction near the jetty end of town. As Vellu slowed to turn left, Quint noticed the Chinese group from the Inn milling about outside what looked like a bicycle rental and repair shop. "Rattletraps," Vellu pointed scornfully. "Whole time break down." The Chinese, however, seemed to have enjoyed a good workout. It was, Quint noted, a Chinese shop.

They passed the toy mosque. Vellu pointed out a sprawling yellowed bungalow standing forlornly among the palms. "Jap headquarters in the war; then Security HQ; now hippie headquarters." He laughed. "Government Rest House, very cheap. Down there," he waved an arm dramatically in the opposite direction, "*kampong.*"

Quint looked with interest. A narrow side road disappeared into the greenery past some rickety-looking bamboo scaffolding. Somewhere down there the anthropologist had lived. He should investigate; but not now, not with Vellu. The Malay captain, perhaps, if he could catch him sober. At any rate not before he'd had a private word or two with Gwendy Jake.

Quint poured himself a second cup of tea he had ordered, adding sugar and a squeeze of lime. Four o'clock tea on his balcony. A hot drink to keep cool. One of the more salutary—he decided—of British colonial hand-me-downs. Strange people, he mused, the British. He had never really grasped them, even after all those years at school in their country. Take Cardew-Smythe, officer and gentleman, so deeply embarrassed when caught in a ridiculous lie most grown men would have sloughed off, and, Quint had a feeling, lying again to cover the lie. What was it Phoebe had said: *Chinese much more Ian's cup of tea.* He sipped his, thoughtfully. *He should have been a tour guide, in Venice.* Schedules. Quint's travel agent didn't like them. She had made that clear enough: the future could not be neatly typed out and Xeroxed. Too many variables. Go with the flow. All very well, but the flow was leading him into a time-consuming investigation of a murder, no, three murders.

Sounds from above betokened the arrival on their balcony of his neighbors—the boys, as Leila called them. Bigoted, besotted, British to the bone. How their forefathers had amassed their dazzling empire was beyond Quint. The sheer mechanics of the operation. Sleight of hand, he suspected. Only now the magic had worn threadbare. A loud pop sounded, like an exploding champagne cork. Quint looked up in time to see a man on the grass beyond the hibiscus keel over, clutching his side.

"Bullseye. Got 'im in the balls!" Sneed shrieked overhead with obscene adolescent glee.

"Teach the sod." Like a hungover foghorn, Miller's voice boomed out across the landscape. The dining-room captain—for it *was* he—jumped up, grinning. Quint heard the clink of glasses. So it *was* a cork. On the lawn the captain danced and weaved and grinned and finally, to three cheers from above, collapsed again, before staggering off to his quarters. What fun they're all having, Quint thought.

"Bloody 'ell!" the voice of Miller boomed out and the fun stopped. "If it's Sir Effing Eff tell him to eff off."

Since the room phones were out of order—permanently, Quint suspected—he guessed there was someone at their door.

The new voice was unmistakeable, etched on Quint's eardrums since he'd heard it at the desk that morning: it was like the sawing of a particularly stubborn plank, or the braying of an ass in a field. "Could'a bowled me over, you could. The guv'ner's come over gugga in his dotage, I says to myself. What's he want hobnobbin' with a brace of criminals the likes of you two? Answer me that now."

"Speak for yourself, Stinki, and drink up," Sneed said. "As to the criminal element, when was he ever choosy?" They laughed.

"Old Stinki never did catch on to much back in them days," Miller jeered. "Ay, Stinki Padinki?"

"Remember at Rose's that time, Mill? 'Come an' get it!' I can see old Milly saying it now, and Stinki standing there like a blooming statue. Whatcher say, Stinki? Drink up now."

"Carved in stone," Miller embellished, "except for a certain vital organ."

"Cut it out." Briscoe had to shout to be heard over the hoots of mirth. "You're looking at the all-new model here. Changed my name and changed my nature. Briscoe it is now, by your leave." He spelled it, "B–R–I–S–C–O–E."

"Oh, Mister Posh, is it? Briscoe. What kind of a name is that?"

"Me muvver's, that's what. Welsh, it is. A good name. Done me proud."

"Got a leek in the goulash, or whatever them Poles eat, ay, Padinki?"

"Right, Miller. And you know what you can do with it."

"Oh, oh. Down boy. Don't get vicious now."

"Hey, Milly," Sneed crowed. "Get this: 'Nicholas Briscoe, Esquire. Tupperware representative for East Surrey. 2, The Warren, Purley.' He made the big time, this kid. How about *Sir* Nicholas, while you're at it?"

"Always said he'd go far, didn't I?"

"A credit to the company."

"Lay off, you guys. Don't mess wiv me. I got a nice little surprise package that I wouldn't want to keep all to myself, now would I?"

"Three guesses, Mill," Sneed sang out. "I say a Tupperware tea set."

Miller said, "Save that for Mildew. The Mrs.'ll go for it."

"Go on wiv you. Mildew? Not here? Our Mildew-Smooth."

"The very same. An' not just him. Here's the bad news: Lance-corporal Craddock. Oh, and Forby's son. Forby's gone, Stinki. Forby is no more."

"Gone where?"

"Kicked it, yer blitherin' idiot."

"Good old Forby," Briscoe said sadly. "Hey, hang on, that's it. Easy patrol! That's the lot of us."

"You know, Stinki, one thing I always admired in you,"—it was Miller—"quick on the uptake. Hasn't lost his touch, has he, Sneedy?"

"What's he playing at, then, the gov'ner? What's it all about?" Alarm crept into Briscoe's voice.

"Just a little—reunion, shall we say, Sneedy?"

"Almost gave up on old Stinki, didn't we?" Sneed said. "Thought he'd missed the boat."

"Now the party can begin. More bubbly?" Miller became the genial host, a part which curiously seemed to suit him, perhaps because he resembled Quint's idea of the florid British publican.

After a slight pause, Briscoe said, "Yeah, well, you know how it is. The business and one thing and another."

"Doin' pretty well for yourself, are you?" Sneed managed to blend envy and disbelief.

"Can't complain, can I."

"Tupperware, ay?"

"Yeah, well, that's one string to the bow, so to speak." He sounded a little edgy.

"2, The Warren, Purley. Been breedin' little Stinkis, then Padinki?" Sneed cackled. "A regular production line, I'll bet. Once they get the hang of it in the warren, there's no end in sight."

"What about you, Sneed? Been keeping out of the slammer, 'ave we? Or they let you out special? Gov'ner stand bail, did he?"

"'Ere, 'owd j'know?"

It was Briscoe's turn to crow. "Shall we say, an educated guess?"

"Stow it, mates." Miller refereed. "Thirty bleedin' years. Blimey. Well, here's to 'em."

"I'll say this," Briscoe added, "I'm a lot less wet behind the you know what than I was then." A tepid silence followed this truism. Briscoe went on, "Reckon he knows a thing or two, the gov. Some spot. How j' get a sea view, then?"

"Put you at the back, did they, Stinki? Heh, heh. Just gotta rate, my boy; show 'em who's boss. Else they're all over you, like them jungle leeches, remember? Blood-sucking Chinks. It ain't like it was, Stinki-me-boy, it ain't like it was."

Another silence while this mournful commentary sank in. Then Briscoe said, "Which reminds me, party's at my place tonight. And believe you me, you won't miss the view."

"You an' your little surprises, eh, Stinki?" Miller oozed patronage. "Well, it so happens that tonight we have a prior engagement. Too bad, eh Sneedy?"

"Tomorrow is another day." A conciliatory note from Sneed.

"Tell yer what. Ask Mildew. Give 'im a break from those kids, poor sod." Miller's suggestion.

"Hitched, is he?"

"Good and proper."

"Shackled."

"Never was one for the three W's, not our Mildew," Briscoe reflected.

"What's that?" It was bait, and Miller swallowed it.

"Wine, Women and you know What."

Sneed audibly perked up: "*That* kind of party."

"What'd yer think? A Tupperware party?"

"Go ahead, Sneed," Miller taunted. "Enjoy yourself. Jitterbug and orange crush; smoochy-woochy in the stalls. Ducktails and drainpipes. Just like old times."

"Like I said, Miller, when you weren't listening: Nick Briscoe ain't Stinki Padinki."

"New, improved, eh?"

"New, yeh. Improved? Debatable."

"Debatable! Hear that, Sneed? His words fit like white

gloves, this one. Better watch your step unless you want a lorryload of Tupperware landing in your lap."

"Well, I ain't exactly come all this way for a tan, Miller, I'll grant you that. We do have sunlamps in Purley."

"Oh we do, do we? Then what 'ave you come for?" It was a challenge.

"Maybe a spot of business, maybe a spot of pleasure. By the by, is our Gwendy along?"

"Lady Gwendoline Jake, and never lets you forget it," Sneed sniffed. "With holes in her soles from running to catch up with her mouth." He giggled in his oddly extracorporeal way. "Christ, I can still see it: Stinki standing there and old Milly here singing out, 'Come an' get it!' and Stinki . . . " He didn't finish, he was giggling so hard.

Quint consulted his watch. He must not keep her ladyship waiting.

CHAPTER SEVEN

The screen from last night's film had not yet been dismantled. Perhaps it would be used again tonight. The sun, streaming in from the right, infused it with the brief, reddish endglow of a tropical day. Quint—from the depths of a rattan armchair ringed by potted palms—saw Gwendy Jake coming at him like a heat-seeking missile with radar-lock on his solar plexus, and wondered when she'd last received an *invitation* to talk. A bit like giving a chocoholic carte blanche at Suchard's. Had it been four days ago from a tall American anthropologist enjoying one last full day on earth?

"Madame, je vous en prie." Quint sprang to his feet and pulled out a chair with an uncharacteristic flourish. French, though not his native tongue, was one he felt comfortable in; he guessed that a little Gallic flair might go a long way with her ladyship.

"Oh, mercy Monsieur," she tittered, and behind her Quint blanched for the murdered words.

"It is so charming of Madame to consent to join me for—how do you say—the down-sunner." He prolonged the act.

"Oh," she squealed delightedly, patting his arm, "Sundowner, Monsieur Quint. Sun-downer. But never mind. Oh, wait till I tell Sir Frankie."

"The noble knight will be joining us, I trust?"

"I'm afraid he's partial to a last dip before supper. Very regular in his habits, he is." She imitated a breast stroke, in case there was any doubt. There wasn't; it was precisely because he had seen Sir Frankie at the pool that Quint had sent his note to their room. A waiter appeared and took orders for drinks.

"Not like the old days." She fixed the retreating back with a stare, part wistful, part peeved. "One does miss the get-up: tarboosh and all. It's all you can do to squeeze a drop of service out of these new boys. And then they're doing you a favor. Only this morning . . . " She was off and running. Quint observed her face under its ever-present fluffy orange topping, the contours reminding him of the small, trussed goat cheeses that shepherds brought down in fall from the high mountain pastures of his erstwhile kingdom. The whole effect, with the headdress—or was it a wig?—would have looked fine stuck up in a melon field, keeping the birds at bay.

He leaned forward: "So you were in these parts before?"

"Beg pardon?" Gwendy Jake seemed surprised at the question, or perhaps it was because Quint had dared to interrupt.

"Were you out here before?" He had no intention of listening indefinitely to complaints against maids, waiters, garden boys, trishaw operators, cooks, the front desk and how the manager's expansive family hogged the best table at mealtimes.

"But that's why we're here now. Surely I mentioned . . . I was married out here. Twice, almost." She stopped abruptly.

Quint waited for the words to flow again, marveling at the power of the thought that could stop that tongue dead in its tracks.

"Frankie wasn't my first love, you know. Of course, I was much younger than he was at the time."

At the time? Presumably the gap hadn't changed. Quint looked at his companion, trying to melt away the overlay of thirty years of life with Sir Frankie; failed, and looked away. The sun had turned the beach pinkish and the distant mangroves a dull copper. He thought of footsteps in the sand. Yes, Sir Frankie had outrun his wife. He wondered if they still shared a bed.

"Your family—they lived out here? Planters, perhaps, or officials?"

She shook her head. "Just me. I was a Red Cross girl, all starched and white; yellow curls, red lips. How their eyes lit up when we went by, swinging our hips, not caring tuppence for any six of them. See," she lowered her voice, "they'd only the darkies besides us, hadn't they?"

The waiter was coming back. Gwendy Jake half-turned in her chair, the better to observe him, as if, at any moment, he might swallow her drink. "The time they take: you'd think we had all night." Yes, Quint thought, it was the gin fizz she cared about. She sipped greedily. "I suppose you know they water the gin? Oh yes, caught 'em at it, I have."

"Cheers," Quint held up his sherry to the last burst of light. "Too bad about that American. Poor chap. I believe you said you'd met him?"

"American? What American? You meet so many these days. They're everywhere, with a finger in every pie. You know what one said to me in Singapore?—I believe he was in fertilizers, or was it the Peace Corps: how much simpler it would be if we did away with governments and all became Americans; at the exact same time, like in countries where they switched over to drive on the right. You know what I replied?"

"But my dear Lady Jake," Quint inserted quickly, "the American you met here at the Inn. The anthropologist."

"*That* American. Why didn't you say so? Well, she was different. Quite prepared to listen for a change, instead of always knowing better. She actually agreed . . . "

"Excuse me, Lady Jake. One moment." Quint held up his hand like a policeman stopping traffic. "She? You are talking about a woman?"

"I am attempting to." She looked coldly at the hand and he dropped it. "Of course I remember her. It was the afternoon we arrived. She was sitting out on the terrace with her drink. I asked—by way of introduction—what it was. A martini, she said. Oh, I said, what a good idea; I think I'll have one, too. You better just taste it, she said, to make sure it's the way you like it. My British friends seem to like it with sweet vermouth; I had to stand over the bartender till he got it right: just a touch of the dry. Well, naturally, I knew all about that from when we were in Honolulu. So I ordered one just like hers."

Quint was hardly listening. How in the world . . . ? Why hadn't Vellu said anything? Surely he'd had the chance. He interrupted again. "Was she tall?"

"Tall?" Lady Jake jerked to another halt, annoyed.

"The anthropologist?"

"Yes. Oh yes." At least he had something right.

"And she *was* an anthropologist?" No more assumptions.

"Studying the natives, she said. Though what they think they can learn is beyond me. Why not study water buffaloes? At least they're good for something. Did you know, Mr. Quint, they have very sensitive skins, which is why they take mud baths?"

"Yes," Quint lied, "I did. What else did you talk about?"

"She seemed very interested in us. Out of politeness, I suppose."

"In you personally?"

"I, er . . . " she fumbled for words and picked up her drink. Quint could almost swear she blushed. "I'd had a little tiff with Sir Frankie. In the room, you know. I was that mad at him. I told her about it. A perfect stranger! I don't know what came over me. Ever so sympathetic, she was."

Quint tried to look sympathetic. He could imagine the glee with which Gwendy Jake had pounced on this listening stranger.

"And it wasn't as if he hadn't promised. Oh, he can be a naughty boy when he wants, can Frankie. Just the two of us, he says, back to Malaya for our thirtieth anniversary. And who goes and gets on the plane at KL? Kuala Lumpur, that is. That man Craddock. I could have killed Frankie. Of course I was all smiles and sweetness—quite my usual self—till I got 'im alone in the room. Then I let 'im 'ave it, fair and square." She began dropping h's in her excitement.

Quint motioned to the waiter for a second round. "So you told her all about Easy patrol?"

She shot him a shrewd glance. "You know about that?"

"Some kind of reunion, I gather?"

"Some kind of reunion," she repeated, changing the emphasis. "That's it in a nutshell. I don't know what got into his head. 'Frankie,' I says, 'you're plumb crazy. What are you trying to prove now?' Always up to something, he is. You'd think after his accolade from Her Majesty he'd have let well alone." She craned her neck and looked towards the pool where a few figures still hovered; it was too dark to make out who.

"Did she seem particularly interested in Easy patrol?"

"Wanted to know all about the old days, she did. Made a big thing about wanting to meet Sir Frankie. He was four years out here, see, after Palestine. Of course I couldn't let her, not then and there, not after our little tiff; I was sure we'd see her again. It's a small enough island, isn't it? Funny thing, though, I was just thinking this afternoon, we haven't."

"Not so funny, I'm afraid." Quint watched the puffy little features carefully. "She's dead. She was in a boat which capsized."

"Oh, how dreadful." Gwendy Jake screwed up her face in horror; then announced loudly, "What a perfectly dreadful country." The waiter placed fresh drinks on the table and backed away. This time she hardly seemed to notice him.

Quint said: "Did the American tell you her name?"

"Her name?" Gwendy's eyes seemed smudged and stupid. She had already gulped half her drink. "No, I don't even know her name."

"How did she look, besides tall?"

"Ordinary. Mousy hair, bit on the long side. No make-up. So many don't these days, do they? She had on one of those wrap-around skirts, batik, in a dark brown. I admired it. The dye was made from human blood, she said. Can you imagine? Oh, and she'd sprained her wrist. Fancy gallivanting about in a boat with a sprained wrist!" The Red Cross persona was surfacing.

"So her arm was in a sling?"

"No." Gwendy sounded disapproving. "Of course I offered to bind it up—a professional job. Never travel without my medical bag; not in these parts." She leaned across, confidingly: "You wouldn't catch me dead in one of their so-called hospitals. Germ traps, that's all they are."

Quint said quickly, "But she declined your offer."

"Be alive today, she would, if she'd listened to me." She shook her head. "That's the trouble with them . . . "

"How old did you think she was?"

"Hard to say. Twenty-eight. Give or take."

"And how did it come up—the sprain?"

"There wasn't any swelling, not that I could see. That was the funny thing."

"I mean, how did the *subject* come up?"

Gwendy Jake thought for a moment, then gave a little squeal, clapping her hands to her head. Her fingers probed the orange fur. "Am I off my rocker? Her name. I must have put it on the card."

"What card?"

"The picture postcard. That's how it came up. She couldn't write too well on account of the sprain, she said. It was her right hand, so she must have been right-handed. She asked me if I'd mind. Had it all ready with a stamp. So I jotted down what she said. It reminded

me . . . " Quint looked into eyes suddenly full of tears.
"Oh, never mind." She fished in her bag for a frilly
handkerchief. "Something, isn't it, the things that stay
with you?"

Quint agreed that it was.

"Now what was that name?" she fussed.

"And the things that don't."

"It's on the tip of my tongue."

"The message—do you recall that?"

"Oh, the usual: wish you were here; lovely to see you. It
was care of the E & O, George Town, Penang. Some
friend or other from home."

"The E & O?" Quint asked, puzzled.

"Eastern and Oriental. Hotel. Though don't ask me
why it's called that. Very grand. We stayed there on our
honeymoon, Frankie and me. We're going to stay a night
on the way back. It won't be what it was, of course, but
auld lang syne, you know. To be honest," she tittered,
covering her mouth with the hanky, "the beds squeaked
even then. How she chuckled when I told her that."

It seemed clear to Quint that the American had got a
wide range of information out of Gwendy Jake—from the
presence of Easy patrol on the island to the state of the
beds at the E & O Hotel in George Town, thirty years
ago. But why this business of the sprain? Far from
rejoicing at finding a trained nurse, she had brushed off
the offer of professional care. Obviously there was no
sprain, not so much as a swelling. Awkward, for her, that
Gwendy was a nurse. Conclusion: the sprain was a device
to have Gwendy write that card. But why not write it herself? Here Quint drew a blank. It was all sheer specula-
tion. "The card; you mentioned it was stamped."

"Yes, I remember thinking what a good idea that was."

"To stick a stamp on a card?"

"To have it all ready to go."

"Of course. And the name—the name on the card—it wasn't by any chance—Gwendoline?"

"But that's me," Gwendy Jake declared.

"Or Gwen? Or any variant thereof?"

"I'd have remembered, wouldn't I?"

"Or even plain *G*?"

"*G*," she repeated. "How clever of you. I asked her what to put and she said, *G*. I remember because I waited, without writing it down. I mean Americans are always saying gee, aren't they? Yes, I suppose her name began with *G*. Funny I didn't remember."

"And you posted it, or did she?"

"She left it with me to post. But as it happened, she could have saved herself the stamp after all. Some people were checking out; going straight to the E & O. They took it."

"That same afternoon?"

"Next day."

The day Quint had arrived. They must have been among the group waiting at the airstrip. Body and postcard traveling together. But even if—as Vellu had implied—the anthropologist wasn't all she seemed—it couldn't have been her card that had brought the helicopter snooping around. The helicopter had come the day before.

"Living alone, unprotected," Gwendy Jake was twittering on, "I can't say I didn't warn her. I did. I said . . . "

"She was in a *kampong*. People all around. Friends."

"That's what I'm saying, Mr. Quint. One minute they're

all smiles—'Yes, *tuan,* no *tuan,* three bags full, *tuan'*— next they're stabbing you in the back with their nasty little twisty swords. Believe me. I know." Her face was grey and rancorous in the fading light.

"Of all you told the American, what seemed to you to intrigue her most?"

Gwendy Jake's mouth shut tight. She looked at Quint as if suspecting, for the first time, that his questions were not wholly born of idle curiosity. Then she finished her drink. Inwardly he cursed his eagerness. Answers, from now on, would not come cheap.

"Oh, look at the time!" Gwendy Jake jumped up. "I must change for dinner. Won't you join us, Mr. Quint? Sir Frankie would insist."

How could he refuse?

CHAPTER EIGHT

S ir Frankie chewed his food as if eating was an exercise prescribed by physiotherapists for the jaws. He chewed rhythmically with the abstract absorption of a cow, more attentive to the comings and goings on the fringes of his vision than to his companions at table.

They were in the Inn's expensive restaurant, so-called because it was air-conditioned, had a glossy menu and its own (sober) captain. As to the food, as far as Quint could tell little besides the language had changed: instead of Fish Masak Lemak, there was White Pomfret Almandine. The expensive restaurant had no view, being directly behind the bar, which opened onto the terrace. But the enclosing glass and chilling hum kept out the noise of a Hammond organ caressed by an individual in a tartan cap who also crooned, in Quint's mind amply justifying the increase in price.

Gwendy Jake seemed in no hurry to reopen the topic of the American, and it wasn't until dessert, while she was absorbed in a choice between the rival claims of banana pancakes and sago pudding, that Quint managed to ask her husband whether he had business in the East or was purely here for pleasure.

In whatever realm Sir Frankie's thoughts dwelt, Quint couldn't help feeling that he, Quint, hardly existed and certainly did not matter. As he probed the other man's world, he fully expected a rebuff. He was surprised when Sir Frankie growled more or less pleasantly, "The gambling instinct knows no boundaries, Quint. It crops up everywhere. What odds would you give, for instance, on Lady Luck ending up with the sago?"

Presumably he meant his wife. "But this is hardly fair," Quint protested. "You know her tastes. I don't."

"Then your money's on the pancakes?"

"I abstain."

Sir Frankie laughed. "You're no bookie's friend, lad. Which means no friend o' mine." His laughter had a disturbing rootlessness about it.

"You're in the gambling business."

"Betting, we call it. More wholesome. Jake's Betting Parlours. When were you last in England, lad?"

"Some time ago."

"I'll say. More parlours than churches there now." The line pleased him: "More parlours than ruddy churches."

In the end Gwendy Jake forswore dessert altogether and called for a gin fizz, her third, not counting the two upstairs. "What's that about churches, my sweet?" She turned to Quint. "He wouldn't know the inside of a church if it was St. Paul's Cathedral and Westminster Abbey rolled into one. Hasn't darkened a church door since . . . " She stopped to think.

"The wedding?" Quint suggested.

Gwendy tilted her head back and cackled so that people at the next table whispered and Quint feared for the orange headdress. "Hitched over the counter, we were. They couldn't wait to see the back of us." She turned on Quint. "Wanted it done proper, I did. A church, bridesmaids, a lace veil. No time for the banns, they said. Out. They wanted us out. If it wasn't one thing, it'd have been another."

Sir Frankie had picked up the menu and was studying it intently. Embarrassed, Quint thought. "What'll it be, then: coffee, tea, something stronger? Hell's teeth," he patted the pocket of his sports shirt, "I forgot my Postum."

Gwendy stood up, sat down, stood up. Clutching her purse, she stayed up. Quint quickly rose, pulling out her chair. "Back in a jiff." She smiled graciously as if he'd asked her to dance. They watched her walk carefully away.

From his pocket Jake pulled a small orange packet and tossed it on the table. The Postum. "Got her knickers in a twist over sommat, has our Gwendy."

Quint smiled noncommitally. "Things were a little bit hectic, do I gather, at the time of the wedding?"

"Hectic? That's good. I like that. You have considerable command of our language, Mr. Quint, if I may say so."

Quint persisted: "But why come back? Why spend your anniversary here? Why? When the years have brought you success beyond that allotted most men?"

"Allotted? Allotted? Now there I must take issue. Success is not doled out like pigfood, Mr. Quint. What line are *you* in, may I ask?"

"I teach government at the moment."

"Government. There you are: a bloody milkmaid. The business of other people's business. Well, keep your fingers out of mine, if you don't mind." He drummed his fingers on the table. "What else she tell you, lad?"

"Easy patrol."

"What about it?"

"She was—ah—concerned to find them all here; a little taken aback."

"Taken aback, ay?" His ferret face registered indifference.

"Memories."

"Memories, ay?"

"So why bring her back?" Quint wouldn't let it go. He wanted a reaction. "Why bring them all back?" Through the glass he saw Gwendy returning. Jake saw her too.

"Because I pay my debts, Quint. I pay my debts. But government wouldn't know about that."

This time they both rose. It was Sir Frankie who stood behind his wife's chair 'like a gentleman.' "Oh, Mr. Quint, you must spend more time with us," she teased. "Frankie's picking up new tricks." She beamed at Quint, who suddenly became engrossed in a search for his napkin. "He must, mustn't he, sweet?"

"Yes, my nymph. Whatever you say."

Quint squirmed. He had made an enemy: Sir Frankie Jake of Jake's Betting Parlours.

A little later, as they were leaving, a restraining hand grasped Quint's elbow. "Don't meddle. There's a good lad." Sir Frankie's lips hardly moved; his eyes followed his wife, who had preceded them through the door. The grip relaxed, then tightened again: "In a day or two, it'll all be over. We'll go our separate ways. Whatever your game is, laddie, lay off."

That's all very well, Quint felt like protesting as Sir Frankie shepherded him out, but three people are dead.

Six or seven patrons sat at the bar and slouched around low tables over drinks. Craddock, Quint observed, was in his usual end spot. At the electric organ, the tartan-topped Malay was committing mayhem. Quint walked straight through the bar onto the terrace, trying to block out the sound. In what sublime synthesis would the silvery trompeta of a good Spanish organ have blended with these moonlit islands, he thought. A power cut was too much to hope for. Out of the corner of his eye he saw, making a rare mealtime appearance, Miller and Sneed, and with them—here the temptation to stop almost overcame him—was a slight, cherubic man with a slicked-back ducktail wearing a burgundy jacket of a shiny material reaching almost to his knees. Briscoe.

Instead of continuing down the steps to the water, Quint branched left past the deserted, but still lit, swimming pool. The frustrations of dinner had induced in him the need to walk. As he strolled across the grass, he was forced to admit that he was hooked: no longer could he pretend that what he was doing was an imposition. He was old enough to know that things generally happen to people because people are open to them happening. And Quint was what they called in Fort Wayne—his place of exile in the New World—'a sucker for a good mystery.' Well, here were two: three deaths by violence involving an American anthropologist; and an ill-matched group of Britons gathered to commemorate an event which few if any of them seemed keen to recall.

The lawn sloped gently towards the bay, dotted here and there with sizable clumps of hibiscus and bougain-villea. By one of these Quint paused, intrigued by the sight of fireflies dancing round it in the moonlight. As he watched, he was seized with a strong sensation that he, in turn, was under observation. Afraid that by looking round he would trigger a response, human or animal, he might regret, he strolled on around the bushes; then, seeing a convenient gap, dived nimbly, noiselessly, in. On hands and knees inside the clump he found he had almost peripheral vision—at ground level. As he waited, pressed uncomfortably against a prickly branch, there stepped into the exact spot that, seconds before, his own feet had vacated, a pair of sneakers. Quint could almost have reached out and untied the laces.

The sneakers lingered for a time, motionless; then, some distance off, above the drone of the crickets, Quint thought he heard his name called. He glanced in the direction of the sound. When he looked back, the sneakers were gone.

A prudent few minutes later, Quint crawled out of his clump and dusted himself off. He seemed to be alone. Instead of returning to the Inn, from where the voice had shouted, he continued on down the slope till he reached the tennis court. Though the lights were off, someone, in defiance of a posted sign, had left the door in the high mesh fence open. Quint stepped inside and sat on a bench and spread his arms along its back. He looked at the stars and felt better. He drew strength from the stars, perhaps as from old friends who are always there. A mosquito buzzed in his ear. He slapped at it, then sat completely still again, listening.

Up at the Inn the movie must have started, because odd snatches of sound filtered through the trees. Closer, he heard the low babble of people going down the steps to the beach. The Chinese group, probably. He imagined them descending for their nightly prowl, and was thinking of taking a look when a rustle, directly behind him, made him turn sharply. Fingers, like live, pink eels, were poking through the mesh; behind them, the grinning countenance of Peter Forbes.

"Sorry if I scared you."

"You look sorry."

"You seemed lost to the world." He walked round till he came to the entrance. "Holding court, I suppose, for the legendary ghosts of Langkawi?"

"Why do you say that?"

"Oh, I don't know." He looked around. "This is a tennis court. And perhaps it was the way you were sitting; like a seigneur receiving tribute. I called to you earlier, but you didn't hear; at least you didn't answer."

"It is the prerogative of the seigneur not to hear."

"Actually, I wanted to say sorry—about this afternoon. Conduct unbecoming. Don't know what got into me."

Quint stood up.

"Tomorrow still on?"

"Vellu will be waiting. Seven-thirty, he insists, to catch the tide."

"Old man Craddock will probably grab a boat and come after us."

"If he finds out."

"He will."

"All the makings of a legend."

"He's going to be a blind, raving lunatic," Peter said, happily.

They reached the swimming pool in silence. The lights

were off now. A figure went scurrying up the beach path, head down, shoulders hunched. "Poor sod," Peter muttered. "Not another flipper!"

Quint asked: "What's the film tonight?" Looking up he could see the bright light of the projector, like a twinkling star.

"Some godawful production with Liza Minnelli. Where do they dredge them up?"

"Old?"

"As the hills."

"Thirty years?"

"Say fifteen. Within living memory."

"But *Tarzan of the Apes*: that's more like thirty years?"

Peter shot him a questioning glance. "If a day," he affirmed. "Prehistoric."

"*À demain,*" Quint smiled. "Don't miss your beauty sleep. You look pale."

"You, too. Take care."

"It must be the moonlight." Peter, Quint noted, was not wearing sneakers.

CHAPTER NINE

The bar was quiet now and almost empty. Craddock, at one end, silently nursed a drink. At the other, Tartan Top conversed in low tones with the bartender. On a stool at the very center sat one other person, looking for all the world to Quint like a heron hunched at the edge of a pond on a drizzly day: Gwendy Jake. Groping in the semi-darkness, Quint installed himself at one of the low tables against the wall. He was pretty sure his entrance had gone unnoticed. Gwendy seemed mesmerized by the long line of bottles back of the bar. As for Craddock, he gave no outward sign of life. Which was fine: for the moment Quint preferred just to sit.

Laughter rippled off to the side: a Malay joke, perhaps. Gwendy Jake, lips moving soundlessly, turned now to the left, now to the right, as if engrossed in some private ceremonial. What stirred in that gin-soaked brain, Quint wondered. A face—the manager's?—looked in and withdrew. Gwendy turned her head towards Craddock. "Stop it," she said, clearly enough. "Don't let him." Then she looked back at the bottles. "Murder." But only Quint paid any attention. "Pleased ta meet ya . . . he's a good man . . . tea in bed on Christmas morning . . . " She began to sob.

How it happened was beyond Quint, but Gwendy suddenly flopped forward off her stool and onto the bar it-self. The stool fell with a clatter and Quint, afraid Gwendy was going down with it, sprang to catch her. She didn't. She stayed on the bar, on her stomach, legs and arms flailing like a child learning to swim. Her objective seemed to be Craddock. One of her feet caught a water pitcher and sent it flying; a row of glasses went down like ninepins, and the two Malays, till now observers, moved into action. One grabbed her legs, the other her arms, and, with a dispatch that suggested years of experience lifting old ladies off bars, subdued the kicking bundle. In the struggle, Gwendy's fluffy headpiece tipped forward and hung crazily over her brow, somehow suggesting to Quint a debauched Roman emperor.

All the while Craddock had watched, fingers twined around his beer glass, as if something mildly boring was playing on television. "You know what they say," he pronounced, when the Malays had departed with their burden; he spoke slowly, sounding even a little pleased with himself; "Once a sergeant-major, always a sergeant-major." The words rolled clumsily off his tongue.

Quint upended the fallen stool and sat on it. Craddock went on: "I wanted her, but he took her." He reached into his shirt pocket, brought out a lighter, and flicked it on. Holding the flame to eye-level, he watched it—Quint thought—regretfully. "Ever felt a coconut, Quint? There's a soft spot you could shove your pinkie through. Am I right? That's what I do: find the spot."

"I see," said Quint, untruthfully.

"I'd have done us a favor, the whole bloody lot of us, if I'd set light to that thing she wears on her head all the time. Wouldn't show herself without it, would she?"

Quint maintained a discreet silence.

"You never saw anything like that, not in the old days. Red golden tresses, she had. Sublime. Worth the price of a drink just to run your hand through." He leaned forward, confidentially. "But where are they? Not there now."

"Tucked up, perhaps. Inside."

Craddock shook his head. Carefully he repositioned his glass. "If you knew our Gwendy, like I knew our Gwendy, you wouldn't say a silly thing like that. People don't change. They may look different, talk different, call themselves some other name, but at some point or other, early on, they get set."

"Thirty years is a long time." Quint took the offensive: "It intrigues me that a man like yourself—a man with his own life, his own concerns—comes all this way, to this place. After thirty years."

"Intrigues you, does it?" Craddock seemed amused. He drained his glass and held it up for more. "I had the best reason in the world," he said. "But I only found out what it was after I got here."

Quint eyed him sceptically.

"Another Tiger, you brown bastard." The bartender, who had returned alone and was repairing the damage Gwendy had left in her wake, approached. Craddock stared at him: "What did you do with her, you dirty bugger?"

"We carried her to her room," the man replied, appending a sullen, "sir."

"And?" Craddock demanded.

"Left her." He backed away. "Sir."

Craddock laughed coarsely and filled his glass. "The

89

noble knight," he attempted old-fashioned obeisance with his left hand, "You know the one I mean? The noble knight did me the greatest favor any man can do another. He gave his life for mine. He put his head in the noose meant for me." He fingered his neck. "So you see, I owe the bastard. I'd go to the north pole for him, wouldn't I?"

Craddock's face glowed purple in the dim light, and Quint saw that what he'd taken before for indifference might more accurately be described as incapacity. He had the inert look of jugged hare. How much beer, Quint wondered, over how long a time, did it take to achieve this effect? Perhaps, in whatever sandy sultanate this man spun out his days wielding whatever power he wielded, some inner demon drove him to imbibe alone night after night.

The bartender brought a Benedictine for Quint which, though unasked for, he'd ordered on a previous occasion. So Gwendy of the Golden Tresses had been going out with Corporal Craddock, but had married Sergeant-major Jake. It surprised him that, attractive as she'd apparently been, she hadn't aimed higher; an officer, for instance. Cardew-Smythe hadn't said, 'Our Gwendy.' Not yet.

"To the eternal triangle." Quint touched the liqueur to his lips. "With a twist: the winner is the loser. Or so you imply."

"Triangle, my arse." Craddock gulped some Tiger. "Hexagon, more like. We queued for the bitch. It so happened I was next."

"After Sir Frankie?"

Craddock shook his head. "He wasn't even in line. Frankie liked his bints brown, 'No spika de English';

probably still does. Was going steady, was our Frankie. Little number from the Sunshine Coffee Shop. Common knowledge." He paused to render an elaborate burp, then, glancing over his shoulder at the door, waved Quint up one more stool, which left only one between them.

The ex-corporal's yeasty breath felt like a warm poultice over Quint's nose and mouth. "Between you and me, the greedy bugger's got his eye on my Leila. Good as made an offer. Of course, I acted dumb. But if he touches one hair of that girl's head, let alone any other part of her anatomy, he's going to have to buy him a new face. And that goes for anyone." Craddock seized an empty bottle, smashed it against the bar, and held the jagged edge within an inch of Quint's vulnerable nose. "I'm talking brand new merchandise. None of your shopworn junk returnable in thirty days." The line of his mouth quivered—an attempt, perhaps, at a smile—"Or years."

Given the man's condition, the precision of the maneuver staggered Quint. "So the sergeant-major pulled rank?"

"Yes and no." The utter neutrality of Craddock's gaze caused Quint to wonder what new trick he was about to witness. "There was a man ahead of me. Corporal, too, as a matter of fact. Corporal Jenkins. To all intents and purposes, they were engaged. Our patrol was ambushed. He was shot. It was Jake's job to break the news. I guess she saw the red sash and hung on, because the next thing anybody heard were wedding bells."

"*Easy* patrol?"

"Easy patrol." Craddock managed to smile, but wearily, as if smiling was a pain. "Last damn patrol I ever went on. Praise be to Allah." He raised his glass. "They didn't

get off scot-free, either, the commie buggers. Soon as the
first shot sounded I opened up with the Sten. Pumped
the jungle full of lead." He swivelled to and fro on the
stool, cradling another empty. At last, Quint thought,
some honest-to-goodness war talk.

Odd that Cardew-Smythe—and to some extent Peter
Forbes through his father—linked Easy patrol with horror, mayhem and shame. Craddock made it sound routine, as if dealing death on patrol was no more murder
than swatting flies.

In his mind's eye Quint saw that jungle trail—the one
to Seven Falls would do as well—and heard the jabber of
bullets ripping the leaves to shreds. He glimpsed a face
under golden red curls, mouthing through Red Cross lips
the single word, *murder*. It could have been the Sten; it
could have been any gun—any stray, or not so stray,
bullet. Result: one dead corporal.

CHAPTER TEN

Quint moistened his lips with the Benedictine.

He had assumed that the reunion of Easy patrol was Jake's doing, that his wife knew nothing of what was in store, was angry when she found out. Had she, in fact, planned the whole thing? Was Gwendy Jake dealing revenge to seven men, any one of whom might have shot her lover, with the same detachment with which one deals cards at bridge?

Craddock was watching him. "Red gold," Quint said at last. "Like Flora."

"Flora?" Craddock's gaze intensified.

" 'Whom to see is to love.' The great Titian did a composite, it is said, of all his mistresses. The result: Flora, and masses of red gold hair; so much more becoming than the pale yellow, the *biondina* tint then the vogue in Venice. But I don't suppose Gwendy dyed her hair, not in those days."

"It was her imagination that was colored. Very entertaining, at times, our Gwendy; and at times . . . Well, take tonight." He tapped his head.

"What was it she said?"

"*Murder.*"

Yes, it would have looked odd had Craddock ignored

93

the accusation—if that's what it was. On the other hand, by drawing attention to it, perhaps he was saying, 'Look at me. I'm reacting normally. I don't know what she was talking about.' Then again, he could be reacting normally, in which case . . . Second guessing was a disease which, given its head, rendered babbling fools of sane men. Quint had seen it happen.

"More Tiger!" Craddock yelled. The bartender approached, bottle in hand. Craddock examined him: "Ever murdered anyone?"

"Beg pardon. Sir."

"You heard. Murdered anyone? You?"

The man's worried frown became a smile. "No, sir."

"Lying bugger." Craddock waved him away. He lit a match and sucked noisily at the stem of a pipe. "I suppose I've wiped out more buggers than bottles drunk tonight. Not one of 'em that didn't deserve to go. Hell, it was her own damn face in the mirror she was staring at."

"They must have been very much in love, Gwendy and this Corporal Jenkins."

"You'd have thought so, the way she carried on after . . . " he sucked and puffed, "after the event. For an hour, at least. No, I wouldn't have bet money on their going through with it. I'd have said the guy was . . . "—he removed the pipe from his mouth, looked at it, shoved it back again—" . . . not that interested in the copulative act, if you know what I mean. In fact, that may have been the attraction. 'Here's one cur not sniffing up my skirt.' She wouldn't stand for that. Not Gwendy. That's the type of girl she was."

"Might that explain Sir Frankie?"

"Uh, uh." Craddock shook his head. "That's one vice you couldn't pin on the son of a bitch."

"I didn't mean that. Just that you said he wasn't standing in line for her. Wouldn't that make him a prime target?"

"Oh, very good," Craddock conceded. "Very, very good."

Quint raised his glass. The English: he despaired. Here were the ingredients for a fiery saga of love and passion and revenge; and what did he find? Ambivalence, posturing, chicanery, and steely, stodgy self-interest. Behind him sounds of scraping and banging had begun; a cleaning man had entered and was hoisting chairs onto tables. The bartender was locking things away. Quint decided to be blunt. "So she really did believe it was one of you in the patrol who shot him?"

"Isn't it obvious?" Craddock banged out his hardly smoked pipe. "And between you and me, old fellow me lad, she still does." The cleaner was upending stools onto the bar.

"And you yourself," Quint asked. "What do you think?"

Gripping the bar with both hands, Craddock lowered himself off the stool. "Anything's possible." He added: "But it could have been an accident." They were both standing now, Craddock still holding the bar.

"He wasn't the first to go down, I take it?"

"It was dark in there. One second you're trotting along behind a phosphorescent blur which is the chap in front, the next all hell breaks loose. Who knows?"

"Where was he in order of march?"

"Jenkins? It was thirty years ago." The bartender waited near them. "It's all right, old boy," Craddock told him. "Not tonight. I've got the disgustingly sober Mr. Quint to give me a hand tonight." He grasped Quint's shoulder and together they made their way onto the terrace. It was deserted, tables cleared and waiting, glass tops gleaming. Craddock said: "They wouldn't let her see the body."

"I thought they were engaged."

"Not officially. Bolshie at times, armies; the British more than most. More scared of setting precedents than of the bloody foe."

"She was distressed?"

"Damn right. If she suspected foul play before, she'd have been bloody certain when they pulled that." He held onto a chair and the grip on Quint's shoulder eased. They stared out across the tranquil bay. The air shrilled to an insect band.

Quint said, "Sir Frankie was on that patrol . . . "

"And he didn't have to be, now, did he? Sergeant-majors have privileges, you know." Craddock seemed to lead him on.

"All the more reason . . . " Again, Quint didn't finish.

"The real poser is this: not why did she marry him, but why did he marry her." He turned on Quint. "Would *you* have married her?" He wanted an answer.

"In the ordinary course of events . . . "

"Exactly." Craddock laughed, or coughed, Quint wasn't sure which. "But we're speaking here of Sir Shithead, crème de la crème of all the shitheads. He smiles, there's a reason. He pees, there's a reason. I tell you." He rapped his ring finger on the table top, beating time to the words. "Frankie Jake is not as other men. Believe me, I know. I've thought and I've thought and I've thought about this. And there's only one reason I can come up with for this marriage."

"And that is?"

"Oh no." Again the coughing laughter, disturbing the night. "Oh no, you don't. I've waited thirty years, Quint. Before I leave this island I intend to know if I'm right. Ask me then." He belched. "You hear what he calls her? 'Lady Luck, My little fortune cookie'? Think about that."

Nymph, poppet, sweet; why not fortune cookie? "They seem very affectionate."

Craddock wheezed mirth.

"How did he get his start? He must have been well into his forties when he left the army, and I don't suppose a sergeant-major made that much."

"Which shows how much you know about sergeant-majors in the British Army." Craddock was enjoying himself. "Though he did make a finer art out of it than most. They're not all millionaires." The chair jerked under his weight and a lizard which had been creeping closer, feeding on ants that were feeding on the crumbs from supper, jumped. "No." He shook his head. "Bloody genius. Bloody nerve, too, of course." Craddock took out his pipe, examined it, tapped it against the table and put it back in his shirt pocket. "But then, who knows the cost. Poor bugger's still paying, for all we know."

Quint watched the lizard once more creeping forward. He felt a bit like a fly trussed in a web of Craddock's weaving; when the lizard shot out its tongue, would he disappear, he wondered?

"He leaves Malaya in a hell of a hurry. No planning

time. And pops up on the other side scrubbed and shiny as a choir boy on Sunday morning, money to burn, his blushing bride on his arm. Think about it."

Because I pay my debts, Quint. I pay my debts. The words sounded so close in his ear, Quint found himself looking round. But the bar door was closed, the lights out, the cleaning man gone. A stealth had crept upon the place. Craddock's hand clamped onto his shoulder. "Time for beddy-byes."

"Is Gwendy Jake behind all this?" Craddock's fingers seemed to squeeze the words out before Quint decided to say them.

"All what?"

"Your being here—Easy patrol—on the island?"

"You're joking."

"Thirty years: time for a celebration. Time to settle up. After all, he owes her: Lady Luck, his little fortune cookie."

The metal chair screeched on the flagstone floor as Craddock pushed it away. The lizard bolted. For a second, hand viselike on Quint's shoulder, he stood rigid. Then the grip eased. "I owe the shithead. He taught me the lesson of life when I was young enough to apply it. Too young, perhaps."

They turned their backs on the grey garden and climbed the stairs, slowly, not talking or touching. Craddock's door was unlocked. Curt, whispered goodnights, and Quint turned away towards his own wing. Ahead of him, as he walked, a door closed on a rear-facing room on the right. A soft closing.

Quint paused on the threshold of the now deserted lounge where, earlier that evening, he'd sat with Gwendy

Jake. The potted palms in the moonlight seemed dipped in silver. Chairs stood in disarray after the film. His legs were poised to carry him through the room to go down to his own floor when something struck him as incongruous: a shape. He approached, curious. Cradled in the branches of a palm was, yes, a machine gun; it looked old enough to have been used by Craddock in the ambush thirty years before. Then he saw—in a chair beyond, sprawled, heaving, asleep, with grey stubbly beard and khaki jacket to which two brass buttons still clung—a man.

At first Quint thought that he'd stumbled on Vellu's sought-after insurgent leader and that the reward was his. His better judgment, however, told him it was the Malay night guard—though the gun seemed a bit excessive. He tiptoed away.

In bed, in his own room, Quint stretched out a hand for the phone to ask for a wake-up call, recalled that it didn't work, and groped instead for his book, his sleep inducer, F. Spencer Chapman's *The Jungle is Neutral*, bought at the bookstall in the lobby the day he arrived. It wasn't on the bedside table. He looked on the floor and—gymnastic feat—under the bed. Puzzled, he padded around the room inspecting every possible surface. The maid? Would she want a book about an eccentric British major who hides out with Chinese guerrillas in the jungles of Japanese-occupied Malaya keeping a diary in Eskimo? She didn't even speak English.

Nothing else was missing, but his gold-tipped pen, instead of being in the usual inside pocket of his blazer, was now in the other pocket. Or had he misplaced it himself after writing the note to the Jakes suggesting drinks before dinner? The idea of someone going through his things not only annoyed Quint, it puzzled him. He climbed back into bed.

CHAPTER ELEVEN

"Behold, Mr. Quint, the Lake of the Pregnant Maiden." Vellu stood with arms outstretched like some Old Testament prophet surveying a promised piece of real estate. "All fresh water," he added, as if it was an extra selling point.

Quint, Forbes and Leila, led by Vellu, had left the boat in an inlet and, because the tide was out, waded ashore. Their path twined steeply among trees whose branches blocked the sky; then magically the sky was below them—through the tree trunks, reflected in the smooth surface of the lake. And in the lake-sky was the sun, having a mid-morning soak, water brimming up into the surrounding green.

A few yards below their vantage point a rough jetty of bamboo jutted into the lake, man's sole mark on the scene. Vellu added, with now a hint of apology in his voice: "There used to be resthouse. Japs burned it."

"During the occupation?" Quint was learning.

"At one time very nice place for picnics."

Peter said, "Still looks pretty good to me."

"Jap soldiers came. Scoffed at legend, according to which a married couple, childless for nineteen years, came here to drink lakewater and afterwards became pregnant."

"How long afterwards?" Leila asked, but Vellu ignored the question.

"One Japanese soldier jumped in naked and all of a sudden disappeared. Then, as his friends watched from bank, his body rose from middle of lake in jaws of white crocodile. Soldiers fired but missed; their comrade was pulled under and it was only next day remains of body surfaced. They must do something, so they burn down resthouse."

Peter laughed: "Frustration therapy; the old resthouse cure." He ran down the path, pulling off his shirt, yelling like Tarzan.

Leila hesitated, then followed.

"Take care," Quint cautioned, feeling old and absurd.

Vellu laughed uneasily. "To scoff, it is not wise."

"So they burned it in revenge," Quint mused, "thereby affirming their belief in the legend. An old trap, much fallen into. No doubt the white crocodile wept for joy."

"In these parts, Mr. Quint, revenge is no light matter." Vellu spoke gravely. "Even today blood feuds smoulder from generation to generation."

"Proving that there's no such thing as revenge."

"I daresay resthouse saved many innocent lives. Who knows?"

"But why has it not been rebuilt? After forty years."

"Superstition, Mr. Quint. Also not to be trifled with."

Quint smiled: "Lest the white crocodile take offense?" He watched Peter Forbes single-handedly turn the peaceful lake into a frothing ferment. He lay on his back, kicking and splashing, daring Leila to jump, his yells crashing round the forested banks. Gone was the doleful wimp of yesterday. The crocodile, if still in residence, would be cowering in some remote corner by now. "Oh, and Vellu," this was their first chance to talk alone since Gwendy Jake's revelation the previous evening, "a little known fact: anthropologists come in two varieties, male and female."

Vellu dropped to a squatting position. He picked up a small stone and began chipping away at a piece of protruding rock. Quint also squatted, causing sharp pains to pierce his knees like darts, a reminder both of the years spent out of the saddle and the maxim of Hegesippe Simon, 'Pain is the body's Hermes.' At last, as though matters of great import hung on a correct response, Vellu said, "If it is a he, it is a he; if a she, a she. What is difference?"

Quint stared through the trees at the lake. "I'd have thought it was obvious."

"When he or she is dead?" The voice beside him was little more than a whisper. "Mr. Quint, I am simple man. I am making living in a certain way. In another way, you are making. You tell me man is woman, I do not argue. You tell me sky is green. OK, it is green. I know what I know. You know what you know. Words will change nothing. That is all I have to say."

Quint dropped the subject, determined to come back to it later. "So this is the Lake of the Pregnant Maiden?" He scanned its surface, as if, in the lucid reflection, he might learn something. He did: that something was wrong. Of course, there was no one in sight in the water, no one on the jetty. His gaze swept the shore. It was as calm and peaceful as when they had first arrived.

"Peter!"

Abruptly, Vellu stood up.

103

Before the echo died, both men were scrambling down
the path. Split bamboo nailed end to end formed the jetty floor. It took their combined weight without a protesting squeak. A little pile of blue proved to be Leila's jeans,
under which she'd worn her swimsuit. Quint had scarcely
taken this in when he heard a splash. It seemed to come
from beneath them. Then, from behind, a great churning
and bubbling made the men turn in time to see not a
crocodile but two human heads pop up out of the water.
Peter's was grinning.

Leila hauled herself onto the jetty.

"Oh, my God." Vellu mopped his face with a large
handkerchief, obviously shaken.

"I say," Peter volunteered a little defensively, "you
didn't really think . . . "

"Don't be absurd." Quint wasn't sure what he'd
thought.

Leila lay back on the bamboo. "Isn't it gorgeous? Let's
picnic right here, can we?"

A movement among the trees by the path caught
Quint's eye: alert faces bobbing among the leaves. Yet
not a sound. The two men followed his gaze. Leila, eyes
closed, said, "It's perfect."

"Was," Peter amended dryly.

"What do you mean?"

"Our Chinese friends," Quint explained, "from the
Inn." He saw plainly now that it was them, streaming—so
it seemed—down the path towards them. And yet no
babble of voices exclaimed in wonder at the sight of the
lake, no giggling, no pointing—as if they had seen it all
before. Odd—the thought flashed through his mind—a
minute or two ago, no movement on the surface of the

water; now, no sound from the Chinese. Absence seemed suddenly significant as in a Chinese painting. No flipper on the beach. No book by the bedside. The pen in the wrong pocket. Things not being where they should be; people not doing what they should be doing.

Leila sat up. Suddenly the new arrivals were laughing, pointing, chattering, doing all the things they should have been doing a few seconds earlier. Some had cameras and snapped pictures, others posed. Quint scratched his beard. Had he been seeing things; or rather, not seeing?

"Bloody tourist trap," Peter cursed.

Some of the Chinese ventured onto the jetty, where Vellu proprietorially began to lay out a picnic lunch; but most still lined the bank or squatted along the path. There were none in the water. They seemed a mixed bunch, some wiry, tough, brown, others pale, studious types, others well fleshed out. All in their teens or early twenties, Quint guessed, mostly men, casually dressed in jeans and T-shirts. And—he noted—sneakers. He smiled a hello here and there, eliciting an occasional shy smile back.

Then, swiftly as they had come, the group left.

"I've just had an idea." Peter struck his brow in a theatrical gesture. "For an escape route."

Leila looked at him, amused, and at the same time, Quint thought, annoyed.

"Dress up *à la Chinoise* and go with them."

"Aha, Nicolette, your knight errant. You have found him." Quint made a little bow in Peter's direction. Peter reddened. "But I wouldn't underestimate the perspicacity of your father, Leila. I spoke with him last night. A most accomplished man. What is his job, I wonder?"

"He calls himself Head Groundsman. That's what the plaque says on his desk."

"Laugh a minute," Peter said. "You're not serious?"

Quint raised an eyebrow: "Head groundsman?"

"Chap who keeps the grass down," Peter chimed in, "muzzles the weeds, rolls the pitch, that sort of thing. Decapitates the dandelions."

"In the desert?"

"The Ruler is most particular about weeds," Leila explained, deadpan. " 'The English,' he always says, 'invented the lawn. Craddock Sahib is English. He is in the lawn-care business.' Which is everybody's cue to laugh."

"Die laughing?" Peter queried.

Quint gestured helplessly. "But then I have never understood the English."

"State security," Peter mouthed. " 'Murder is our business.' "

"Ah yes. Murder." Quint gave the word a ruminative ring. "Your father mentioned that, you told me, Peter. It was on his mind."

"What's that got to do with anything?" Peter snapped. It was all right to discuss Leila's father in these terms, but not, apparently, his own.

"Just a passing thought. Your mother sensed there was another woman, you said. And women are so rarely wrong in these matters."

"You're crazy," Peter hooted. "My old Dad never looked at a woman in his life except for my old Mum. They were sweethearts from childhood. Ask anyone." He paused. "Ask Cardew-Smythe."

" 'My old Dad,' " Quint mimicked. "Sometimes we think our fathers were born our fathers. There should be

106

a word—the equivalent of patronizing—for the way sons
see fathers."

A faint sound of singing was born to them on the
breeze. "Oh, no," Leila said anxiously.

Peter wailed, "Not another invasion."

"From the West, this time. Your compatriots," Quint
remarked, as the figure of Sneed hove into view among
the trees, followed closely by that of Briscoe, a.k.a.
Padinki. They were warbling throatily and, catching sight
of the others, redoubled their efforts:

Don't forget to wake me in the morning,
And bring me up a nice hot cup of tea:
Kiss me goodnight, Sergeant-major,
Sergeant-major be a mother to me.

Halfway down the path Sneed stopped, turned and
shouted through cupped hands, "Ahoy, back there.
S.O.S. Chop chop." He brandished what looked like a
beer can.

Briscoe croaked a heartfelt, " 'ere, 'ere." And they
stumped on down the path.

"Birds of a feather, great minds seldom differ, it never
rains but it pours." Sneed halted in a babble of platitudes
at the jetty, waiting, perhaps, for an invitation to proceed.
"Might as well raise the Titanic," he confided to no one in
particular, jerking his head in the direction they'd come
from. Then he turned and started back towards the trees.

Briscoe stepped gingerly, as if on sore feet, onto the
bamboo and Quint saw him close up for the first time. He
gave the appearance of having been plucked off a street
in Surrey and plunked down here in the East by accident.
He had a pallor about him, a softness quite unlike the
softness Quint sensed in his two cohorts. Theirs was the

necrosis of the white man too long in the tropics that Conrad had captured in *Lord Jim*: 'They loved short passages, good deckchairs, large native crews, and the distinction of being white . . . They talked everlastingly of turns of luck . . . and in all they said—in their actions, in their looks, in their persons—could be detected the soft spot, the place of decay, the determination to lounge safely through existence.'

Briscoe held up his beer can. "More where this came from," he announced, with an inviting wink. He exuded the perkiness of an encyclopedia salesman, and something of the melancholy, too. He wasn't a lounger. As far as Quint was concerned this voice—first heard in the Inn lobby—would always be the measure of the man: wheedling, provoking, soothing; by no means at ease with itself.

Even as Briscoe spoke, a string of ribald oaths issued from the trees and ricocheted round the green bowl of the lake. Miller appeared above them staggering under the weight of a sizable white beer cooler. Sneed, stronger than his weedy frame suggested, hoisted the cooler onto his own shoulders and preceded Miller towards them down the path.

"So where are they, then? What did you do wiv 'em, Sneedie?" Miller demanded between elaborate wipes of his flushed face. His trousers, rolled to the knees, were soaked. His shirt—a flamboyant, loose-hanging affair that barely met across his middle (and Quint recalled from the day before and the day before that)—revealed the blue pricks of the needle of some soldier-frequented tattoo parlor. He'd noticed earlier that they were traveling light, Miller and Sneed, with one tiny cardboard suit-case apiece.

"Out wiv it," Miller persisted. "What about them maidens?"

"Don't ask me," Sneed protested. "You were the one that told me."

"It was that so-called captain told me. Wait till we get back. I'll bust his balls for him, I will."

"Excuse me," Vellu ventured, "but maybe some honest confusion can explain all. This lake is named after certain so-called maiden, who, many years ago . . . "

But no one was listening. Miller was down on hands and knees rummaging in the plastic cooler. Sneed lay prone on the jetty, a beer can heaving gently on his stomach. "Sneed's Golden Rule of Survival Number 2," he threw out. "Thou shalt at no time be more than an arm's reach from a cold beer."

Briscoe tittered girlishly. He was looking at Quint. "Briscoe's the name. B-R-I-S-C-O-E. Glad to meet you."

"Q-U-I-N-T." Quint shook the proffered hand. How well he knew that look: how much can I take this one for?

"Name your poison, Quintie: beer, beer or beer?"

"Beer."

Briscoe snapped the top on a can and passed it over. "Beggars can't be choosers." Again the ingratiating leer. He gestured to the others to help themselves.

Quint held his can gratefully to his cheek. To be that cold, even in the cooler, it couldn't have been long out of a refrigerator. They must have come very fast from the Inn. The vessel Vellu had furnished—a creaky wooden fishing boat—had taken two and a half hours. It dawned on him that no one was eating. "Vellu, the food. You're sitting on it."

Vellu was indeed smothering the picnic hamper like a broody hen. "Mr. Quint, please, a word."

"Can we drink this good beer and deny our benefactors food?"

Peter Forbes stood up. "Three Brits beats thirty Chinese, I suppose. Still, I think I'll explore. Coming, Leila?" She scrambled to her feet and they ran off.

"What's he on about—thirty friggin' Chinks?" Miller seemed suddenly apprehensive. He eyed the retreating pair with puzzled hostility.

"Surely you passed them, or at least saw their boat?" Quint insisted. "They were here only a few minutes ago."

Miller scratched his head. "Did we boys?"

"Islands are full of hiding places," Vellu said appeasingly.

"But thirty Chinks in a boat," Miller pondered, helping himself to a vegetable samoza.

"Hell's teeth, Milly; for all *we* know, the Yankee Sixth Fleet is out there." Sneed turned to Quint: "Last night was a bit of a blast."

Briscoe sauntered over to where Quint was now sitting, dangling his legs over the water. "Reckon you're a pretty choosy sort. What might be called discriminating . . . " He squatted down, half glancing towards Miller and Sneed. "Unlike some among us."

Over Briscoe's shoulder, Vellu's mustached face registered acute distaste, reminding Quint—no doubt the intention—of his warning of the day before. As much for his Indian friend's benefit as his own, he asked: "You arrived only yesterday, I understand? From Thailand?"

"Right you are. By boat, as a matter of fact. Not a question of expense, naturally. A spot of business to attend to in that neck of the woods. Combining business with pleasure, shall we say."

"A trader, I take it?"

With a flourish, Briscoe produced his card. "At your service, sir."

Quint read it. "I trust the market for—er—Tupperware is booming in Thailand, Mr. Briscoe."

"Nicky's the name, tricky's the game." He smirked. "Virtually untapped. Virgin territory, if you take my meaning." In the background, Vellu's facial barometer moved from 'distaste' to 'intense wariness.'

"And your traveling companion? Forgive me, but I happened to be passing through the lobby as you were checking in. She is enjoying her stay? Perhaps not caring so much for the sea crossing?"

"Oh, we are a sly one, aren't we?" Briscoe patted the plank beside him. "No flies on Mr. Quint. No, she never was partial to the sea. Laid up. Took to her bed, didn't she."

"I'm sorry to hear that."

"Not so as she can't receive the occasional visitor, of course . . . " He looked at Quint coquettishly, mouth partly open. Quint saw a tongue appear in one corner, moist, pink and wiggly. "Maybe we can do business." Behind him, Vellu's facial barometer registered off the scale.

"Well now, Vellu. Should we be getting a move on?" Quint looked round. "Where did our young lovers go? Don't say we've lost them again."

Vellu stood up, hand shading eyes. "I myself will look."

"Bloody Pakis," Briscoe groused when he'd left. "Can't shake them, can I? All over bloody Purley. Once they get their hooks into a place . . . Makes you feel good sometimes, just to see an honest English face."

"Who's talking?" Sneed called over. "Not a drop of English in him, Mr. Quint. Regular mongrel, ain't you, Stinki Padinki?"

From above came a noise like the biblical rushing, mighty wind. All four looked up, but saw nothing. Then suddenly, over the jungle, looming against the blue sky, the helicopter hove into view; a huge, throbbing dragonfly. Sneed waved, but there was no answering salute.

"Get lost," Briscoe screamed, hurling his empty beer can.

The chopper held course, its shadow careening sideways across the lake like a great crab. Then it was lost to sight behind the encircling heights.

CHAPTER TWELVE

"What was all that about?" Briscoe asked. The helicopter was a distant buzz.

"Just the postman," Sneed scoffed. "Expecting a Christmas parcel from Purley, are we, Stinki?"

Miller said, "Why do they come snooping round out here?"

"It's Stinki they're after," Sneed joked. "What 'ave you been up to, Stinki?"

Briscoe smiled thinly.

"They're looking for a man who's a kingpin in the Thai opium business," Quint said authoritatively. "A man with a price on his head."

"How much?" Miller threw out, casually.

"Quite a lot." Quint saw that Vellu was returning, and with him Leila and Peter.

Taking leave of the new arrivals, the four of them walked back to the inlet to find the tide practically at its lowest ebb and the boat riding at anchor farther out than before. Vellu, who could not swim, was floated out to it on an inflated rubber tube, clutching the hamper. A delighted Peter somehow inveigled Leila onto his back, but they hadn't gone very far when he let out a hair-raising yelp. Quint, wading behind under a pile of garments which had somehow found their way into his arms, saw

Leila pitch into the water and strike out for the boat to the cheers of the crew who crowded to help her up over the side, broad smiles creasing their weathered faces.

It was generally assumed she had provoked the incident, but Peter swore he had stepped on something sharp. And a gash on one side of the instep bore him out. Leila knotted it solicitously in a handkerchief to stop the bleeding. Intriguing, thought Quint, the sea-change wrought in this young woman in the few hours they'd been away. Though the idea that Peter had anything to do with it rather rankled. It wasn't Peter's presence as much as Craddock's absence, he suspected, that had worked this magic. Absence: there it was again. Where were the war stories? Where was Gwendy Jake's hair? "Truth, like falsehood, is recognizable by its attempts to conceal itself"—Hegesippe Simon.

Quint cast an envious eye at the little speed launch bearing the Inn logo that the others must have arrived in. The hammerblow thud-thud-thud of the engine of their own boat made even the barest conversation difficult. And no sooner was it clear of protecting banks than the wind pounced from nowhere thwacking at the fragile craft like a giant invisible cat's paw, smothering Quint in a pall of diesel exhaust. Communication on deck all but broke down.

Peter and Leila sat in the prow, braced against the gunwale. When the wind let loose and the waves rained plumes of spray they huddled close. Soon his protective arm girdled her bare shoulders and his mouth stayed close by her ear, shouting words of encouragement, no doubt. Cleverly planned, superbly executed. Quint had underestimated Peter's resourcefulness.

Shadows made dark sockets of the captain's eyes. A slight, supple-limbed Malay, he seemed to have entered some seaman's world of his own, a hand clasping the tiller, face tilted sideways to see past the hulk of the cabin. To their right a forested island rose massively to a peak. Quint stared at the fixed point of the peak—a seafaring trick he'd learned—and gradually surrendered his body to the elements. Vellu, poor soul, had vanished, probably into the cabin.

The mystery of the disappearing Chinese was presently solved. Not far from the inlet where they had anchored, two islets raised themselves from the sea like slabs of greyish cake with green icing. Quint had noticed them earlier as they sailed by; but now, coming from the other direction, he saw that in the lee of one was a cleft in the overhanging rock wall. Here, sheltered from the wind that elsewhere whipped up waves, a boat lay at anchor, a fishing boat of standard size, like their own—wooden, some thirty feet long, paint faded, low flat-roofed cabin amidships having space for little besides the motor. Hanging over the side of the boat, apparently staring into the depths, were the Chinese. Then Quint realized they were fishing—not with rods, just reels, dangling their lines straight down. In all the stillness, it could have been a ghost ship. And something else struck him: there weren't enough of them.

The sun was behind them now, and soon the two islands were stark crags of shadow in the bay. The boat rounded a point and they were lost to sight. Quint half sat, half lay in the stern, looking back. The skipper had relinquished the helm to one of the crew who stood nearby, also seemingly lost in thought. The lethargy of afternoon claimed everything. Peter and Leila were in the prow, spray breaking over them like chrysolite confetti. Vellu inched his way towards Quint clutching the cabin roof with both hands. Safely past that obstruction, he waved to his left at the great mass of an island, shouting something Quint didn't at first catch. "Cave of Banshee," Vellu pointed again. "You like to visit now?"

Quint saw a small beach set among mangroves. In a cliff face back of the beach he fancied he saw a darker patch, a cave opening perhaps. "Another day." He shook his head. Vellu shrugged. How many other days do you have, he seemed to say. Three was the answer to that, not counting Sunday, the day he was due to leave; the day they were all due to leave. He hoped Gwendy Jake would cooperate. He had something he rather urgently needed to ask her.

At this moment the white speedboat flashed by, trailing a bridal train of foam, its three passengers hurling epithets and beer cans with equal ferocity, drunk as lords.

If Quint had visualized a Christians-to-the-lions type reception he was pleasantly surprised. It was getting on for four before the boat tied up at the jetty—the Inn jetty, at Vellu's insistence—in full view of anyone who might be on the lookout.

As he clambered up the vertical wooden steps nailed to the side of the long pier, Quint found himself glancing anxiously in the direction of the white edifice whose comfortable spread wings and red-tiled roof submitted blandly to the glare of the afternoon sun. His own balcony, at the nearest point to the jetty, was as blank as the eye socket of a skull. On the balcony above there was movement, but, given the distance, he couldn't see who.

Miller or Sneed, no doubt. It was their room. The speed-boat with the Inn logo on its side was already snuggled safely inside the boathouse. A line of flapping laundry and the sound of women's voices raised in gossip were a reminder that half the boathouse building housed Inn staff.

Vellu excused himself, staying on board for the short ride back to town, promising to stop by after supper to discuss the next day's plan. At the last minute, Quint had drawn him aside. Could Vellu, at a pinch, Quint asked, communicate by phone with the cousin in Penang whose daughter—or was it niece—was betrothed to the clerk in the police morgue? "If line is not down," Vellu looked alarmed and unhappy, "and landlord is not away whose shop is only nearby place with phone. But why?" he appealed. "Never in my life have I rung him from here. Long distance, it is. He would think something terrible had taken place."

"And might not be far from the truth." Quint smiled reassuringly, "But don't worry, it probably won't be necessary. One merely likes to know one's options." Vellu looked more worried than ever.

Quint, Leila and Peter chose a frontal assault on the Inn rather than an outflanking movement. They could have avoided the brick path along the slope which joined the steps that led from the beach past the pool up to the terrace, where tea was doubtless being served. They didn't. Peter walked ahead, Leila and Quint side by side behind him.

"Peter," Quint called to him, "it was your left foot you injured, wasn't it? Let's see you limp."

"It's all right now." Peter half turned.

117

"Nevertheless, limp," Quint commanded. "Limp as if your life depended on it. Which," he whispered to Leila, "it may."

"Limp," she pleaded.

Quint surveyed the effect. "That handkerchief, the bloody one, you still have it? Tie it on again." Leila tied it.

Peter shrugged. By the time they reached the steps, he was convincingly into his limp. Craddock and his wife and the Jakes were sitting at a table under a sunshade near the pool. There were drinks on the table. Their combined gaze, as they saw who was approaching, would have seared the down off a goose.

CHAPTER THIRTEEN

"**O**ur young friend here has gashed his foot." Quint grasped Peter solicitously by the arm. "We are on our way to the clinic."

"That's what you think." In a trice Gwendy Jake was on her feet and moving. "Clinic," she scoffed. "Seen perfectly clean cuts turn gangrenous overnight in these so-called native clinics, I have. Come on. Let's have a look."

She marched ahead up the steps, scrawny legs and fuzzy orange headdress at either end of a flowery beach dress which swayed in what once might have been a provocative manner. Peter, leaning heavily and perhaps a little vindictively, on Quint, hobbled after her. Leila was left to face the lions alone; not even a Christian.

The Jakes occupied a suite of two connecting rooms, each with twin beds, a bath and balcony looking out towards the pool. Gwendy delved around in a closet and came up with a white metal box with a red cross painted on the lid. "Don't just stand there," she fussed at Peter, pointing to the bathroom. "Run and wash it." She laid the box on the nearest bed. "Goodness knows what's got into it by now. Jiggers, most likely. I'm surprised at you, Mr. Quint, a grown man, sneaking off like that; and then look what happens. Sir Frankie is ever so upset . . . "

"They're not exactly children either, remember," Quint protested; mildly, he thought. The night before at the bar might never have happened. Perhaps, in her mind, it hadn't.

"I don't mind telling you that Sir Frankie spent a tidy sum on this trip. All expenses paid, mind you. He'd be very concerned if anything . . . Well, if anything *happened*, you know what I mean." She dropped her voice: "You'd think they might show a little gratitude. He didn't have to do it, now did he? And he does so love all being together."

"Then why didn't he hire a coach and take us to Butlins Holiday Camp?" Peter hopped out of the bathroom. "Clacton: Mecca of Togetherness. Hey. Now there's an account worth stealing."

Gwendy, wielding a bottle of antiseptic, dabbed at the wound with a swab of cotton. The room began to reek. Peter, prostrate on the bed, groaned. "Trouble with you lot," Gwendy huffed between dabs, "you've never been to war. Not a proper one. Don't know the meaning of pain."

"You and Florence Nightingale," Peter retorted.

Gwendy bridled: "The Emergency was war—war in all but name. Your Dad never tell you?" She slapped a dressing over the wound. Peter yelped. "Keep still!"

"Then stop tickling my foot."

"That's better. Just like his dad." She winked at Quint. "Ever so ticklish his feet were."

"Oh yeah?" Peter started to sit up.

Gwendy pushed him down. "We go back, young man, your dad and me. He didn't let on, ay?" Another knowing glance at Quint.

"As a matter of fact, no."

"No, I don't suppose he would, would he? Never was one for words, your dad; not like some of 'em." She picked up a roll of bandage and measured off a length with her eye. "Do us a favor, ducks." She looked at Quint. "Snip, snip. In the kit."

He'd been called some strange things in his time, but never ducks before. Quint found the scissors and snipped. "Yes, I imagine you could make a good sling out of that." Here, at last, was his opening.

"Heaven help us." She had lifted Peter's foot and was readying the bandage. "Whatever put that idea into your head?" In an attempt to be useful, Quint leaned over and held the patient's leg. Peter craned his neck to look. "Keep still," Gwendy snapped. "Who said you could move?"

"Jesus flipping Christ," Peter flopped back. "You owe me for this, Quint."

Quint answered her question: "I was thinking of that American—the anthropologist."

"What about her?"

"She needed a sling, you said."

"So she did." Gwendy had a safety pin held in her lips and another one poised with which to fasten the bandage. It occurred to Quint that his timing was off. "I don't suppose," Gwendy addressed Peter, "you have such a thing as a clean sock?" She stood up to survey her handiwork. "Otherwise I'll fetch one of Sir Frankie's."

"Oh, I'll find something." He looked ruefully at his now bulging foot. "Thanks. Thanks a lot."

"We don't want to get it soiled now, do we?" She disappeared through the connecting door with a determined look on her face.

121

Peter shook both fists, not after Gwendy but at Quint.

Smiling, Quint strolled to the window. The shouts and screams of swimmers drifted up. In a voice slightly louder than necessary, he said, "No bathing, of course. No more disporting in the pool, you understand." He raised an eyebrow, "Jiggers."

Gwendy reappeared with a sock. "Can't be too careful, not in these parts. Here, try this for size." Grasping Peter's hairy calf, she eased the sock over the bandage. "There," dusting her hands. "Be off with you." She beamed at Quint. "Good to be back in business."

They watched her pack up the precious box. "I don't suppose you get much practice these days," Quint remarked. "Sir Frankie seems disgustingly healthy."

"Should have seen him last year in Honolulu: turned bright blue, he did, right at the casino. Nasty scare. Been watching himself since then . . . "

Peter edged towards the door. Quint coughed. "We mustn't keep you. And please excuse my ignorance in the matter of the sling. Unforgivable."

"This—" Gwendy plucked a roll of black cloth from her box and let it unfurl dramatically,"—is a sling. This," she whipped out the bandage, "is a bandage."

"In black and white, there you have it," Peter said from the door.

Quint ignored him. "And to think, the life of that woman hung on so delicate a thread, so to speak." He picked up the sling and let it fall on the bed.

Gwendy looked annoyed. "What are you saying, Mr. Quint?"

"My dear lady, it's quite simple. Had you insisted on putting that sprained wrist of hers in this sling, she would surely have had second thoughts about gallivanting off in a boat that very same night."

"She knew her own mind, that girl. As I said," she glanced at Peter, "you can't tell 'em anything these days."

"One more thing," Quint said, "I need to know the name of the person to whom you gave that postcard."

"And what if I don't remember?" She looked at him coyly.

"Lady Jake," Quint sounded exasperated. "If you don't want to be frank with *me*, I'm afraid you may find yourself talking to the local police." He hoped she didn't know there were none.

The effect was magical. "Well, I never did," Gwendy patted her head in an attempt to recover her poise. "How did I know you were involved in any sort of—investigation, is it, Mr. Quint? But I might have guessed. The Americans are always investigating and being investigated. If it's not one thing, it's another. Well, I never." She looked conspiratorially at Peter, who had removed his hand from the door, clapping her hands in a parody of girlish delight. "Can't wait to tell the others."

"I'd prefer not," Quint said sternly. "In fact, for the time being, I forbid it absolutely. And that goes for you, too, Peter."

"Cross my heart and hope to die," Peter whispered.

Quint turned to Gwendy: "Now perhaps you'll give me an answer."

"It was that nice Swiss couple—remember? No, of course, you wouldn't. Can't say I know the name, though. The desk should, but whether they do or not's another matter."

Quint moved to the door. "You've been most helpful." He made a little bow. "By the way, a *picture* postcard, you said. What was the picture?"

"Just a postcard, like you buy in a gift shop."

Quint stood by the door, which Peter had opened. "Remember: not a word." She screwed her face into a wink. The door closed.

"Phew. Heavy," Peter breathed as they walked down the hall.

Quint put a finger to his lips. "Limp," he commanded softly. Then, when they reached the lobby: "There is a saying, 'Walls have ears and women can't control their tongues.' "

"Suspiciously sexist. Are you some kind of spook?"

Quint stopped and faced him: "Meaning?"

"Private eye, sleuth, gumshoe, flatfoot, bloodhound, dick, tec; in a word—detective."

"In a word, no."

"Then why the big act? And—by the by—talking of women's tongues, you realize the first thing Our Gwendy's going to get up to after that imperial edict of yours? So don't blame me when the weird looks start."

Quint laughed. "You do have a way with words, Peter."

"You should see me when I'm getting paid for it."

"Then I shall make you my Fool. A man feels naked without a Fool. I miss not having one around."

"Thanks."

"No, no. It's a high compliment. The Fool intercedes for the people. He is the conscience of the ruler. Injustice, pomposity, cant—his wit reduces it all. He has the ruler's ear, Peter. His head is safe on his shoulders."

"While the ruler's is on his. What's the salary?"

"The odd purse of gold. But to get back to the fair Gwendy." He lowered his voice, though the lobby was large and empty. "If she can keep a secret, I'll be disappointed. I went to bed last night with an unpleasant opinion of her. Our little mise-en-scène today was by way of helping me revise it."

"To an even more unpleasant one."

"I hope not. Let's buy a few things here at the gift shop." He took Peter by the arm. "If you don't object."

Peter let himself be led: "So Gwendy tells all: our Mr. Q—far from being the genteel though foreign tripper he pretends to be—is at the hub of an international investigation into wrongdoing—marvelous American word. And so on, and so forth, and so what?"

"In a firing squad, one man only has the live round, am I right? The rest are blanks."

"You'd better ask Craddock. That's his line."

"In order to draw the fire of the man with the live bullet, to render him harmless, we need a target . . . "

"And you—dare I ask—are it?"

"Come and look at postcards."

They bought one each of all the island scenes. Quint asked the Indian behind the counter if he recalled an American woman—tall with long brown hair, not a guest at the Inn—buying a card. The man was positive: "Only guests are buying here. Other shops in town."

"I see you have a number of copies of that book you sold me."

"Oh, yes, sir. *Jungle Is Neutral*, is it not? Very good buy at old price as marked. New shipment twice the price. Perhaps your friend . . . " he glanced at Peter's foot, "has time hanging heavy on idle hands?"

"A funny thing," Quint remarked. "That book was filched from my room sometime yesterday. Perhaps my friend already has a copy." He nudged Peter. The Indian laughed. They walked away. "I wonder how Leila is doing among the lions. Cruel of you to throw her to them, I thought."

Peter growled. "You know, Majesty, if you weren't quite so genteel and your beard wasn't turning grey, I'd . . . " He flexed his fingers. "As things stand, the first thing I'm going to do with my idle hands is rip this off," he waved his foot, "this club."

"Peter, Peter," Quint shook his head sadly. "A Fool does not have to be an idiot. That club, as you call it, is precisely the weapon you need. Craddock's guard will be down. How—in that state—could you possibly carry off his daughter? Not, of course, that that is your intention." As Peter started away, he added, "One other favor: lend me your tour schedule. And Peter," Peter looked back, "limp."

As soon as he'd gone, Quint approached the desk. The clerk on duty was the woman Briscoe had tried to bully when he checked in. It irritated Quint to think that, in the woman's eyes, he and Briscoe were two of a kind: tourists, white, trouble. He smiled hopefully at her. "I would like to telephone the E & O Hotel in Penang, to that Swiss couple who were staying here. They left on Monday and I'm sorry to say I don't even have their name."

"Mr. and Mrs. Bauer." She didn't bat an eyelash.

"How clever of you."

She in turn, smiled: "I'm afraid, sir, the lines to Penang are down."

CHAPTER FOURTEEN

Quint sat on his balcony wishing Craddock would go away. The banging was muffled now by the closing of door and window so that he no longer heard his name. But he knew it was a summons. No doubt, in Craddock's adopted land, this kind of work was farmed out to lesser fry; not on for The General himself to go knocking. Of far greater import was an argument that was taking place above him.

Miller was hammering away at Sneed, the bone of contention, so far as Quint could tell, being Briscoe. Quint caught the words, "You heard what he said . . . he saw us. He was there all right . . . " In keeping with 'Sneed's First Law of Thermodynamics,' expounded to Quint earlier in the grueling heat of midday—'Heat rises, therefore keep your head down'—Sneed lay low.

"And another thing: the one with the beard,"—Quint fingered his beard—"rum customer. You gotta watch him, too. Big flappers." He felt an ear.

Sneed chimed in. Overenthusiastically. "Odd geezer."

"Busybody." Miller pronounced judgment.

"Gotta watch them sort," Sneed echoed. After a pause, he said: "Milly?"

"Yeah?"

"What's old Stinki on about then? You think he's got

127

the goods up there? You think he's got the crown jewels,
like he said?"

"Nah. Stinki? That con-merchant?"

"Why would he keep on about it?"

"Bit of bluff, ain't it? For the consumption of Mr. Gullible here. What you would do without me around is anyone's guess." In response to Sneed's feeble protest, Miller exclaimed, "All right, we're gonna go for a look-see.
Come on. Now. Move it."

"What? Now?" Quint heard chair legs scraping and
Sneed's imbecilic giggle. Then a door slammed. Silence.

With easy agility Quint stepped over the balcony rail
and lowered himself into the hibiscus: there was always
the risk that Craddock still lurked outside his door.
Ducking round the end of the building he arrived in a
very few minutes at the front of the Inn and entered the
lobby. Briscoe, he gathered, had a rear-facing room, and
Sneed had said 'up.' Quint crossed the lobby, keeping a
weather-eye out for Craddock, climbed a short flight of
stairs, passed a billiard table, a ping-pong table and a TV
set (on, no one watching), and reached the lounge area
where films were shown. Here he turned left through an
open doorway.

He was, he realized, in a foolishly exposed position.
The Craddocks' suite was a few doors down on the right.
Craddock could bottle him up in the hall. Of Miller and
Sneed there was no sign; either he had missed them, or
Briscoe's room was in the other wing. Quint turned to go
back, and as he did so a man charged out of a room behind him, slamming the door. It was Miller, and his face
in the dim passage gave off a ruddy glow. Later Quint recalled the eyes: white and staring as an epilep-

tic's. He wasn't sure that Miller had seen him, close as they'd come, almost to touching.

For a moment or two after Miller disappeared into the lounge Quint stayed put. And as he stood there, it dawned on him that it wasn't the first time he'd seen that particular door close. It had happened so softly the night before—in such total contrast. He listened. Giggles? Sneed's or a woman's? He couldn't be sure. At any moment Craddock might appear. He opted not to wait to find out.

A bit later, back in his own room, Quint's stomach insisted it was dinnertime. When it came to food, this stomach of his had a mind of its own and over the years Quint had let it bully him into submission. Its penchant for eel pie, sardine omelets and other indigestible morsels had been the despair of successive doctors. Just as Quint was calculating his chances of slipping safely out for a bite, there came a tap at the door. Tapping surely wasn't Craddock's style.

"The general is on the warpath," Peter whispered as Quint beckoned him in. "Leila has been sent to her room and the prison matron posted. She's no mother, that woman; she's a jailer. I'm going to report the pair of them to Amnesty International when I get back; see if I don't." He produced a Xeroxed paper. "Here's this." It was the schedule.

"I'll return it."

"Don't bother." He swung the still-bandaged foot. "Doctor says off games for a week. Can't thank you enough."

"And the general—he was mollified at the sight?"

"Saved me from the firing squad. Of course I shunted

the whole affair onto your capable shoulders: led astray, elders and betters, that sort of twaddle. Afraid you're rather in for it, old chap. Pistols behind the air-conditioning plant. If you're stuck for a second, let me know."

"Is the coast reasonably clear?" Quint stuck his head into the hall. His particular favorite, beef *rendang*, was on the dinner menu.

"There went out a decree from Sir Frankie summoning the troops to a communal bash. Command performance. Flap, flap." Peter looked at his watch. "Late already. You're probably safe for an hour or two. Last meal before the lynching, eh? Enjoy." He clutched at his throat, gurgled, and disappeared.

Typically English, Quint thought: that distorted sense of the comic. He wondered again what Leila saw in the man. Just a means of escape? Perhaps. She seemed pretty sensible. He looked at the schedule. Three days to run: Thursday—'Visit to Rubber Plantation and Authentic Native *Kampong*,' Friday—'Idyllic Tanjong Rhu Beach,' Saturday—'Fresh Water Lake of Pregnant Maiden,' followed by 'Fishing.' Predictably, the writer waxed effusive over the legend of the maiden, adding an eerie punchline: 'For all who do not believe, the white crocodile lurks in wait. It is said that those who are sucked in his crunchy embrace emerge in some subterranean cavern where ghosts of all victims glow white in darkness.'

Quint's appearance on the terrace for dinner caused a minor stir at the Jakes' table where Sir Frankie and Gwendy presided at either end. He chose a peripheral table, the better to observe without seeming to stare, and settled down to enjoy the meal. The most cursory of glances revealed that Gwendy had lost no time in betraying his 'secret.' It might, Quint reflected as a waiter took his order, be the last time he would truly relax in the presence of Easy patrol.

They were all there, even Leila—flanked by her jailers. The Turk glowered at him with unconcealed disapproval, a true daughter of Suleiman the Magnificent, and Quint wondered what depths of depravity her husband had ascribed to him. Craddock himself seemed at pains not to acknowledge Quint's presence, as if to do so would necessitate the immediate issuance of a challenge. He had picked on a waiter instead, and was roundly berating him, and had already accumulated an impressive number of Tiger bottles. Leila eyed her plate, thinking, perhaps, of the impending escape attempt. When would it be? Further down the table, Peter was talking to Sir Frankie. His back was to Quint, but by the movement of his shoulders and the way Sir Frankie's eyes flicked in Quint's direction, it was obvious whom they were discussing. He didn't wholly trust Peter. There was an intrinsic weakness about him that he couldn't put a finger on. When it came to the crunch—the white crocodile flashed into his mind—Peter might not come through. In a gentle way Leila should be warned.

Miller settled his eyes on Quint as soon as he walked in, and kept them there; a frown so knotted that Quint toyed with the idea of holding up his glass in a toast. Perhaps the man was daydreaming. Eventually Quint shifted, and when the frown failed to follow, he wondered if, after all, it hadn't been aimed at Briscoe across the table, who was chatting with Sneed. The veiled companion had still not showed; nor had the Cardew-Smythe children. Their parents flanked Gwendy Jake, Ian picking at his food in studied attentiveness, Phoebe only needing a book propped open in front of her to accentuate the boredom she doubtless intended to convey. Gwendy's words washed around them like the sea around two rocks, imperceptibly diminishing. As soon as she spotted Quint her lips pressed together, squeezing off the sound-flow, and her eyes darted around the table. When they returned to him as he knew they would, he was ready with a stiff little bow and an air of deep gravity that confused her for a moment.

As Quint applied himself hungrily to his shark's fin soup, the Chinese group filed onto the terrace and sat at a clutch of tables reserved for them not far from Quint's own. They seemed in a talkative mood, as if they'd enjoyed their day and looked forward to tomorrow's adventures. He wondered how long they were staying. When next he looked at the Jakes' table, one place was empty. Miller's. Quint glanced about but did not see him. He was enjoying his spicy *rendang* when a familiar voice sounded at his side. "I hope you are having a nice day, Mister."

For a moment he didn't recognize the captain out of uniform. But the breath still cried beer, and the bloodshot, shifty eyes said, 'No problem.' "Tonight, very special Langkawi conducted tour. You'll participate? Swell." The gold in his teeth gleamed brighter than ever. His day off, Quint surmised.

"Special? In what way?"

"Super hush-hush special. No frails need apply."

"No what?"

"Frails, Mr. Quint. Stag party. No frails tour."

There were things Fort Wayne hadn't taught him. "You

mean, 'No frills tour?' " Quint asked. His agent specialized in them.

"Sure. You got yourself a deal, partner. You like to bet
a little loose change, maybe win big." He held out his
hand. "Put it here, buddy boy."

"What exactly is it you're offering?" Quint said stiffly.

"National sport of Malay people, Mr. Quint. Cockfight."

"Why at night? Why hush hush?"

"Because," the captain scowled at the table where the
manager's family sat, "Bigshots say no dice."

"In other words, it's against the law?"

The Jakes' party was breaking up. Quint kept an eye
on Craddock, but Craddock was shepherding his women
away and didn't even look round. "When do we leave?"

"Midnight. From the end of the building near your
room. Climb over your balcony."

No one will see me leave, Quint thought. He watched
the captain dissolve into the night. Convenient. Very convenient. Well, he had asked for it, hadn't he?

A hand brushed the back of Quint's chair and Ian
Cardew-Smythe's worried face came into view. "Do
forgive me for butting in like this, but I rather gather you
were out with young Peter today. I couldn't help noticing
that gammy leg of his. Am I right in thinking he's—well,
shall I say—overdramatizing? I do hope you don't mind
my asking, but it could be rather important."

"Not at all." Important seemed an odd word to use,
even for a schoolmaster. "But why not ask Lady Jake?
Red Cross nurse, I understand; but, of course, you'd
know that. She fixed him up."

133

Cardew-Smythe colored. "I was afraid you might suggest that. Well, as I say, sorry to butt in . . . " He backed away.

Afraid? Quint toyed with the thought of asking the man for his company that night. No; cockfighting wouldn't be up his alley. And how would he explain it to his wife? It was Englishmen like Cardew-Smythe, no doubt, who'd tried to stamp out cockfighting in the colony, but obviously hadn't quite succeeded.

"Oh, one other thing." Cardew-Smythe hurried back. "Sir Frankie made a special plea to us all just now to stick together these days and not go charging off on our own if we can possibly help it. Means an awful lot to the old chap, you know; and, after all, he is footing the bill." He gave a nervous hiccup. He knows he is talking hogwash, Quint thought, and he knows I know he knows.

"But why are you telling me?"

"I just thought," Cardew-Smythe stammered. "It did occur . . . One really has no right to *think* this sort of thing, let alone *say* anything, but . . . " He floundered to a halt.

Quint observed him for a moment, then stood up and pulled out a chair. "Do sit down."

"No, no. Really." He appealed to the ceiling; a sound—could it be music?—was filtering down. "Phoebe did seem rather keen on the film tonight. I promised I'd deal with the children." He was halfway across the room before Quint had resumed his seat.

Quint lingered over coffee, expecting Vellu to put in an appearance. He didn't. A short while later, back in his room, he was intrigued to find his missing book sitting on the bedside table exactly where he'd left it. His marker—

an airline baggage receipt—still kept the place. Only in with it was another scrap of paper, an Inn 'Do Not Disturb' sign. Someone, in a child's block letters, had scrawled across it: 'LEAVE WELL ALONE. BECAUSE OF YOU PEOPLE IS DYING.'

*B*ecause *of you people is dying.* Quint sat in the darkness of his balcony turning the words over and over in his mind. He thought of Vellu. It was unlike Vellu neither to come, as he had said he would, nor send word. He thought of the fisherman in the back seat of Vellu's car. He thought of the blue plastic bag containing the body of the anthropologist. No one could blame him for *that*: the American was dead before Quint had ever set eyes on her. He need not feel guilt over that. But Vellu . . . He held up his watch to catch the moonlight: a quarter past twelve. He'd give the captain another fifteen minutes. What had Phoebe Cardew-Smythe said: *the Malay has no notion of punctuality.*

Quint peered out into the silence of the bay and began to feel slightly ridiculous. He had psyched himself up for the occasion, convinced that the trap had been sprung, that the mystery would begin to unravel. Such a delicate process where human beings were concerned. Nature at least had laws, however little understood; forces dictated actions. Man was unpredictable, mysterious. Man's made laws can be evaded, nature's cannot.

"Psst." It was the noise peddlers are reputed to make on the street corners of tourist-infested towns. "Psst," it came again. Quint leaned over the balcony and saw a hand, waving, the way drivers wave when slowing down. It projected from the corner of the building, just a few feet away. It had a ring on one of its fingers. He dropped over the railing and pushed through the shrubbery towards it, stepping high to avoid the entangling growth. He wore black. The captain, too, was darkly dressed. They resembled a couple of cat-burglars. Quint peered past Hilton into the night. He was alone. "Come." The captain beckoned. "They are waiting."

In the road at the end of the drive, Quint saw the shape of a car. It crouched like a tortoise, low to the ground. Quint fancied it was empty till, on their approach, the engine came alive and the glint from the dash lit up a young Malay face unknown to him. The captain, smiling, opened the rear door, and as Quint bent to climb in he saw he had a traveling companion: Miller lounged along the seat. He seemed in no hurry to move.

"Just the two of us?" Quint wasn't altogether surprised. The car crept forward.

Miller didn't answer. He sucked a last puff from a cigarette concealed in his fist and tossed the stub through the window, keeping his eyes off Quint.

They drove through the town at a funeral pace, a reflection on the car, Quint suspected, which was old and infirm. The street was empty, shops and houses shut tight, not a chink of light anywhere. People slept—to be up with the sun. From the front seat came soft little bursts of language. Malay, he assumed.

They were heading out on the airstrip road when Quint picked up a change in the tone. The driver fussed with the rearview mirror, but it was tied with string, and hung useless. The captain turned and stared through the back window. He made some remark and the driver laughed. Miller fumbled for his cigarettes, and in the flare of the match Quint saw his face: the rigid neck muscles, the damp locks, the unhealthy sheen of the flesh. It was not a sight he had expected. Miller looked afraid.

They kept going. The Malay dialogue continued, punctuated every so often by backward looks. The tobacco had an unpleasant acrid smell that tickled Quint's nose. He wondered what he'd expected to see on Miller's face: smugness, a scowl, indifference? Almost anything but fear.

Some three or four miles beyond the town the car turned left onto a narrow, leafy track, and then, immediately, left again, bumping a little way over bare earth. The driver cut the lights and killed the motor before stopping so that they rolled for a few yards into what seemed like someone's garden. Flowering bushes, a sagging rattan chair, and the tubular pale trunks of palm trees rose around them at crazy angles into the night. A hanging plant obscured the view on Miller's side. Odd place for a cockfight.

For a few seconds they sat in silence, then Miller, in a voice in which exasperation got the better of fear, blurted, "What the bloody hell's going on?"

The captain waved an excited hand at him over the back of the seat, commanding silence. The Malays were on edge, listening. Quint heard a noise like a slow swoosh. Something passing on the road? The captain nodded at the driver who laughed. But whatever the joke was, they weren't telling. The car was started again, the lights came on, and as they reversed Quint saw a small thatched wooden house with closed shutters.

Back on the main road, all went as before: the Malays chatting, Miller sucking nervously on his cigarette, Quint watching, taking it all in. Another couple of miles and the captain leaned back, touched Miller on the knee, and pointed. Up ahead were the taillights of a car. The car was pulled over to the side.

Slowly as they were going, the driver slowed still more. They crawled past the stationary vehicle. Quint's impression was of a battery of young faces—five, six, maybe more—intent, expressionless. "Chinese," Hilton said, scornfully.

Miller pulled back sharply. "Bloody Chinks. What do they think they're doing?"

"No problem," said the captain.

"I'll give you no problem," Miller threatened. Quint looked back through the rear window. "They comin'?"

"No." There was no one behind them that Quint could see.

"Bloody Chinks," Miller repeated.

They passed the end of the airstrip behind its wire fence, and, a half mile further on, turned left down a bumpy lane by a collection of huts. Quint took a last look back but saw no following headlights.

"No more bloody damn Chinks," the captain blurted, and said something to the driver.

"Cheeky bugger," Miller growled.

"Yes, *tuan*."

"I'll tuan you, yer brown bastard." Miller seemed to have regained a measure of self-confidence.

They bumped and lurched along, the path snaking in and out among the trees. Once or twice the wheels spun in loose sand and the engine whined. Eventually they stopped altogether in a small hollow. Whether they'd arrived or were simply stuck it was hard to tell. The captain got out and opened the door on Quint's side. "OK," he announced cheerfully.

Quint looked around. Where were the people? A cockfight surely implied people heading towards it. There was no sign of life at all, only moonlight filtering through the coconut palms, and grey sandy soil and a starlit sky. Miller stretched noisily. He had with him— Quint saw for the first time—one of those small airline shoulder bags, without much in it by the look of it. He'd been taking great interest in their surroundings, Quint had noted, since they left the road; twisting this way and that to see through the windows, letting his cigarette burn out. Now, as the captain and the driver—who'd stayed put—exchanged some words, he breasted a sandy mound and reconnoitered some more. Quint joined him. How winded, even after such slight physical exertion, the man was. If it came to a struggle between them, Quint had a good chance of winning. Unless Miller was a black belt. "This was your idea, I imagine."

Miller didn't answer directly. "That reward," he said. "You seem to know all about it. Then at supper it was going round you were some sort of tec."

"Tec?"

"Detective."

"Ah, yes."

"I thought p'raps maybe I could help."

"In what way?"

"That reward money. It's as good as mine."

"You mean you know where this man they're searching for is?" Quint sounded sceptical.

Miller didn't respond at once. He was looking through the trees to where the night seemed to flatten out into a broad, dark pan: the sea, Quint realized. Behind them the car started, then ground its teeth as the driver found reverse. Quint watched it slink away between the trees, a vast black tortoise, exhaust tainting the limpid air. Miller hadn't looked round. "Tide's out," he remarked casually. Then, turning to Quint, "Yeah, reckon I could point him out."

A short, shrill whistle sounded. Hilton was beckoning. They hurried after him along a much trodden path. Bulky shapes, looming among the trees, were thatched wooden huts on stilts. Under one glowed the embers of a fire. Quint savored the warm, sweet smell of a *kampong* night. Behind them, at a safe distance, trotted a dog. It stopped when they did, assuming an air of bored innocence and somehow bringing to mind the carload of Chinese.

The captain left the main path and struck off on a smaller one, less well defined. Quint found himself stepping into pools of blackness, hoping to touch bottom, and slithering on fallen palm fronds. Miller, in front of him, cursed and stumbled and seemed to have difficulty with even the smallest obstruction. The captain waited for them to catch up, then led the way through bushes and trees towards a hut little different from others they'd passed except that the poles it rested on were enclosed with *attap*.

Just as they reached the door, a man stepped out through it. He greeted the captain perfunctorily, not so much as glancing at the others, and, after a brief conversation, went back inside. It was at that moment that Quint heard one of the sweetest sounds to reach his ears

142

for some time: the crowing of a cock. A rather stifled crow, coming—as far as he could tell—from inside the building. As if on cue, the captain turned to his charges and, holding up both hands in a gesture of surrender (which, as Quint was to discover, was anything but), declared: "OK. Bets are on. I handle. No problem."

"No bloody fear." Miller gave a hollow laugh. "I make my own bets." He seemed to know something that Quint didn't.

The captain shrugged, and smiled his dining room 'may I seat you?' smile. "As you wish." He turned to Quint. "This is your first time, yes, Mr. Quint? Believe me, you are in good hands."

"Good and sticky." Miller pushed his way past.

Quint followed him through the door which the captain held ajar. A warm, stable smell, not unpleasant, filled his nostrils. The space was small, made more so by the crowd, twenty or thirty strong, squatting and standing in a tight circle, brown faces barely illuminated, even to Quint's night eyes. A few glanced up, but most did not, whether from politeness, shyness, or disinterest, he couldn't tell.

All eyes were on a patch of smooth mud floor where, in the center of the room, two paraffin lamps glowed yellow. The scene resembled medieval nativity paintings in which all gather round the Christ child who is the source of light. Only here the cocks took center stage, crouched in their handler's grasp, archnecked, feathers rising, facing each other across five feet of space. Quint watched, as, held firmly by their tails, they were allowed within inches of striking distance, as if not mortally aroused already. Here and there shouts erupted from the crowd, guttural cries of praise for one or other contestant. All men, Quint looked around, wrinkled and smooth, toothless and hairy. The captain spoke in his ear. "Take your pick, Mr. Quint. Name your bird." He held out a hand, and Quint put something in it.

Miller whispered, "The near one," and squeezed around the edge of the room after the captain. A moment later he came back, alone. Another hush, and the handlers let go their birds.

Quint did not share the lust for spectator sports that infected so many in his adopted country. He watched dispassionately as the cocks hopped about in their dance of death, eyeing each other, maneuvering for the downward slash of the metaled claw that would rip a six-inch gash in one puffed-out feathered breast or the other. Beautiful specimens, glinting gold and silver in the light. Gold and silver. Quint smiled. He would call them Francis and Henry, these vain, prancing beasts. Which had the captain backed for him, he wondered. Francis or Henry. Most likely Miller was right: he would pocket the money, or most of it, counting on Quint's not knowing the difference.

As the first bout ended, Miller said, "Toss up, ay?" The handlers were on their knees fervently spraying water from mouth to beak. "Could go another two or three. Long night at twelve minutes each." He seemed uncommonly chummy. "What say a breath of air?" The captain was nowhere to be seen so they stepped outside. "Blimey," Miller waved a hand about his nose, "what do they eat? No bloody self-control, the wogs. Look on the bright side," he continued, "no Chinks. Not down here.

More than their life's worth. A Malay doesn't trust a Chink any more than you or me."

"Why are you so concerned about the Chinese?" They were alone under the trees. From the hush inside, the second bout was getting under way. Miller seemed in no hurry to go back.

A little way off a dog whimpered, the dog that had followed them. The hut, it seemed to know, was out of bounds. "See that mutt?" Miller pointed. He picked up a coconut husk, aimed and threw it. The dog jumped aside, looked at Miller, looked at the missile, and tentatively wagged its tail. "Don't let any Chink closer to you than that. Ever. Take it from me. Chinks are trouble."

"Trouble?"

"Do we have business to discuss, or don't we?" For the first time that evening, he looked Quint firmly in the eye.

Quint's keen, cold eye stared back. "You tell me."

Miller's gaze wavered. He bent down, picked up another husk, examined it and tossed it over his shoulder. "Don't say I didn't try," he said, and went back into the hut.

After a while, Quint followed.

CHAPTER SIXTEEN

Knocking. At first it was part of a dream Quint was having, of two kings tilting at each other, in silver and gold. Now there was a boy standing beside him, bending over him, talking to him, imparting a sense of urgency. Quint tried to turn over and go back to sleep, but the boy wouldn't let him alone.

"Please sir, Mr. Quint sir, very sorry sir. Mr. Vellu send very urgent message. Mr. Vellu very ill, sir. Cannot come today. Maybe tomorrow." Having delivered his message, the boy—wasn't he Vellu's nephew who'd brought lunch that day to the plantation?—watched Quint's face for a sign that it had been received so that he could bolt from the room with a clear conscience. Receiving no such confirmation, he began again in the same piping falsetto: "Please sir, Mr. Quint sir, very sorry sir . . . "

"Enough. I hear you." Quint started to sit up and thunder crackled in the area his head usually occupied. He closed his eyes, and when he opened them again the boy was gone. No doubts now about where he was. In his hotel bed. The question remained: how had he got there? And why was he lying under the purple sheet clad all in black? As if laid out. He wiggled his toes. At least his shoes were off. He leaned sideways. They were lined up neatly beside the bed.

Sunlight shining through the thin curtains made weird patterns on the opposite wall: it was morning, early morning. Quint lowered his feet gently to the floor and sat for a moment on the edge of the bed. So far, so good. He reached out, removed the 'Do Not Disturb' sign from the book on the bedside table, got to his feet and shuffled over to the door. By balancing his head on his shoulders as if it were a full flagon of wine (why did the word make him wince?) he was able to reduce the pain to a dull buzz. He opened the door, hung out the sign, closed it, locked it, went into the bathroom and stood in front of the mirror. No outward signs of damage presented themselves. That was something. He took off his clothes and stood under the shower, and though the water ran luke-warm, then cold, after a while he felt able to think. He got out, put on his flannel bathrobe and went and sat in the easy chair. Only then did he permit himself a smile.

The cockfight had gone to four rounds. Henry—in silver—had been the victor; and Quint, to his surprise, had backed him; or rather the captain had backed him with Quint's money. Especially impressive had been the size of the bet. Instead of passing the man a small bill, Quint mistakenly had pressed into that practiced palm one hundred Malaysian dollars. Thinking back, it was the sheer sum involved that had thwarted any dishonorable intention the captain may have had, because Quint's stake in the fight soon became widely known, adding to the excitement and earning him an enviable reputation; a gambler's gambler. Miller's paltry ten *ringgits*, on the other hand, bought neither fame, nor, as it turned out, fortune. Miller went for the gold, and Francis, in the end, let him down.

With his winnings—a wad of greasy bills he hadn't bothered to count—Quint recalled paying off the captain, though doubtless the wily rogue had already deducted a commission. Then, the center of attention, he'd called for drinks all round. *Drinks*. His body cringed at the thought. What on earth had they drunk? And how much? Never again, he swore, would he raise a drink to his lips. To cap it all, hadn't he lent Miller money, a thing no sane man would ever do.

Quint sat for a while like a man at the edge of a dark, deep well into which he'd dropped a line on the off-chance of catching eels. Miller? The captain? The journey back? He felt no twitch of memory. He stood up, eased his body into some fresh clothes, and stepped out onto his balcony.

The sun in the east stretched long shadows across the garden. Quint's watch had stopped, but it couldn't, he reckoned, be much after seven. It was still not hot. He filled his lungs with fresh air and breathed slowly out. For all the signs of life, he might have had the place to himself. Two figures were walking along the path to the steps which led to the terrace; waiters, perhaps, on the breakfast shift. He went back inside, pocketed his key which was on the bedside table, and emerged again, closing and locking the balcony door just as he'd done the night before. Soon he was strolling in leisurely fashion across the lawn and down the hill towards the boathouse.

It wasn't the boathouse itself, but a sort of clubhouse attached to the back of it, that housed some of the Inn staff. Not wanting to barge in at this early hour, Quint sauntered past, towards the water, and stood looking out at the dark, distant shapes of islands ringing the bay. A

movement at the far end of the pier—a flicker of white—
caught his eye. He screwed up his eyes, shading them
with his hat to see better, just as a man came out of the
clubhouse and started to run in the direction of the Inn.
Quint called after him and he stopped, still buttoning his
brown waiter's tunic. "Good morning. Is Hilton, the captain, up yet?" The man looked blank. "The captain,"
Quint pointed at the clubhouse, "is he there?"

"Captain? Captain not here. Day off." He gave Quint
an oddly searching look. Quint was about to point out
that yesterday had been the man's day off, but thought
better of it. The waiter hurried away. If Hilton wasn't
there, he wasn't there.

Unwilling to give up so quickly, loath to confront Miller
without knowing what had happened, Quint mounted the
pier and meandered along, keeping an eye out for loose
planks, projecting nails, gaps and other impediments. A
soothing breeze was blowing and he saw that what had
earlier caught his eye were the pages of a book ruffling in
it. Stretched out nearby were a pair of legs, one over the
other, ending in a rather whiter pair of tennis shoes than
it was usual to see these days. Where had he seen a very
white pair of sneakers recently? He moved nearer on soft
rubber soles. The old canvas kind, too. The rest of the
body, presumably propped against the guardrail, was
hidden by a thick pier support post. An arm dropped—
thin, pale—onto the book, stilling its pages, and the next
thing Quint saw was the brim of a floppy hat. He was glad
it was Cardew-Smythe, the only person, apart from Vellu,
he felt he could talk to about his nocturnal egression. And
Vellu was ill.

By the time Cardew-Smythe woke up to the fact that

he was under observation, only a few feet separated the two men. "By Jove," he cried, "you did startle me!" Then, as if it were his own fault that he'd been startled, he assumed a sheepish grin. "Dear me, Quint, you're probably wondering what on earth I'm doing out here like this at this hour of the morning." He picked up the book and clutched it rather guiltily to his chest. "Actually it's the one time I find I can buckle down to a spot of work. Before the children are up, you know."

It pained Quint that Cardew-Smythe seemed forever to be explaining himself to him, as likely as not apologizing. The man's conscience must be an ogre. "I'm the one who should be embarrassed," he protested. "To be honest, I didn't realize it was you till just now, though the shoes did have a familiar gleam that drew me on."

"Oh," Cardew-Smythe looked at his shoes. "Blanco." He sighed. "Old habits die hard."

"Army habits?" The other man nodded. "Only in those days you had someone to do it for you. Young Peter's father, wasn't it? Well, I'll leave you to your reading."

"Take a pew, won't you?" Cardew-Smythe looked at his watch. "Have to be heading back soon, anyway. I did rather promise Phoebe breakfast in bed."

Quint sat down on a sheet of paper Cardew-Smythe tore obligingly from a notebook. He leaned against the railing, stretched out his legs and felt better. The sun was to their backs, as was the Inn. In front, a point of land hid the town and its jetty. A few small boats bobbed on the glinting water. "What's the book?"

Cardew-Smythe read the title: "*The Malacca Straits: Economic Imperialism in the Far East, 1521–1957.*" His voice held a distinct note of scepticism. "In galley still.

An editing job I picked up. Pay isn't bad, and frankly we need the money. Takes genius for five people to get along on a schoolmaster's salary." Quint accepted the book. "New series they're doing for schools out here. Rewriting history." Cardew-Smythe smiled enigmatically.

Quint opened the proofs to page one. " 'Once did they hold the gorgeous East in fee. William Wordsworth, English Poet Laureate,' " he read aloud.

"That's a case in point. Completely out of context," Cardew-Smythe waxed indignant. "Wordsworth was talking about the Venetian Republic, not the British Empire as is implied. He was writing in 1812, unless I'm very much mistaken long before he was poet laureate. One simply can't let them get away with it. All right, we've had our innings. Now it's their turn. I'm not discounting that. All I'm saying is that scholarship mandates certain rules, a certain etiquette. Or am I wrong?"

Quint agreed. "And surely this is why they need your services?"

"It gets worse, much worse," Cardew-Smythe said dryly. He stared mournfully at his white shoes and this seemed to put him in mind of something. "We've a rather interesting program on today. Visit to a rubber plantation, followed by a *kampong* tour in the afternoon. Perhaps you'd care to come along?" He added, "I'm sure Sir Frankie would be delighted."

"Very kind, but I fancy I've done my *kampong* tour." Quint gently probed his temples. "Besides, Sir Frankie doesn't approve of me."

"Oh, I'm sure that's not the case."

"He told me so, more or less."

"Oh." Cardew-Smythe was quiet. Again the shoes

seemed to spur him on. "I do hope young Peter Forbes will see fit to join us. It really is rather crucial. By the way, I do apologize for rushing off as I did last night. Unforgivable. How's that leg of his getting on, I wonder? Perhaps you *could* put in a word. I don't seem to have much luck with him myself."

"I'm sure wherever Leila Craddock goes, Peter will be able to follow. More likely it'll be Miller who doesn't show."

Cardew-Smythe shot him a worried look. "Dear me, I wonder why?"

"He, too, did his *kampong* tour last night."

"Last night? But what could you possibly see at night?"

"A cockfight, for one thing, although it's not my favorite diversion."

"Yes, that would be more Miller's line. I suppose he talked you into it. Isn't it against the law?"

"It was all very clandestine. That captain in the dining room—the one with the gold teeth—laid it on. I think at Miller's instigation. Miller seemed keen to have a private word."

"Seems a bit rich; a cockfight, at night, in a *kampong*. Easier just to go to your room. Rum customer, Miller, I'm afraid."

"Has he changed much in thirty years?"

The other man considered. "I remember a boy at school: had an air of the illicit about him. All very thrilling to a twelve-year-old. His specialty was placing bets on the local races, although, at a pinch, he could procure anything from a cigarette to the headmaster's daughter. And he was never caught. He kept wheels oiled; his hair, too. I imagine he turned out like Miller."

"Were Miller and Sneed close in those days?"

"Sneed was the disciple, did the dirty work, took the rap, and generally lay around at Miller's feet. Always looked on the bright side and ended up on jankers."

"This new fellow," Quint went on, "Briscoe. Seems to have set himself up as the competition. Keeps something rather appetizing under wraps in his room. Miller's mood was very black yesterday."

"In his room? Oh dear ... odd about this fellow Briscoe," Cardew-Smythe went on hurriedly. "Hardly seems the same chap. Padinki, he used to call himself; sad-faced little blighter. Pole, I gather. Refugee. Wouldn't say boo to a goose. I used to feel quite sorry for him. By the way, why did Miller say he wanted to see you?"

"Something about the Chinese. He seems to have an inordinant dread of them, thought they were following us at one point. He didn't breathe easy till we were in a *kampong*, inside a hut, cheek by jowl with thirty Malays. Malays and Chinese don't mix, he said, especially at cockfights. Seemed quite glad of it."

Cardew-Smythe laughed. "He'd have a high old time in Singapore—nothing but Chinese there." But behind the quick riposte Quint detected something else: an alarm had gone off.

"But why this—sinophobia, if that's the word?"

Cardew-Smythe stared into the bay, head slightly cocked. Eventually he said: "I suppose it could be his conscience. Interesting to know if he has one."

Quint looked at him. The words had a strange, forced sound. "Meaning?"

Again, silence. "I've never seen a cockfight, Quint. I

don't think I ever want to. But in time of war, soldiers are primed like fighting cocks—to kill. Kill or be killed. Just as the cocks are given long, sharp metal spurs, we are decked out with weapons, fed with hate, fear and prejudice by our handlers, and brought into confrontation with 'the enemy.' Mistakes are bound to happen. Innocent people will suffer. Easy patrol was one of those mistakes."

CHAPTER SEVENTEEN

"As far as the brass and the authorities generally were concerned, it couldn't have come at a worse moment."

Cardew-Smythe uncrossed his legs and crossed them again in the other direction. To Quint's surprise, he seemed suddenly almost eager to talk.

"The high commissioner of Malaya had been ambushed by communist terrorists—CTs we called them—and shot dead as he ran from his Rolls-Royce to draw the fire off his wife. Templer, the new commissioner, was on his way out to take over. From our side's point of view, nothing seemed to be working. Morale was zero. If the papers had got hold of what really happened to Easy patrol that day, all hell would have broken loose. What it boiled down to was that we couldn't protect our own people, even from ourselves. A short fuse to a barrel full of gunpowder. And in the middle of it all, Sergeant-major Jake decides he has to go and get married."

Quint, glancing up, was surprised to see Ian Cardew-Smythe's lips twisted into a smile—or was it a grimace? It was hard to say. "And Miller?"

"I don't know why what happened should have left its mark on Miller more than on anyone else. I suppose—due respect to the Bard—that conscience makes cowards of some and not of others. You see, there weren't ten of us on patrol that day; there were eleven. The eleventh man was Chinese. And thereby hangs a tale.

"It was held by the powers that were that if the CTs could be cut off from their sources of supply—primarily the Chinese squatters who lived in scattered compounds on rubber plantations and along the fringes of the jungle—they could be bottled up in their jungle hideouts and starved into submission. By this time some half a million of these wretched squatters had been rounded up and resettled in hundreds of so-called New Villages. These consisted of lines of identical wooden huts surrounded by barbed wire and patrolled by the largely Malay Home Guard.

"In most New Villages, at the lowest level of intelligence gathering, there were one or two detectives. These were invariably Chinese, as often as not CT deserters. They worked in civies and lived in the security of the Village Police Post compound. They were paid for their information; pretty well, actually. If it led to, say, the capture of a terrorist on the wanted list, depending on the chap's place in the CT hierarchy and so on, the reward might be as much as $60,000 Malay. Enough to retire on, or set up in business, and many did. The average rubber tapper earned $100 Malay a month.

"One morning the company commander called me into his office. 'I've a little job for you, Ian. Nothing very strenuous,' he said. The IntO—sorry, that's the intelligence officer—chap called Radici, was there, too, with a smirk all over his face. I soon found out why. At that time the battalion was based in Perak, a hundred plus miles from here down the coast." He waved a hand. "We'd been sitting there for a year, but the regiment was being posted south to Johore. So we were putting on a bit of a last minute spurt, trying to up our grand total of CTs killed or captured which was pathetically low. My platoon had just staggered in the night before from a three-day jungle patrol where the only enemy encountered were leeches, boils, prickly heat, dhobi's itch, eczema and footrot; in fact, the usual. And rain. It had rained non-stop. Three sopping days and three soggy nights. It was Saturday. I'd promised the men some R & R over the weekend, a day at the beach or something. Anyway, 'Carry on, David,' the company commander said, glancing at Radici.

"Apparently—info just in—the CT had buried a cache of small arms near the edge of a rubber plantation just inside the jungle at a point about an hour's drive away. We were supposed to go and dig it up. Radici didn't say in so many words how he knew it was there, just the 'acting on information' bit—he liked to play mystery man—but he did say he would send along one of the Chinese detective chappies from our local New Village as our guide, so I assumed the gen had come from him. We were to leave at 1500 hours, take up positions, and go in—aiming to be out by dusk. 'Oh yes, and take young Reid with you,' the major drawled. 'Show him the ropes.' Reid was a National Service lieutenant, like myself, but fresh out of Officer Cadet School in England. He'd arrived at the base while we were away. I had met him for the first time at breakfast. He seemed like a decent chap.

"Naturally, I wanted to pick the most rested men in the platoon for the job. I talked it over with Jake, my sergeant, and, to my surprise, he volunteered himself, and

Corporal Jenkins and Lance-corporal Craddock. Said it would set an example. That made five. I needed five more, I reckoned. My batman, Forbes, hadn't been out in a while and needed a little rough and tumble, so I chose him, and Private Miller who'd been on sick parade but was up and all set to go to the beach. Private Sneed had it coming to him for sitting down on a forced march and refusing to get up, and Private Padinki, for his own good, needed to be kept busy. As radio operator I took Private O'Rourke who was built like a bull. The platoon had been split into four patrols over the preceding days—Able, Baker, Charlie, Dog—so I decided to call this one Easy. Easy patrol. And from the sound of it, that's what it was shaping up to be.

"We set off in the lorry—the Chinese guide and myself sitting up front with the driver. No escort. It was broad daylight, a well-traveled stretch of good road. I anticipated no problems; though you could never tell and we were all inclined to be jumpy after what happened to Gurney, the high commissioner. The guide seemed a nice enough fellow. Quiet. Spoke a little English. I remember asking him about his family and being quite surprised that he had teenage children. He didn't look much older than I, and I was pushing twenty. Sitting next to the engine was like sitting beside a turbine: after a mile or two I gave up shouting.

"By that time in the afternoon the rubber tappers had all gone home to their evening meals, which we'd counted on. The fewer witnesses, the less risk of a surprise attack. We split into two groups and arranged a rendezvous at a point just inside the jungle. I sent the guide off with one party under Lieutenant Reid and Sergeant-major Jake, and took the others in myself. From the rendezvous, according to our guide, it was only a ten-minute walk to the cache.

"I remember thinking what a hell of a nerve the CTs had burying their arms in what had been considered 'our' territory. Later, I heard that the IntO—Radici—suspected it indicated a major CT offensive in the area, and there'd been talk of staking out the site to see if anyone showed up; but as this might mean weeks of waiting, and the battalion was pulling out in days, the idea was dropped. Anyway, we re-formed at the rendezvous and set out single file along a pretty well-defined track. The ten minutes were pretty well up, when . . . "

"Excuse me," Quint interrupted, "but what order were you in?"

Cardew-Smythe pulled his legs up to his chest and rested his head on his knees. He seemed to stare out from behind a bony stockade. "Well, the Chinese guide was in front, of course, with Corporal Jenkins directly behind him. I was in the middle, with O'Rourke, the radio man, behind me. Reid and Craddock brought up the rear. Craddock was back marker with the Sten. I'm pretty sure Forbes, my batman, was just ahead of me, and Jake was up there, too. Yes, I remember, I put Sneed in as number three with Jake right behind him to prod him in the buttocks if necessary. That means the other two—Miller and Padinki—were behind me, which makes sense because I think they had the Bren between them."

"That's good—for thirty years."

"Except I've patrolled that jungle track I don't know how many times in my mind since. Hundreds." Cardew-Smythe's voice dropped, almost as if he were talking to

161

himself. "It seemed as if they were lined up waiting for us, like a firing squad, waiting to pick us off. They knew we were coming. They knew exactly where we would pass. There was never any doubt in my mind about that. The first shot came from behind. I'm pretty certain, because I was half-turned around when all hell broke loose in front. Whoever fired it must have had Reid square in his sights. He was killed outright. Never knew what hit him. A couple of weeks before he'd been bayonetting clumps of bracken on the Welsh hills. Then this.

"When the dust settled, Jenkins was dead, too, and O'Rourke was dying. While the others were chasing shadows through the trees, and Forbes was doing his best for the wounded man, I radioed back to base for a helicopter to get him to hospital. Then, as it was pretty dark in the jungle, I called off the chase, which had anyway proved fruitless, and we carried the bodies back down the track to the plantation, where the chopper could see us. It was only then that someone noticed the guide was missing.

"There was only one thing to do: send back a search party. Three men volunteered—Jake, Craddock and, surprisingly, Padinki. I could tell by the look in their eyes they weren't on any mercy mission. We'd all had the same thought, though no one voiced it. I said—and I remember thinking how sanctimonious it must have sounded—'Alive and unharmed, is that clear?'

"They didn't find a trace. While they were searching, O'Rourke died. He was looking at me at the time, conscious to the end. I can see him now. He had blue eyes. I hadn't noticed before. The chopper came down through a gap in the rubber and left with a full load: three dead bodies.

"Going back in the lorry, I sat up front again, alone with the driver, an enormous Sikh. This time I was glad of the noise. Somehow it deadened thought.

"By the time we reached the town—if you could call a collection of bars and brothels and a bank a town—it was dark. The New Village was a mile or two beyond, maybe half a mile before the base. I could see as we drove along the barbed wire perimeter fence that the Saturday night film show was under way. The mobile film van which belonged to the base propaganda outfit was set up on the Police parade ground and the screen flickered merrily. It looked like one of the shorts that went before the feature: *Sheep-farming in Yorkshire*, *The Royal Family at Sandringham*, that sort of thing.

"Suddenly there came a terrific hammering, metal on metal, on the partition behind me. I had the driver pull over, and was about to jump out to see what all the rumpus was, when Sergeant-major Jake appeared at the window and crashed a salute. 'Permission to dismiss and attend the film, sir!' He fairly trumpeted it.

" 'What do you think, Sergeant?' I asked, a bit taken aback. Frankly, it was the last thing I'd have wanted to do myself, under the circumstances. It always amazed me how different one's reactions were from the men's, as if we belonged to separate species.

" 'I don't see why not, sir. The men seem keen.'

" 'Oh, very well, Sergeant,' I said. 'You're in charge.' It wasn't unusual for men to get permission to attend the Saturday night film in the New Village. In fact the CO encouraged it. Came under 'fraternization,' along with the occasional football match and the Christmas party for the small fry which had taken place the week before, and was a lot healthier than other kinds of fraternization that went on on Saturday nights in town. British tommies sharing chewing gum with Chinese youngsters was the sort of image our side wanted to project. 'They can leave their gear. I'll have it dealt with.'

" 'Sir!' Jake snapped another salute. Two bangs on the side of the lorry were the signal to proceed.

"Back at base I rounded up a couple of men to unload, so the driver could take off, and was a little peeved when, along with the field packs and picks and shovels and so on, they dragged out two crates of Tiger. Empties, the lot of them. I knew at once who to blame: Miller and Sneed. They'd laid in a supply, for the beach. Six into twenty-four: four each on empty stomachs. Sergeant-major Jake had looked a bit flushed. But, at that moment, I had other things on my mind. The major would be wanting a full report.

"The more I thought about those three dead men and that missing guide, the more convinced I became that the IntO, Radici, was to blame. Certainly nobody in that lorry, besides myself and Jake, had the first idea where we were going and why. The sight of his smarmy face in my mind's eye made my blood boil. I'd have willingly disfigured it for him. I mention this," he looked apologetically at Quint, "because much later it helped me understand what was about to happen.

"The company commander was his usual passive self. This time we were alone together. I gave him a complete report, and at the end he asked for my opinion. I said there was no doubt in my mind: there had been an intelligence leak, and sending us in there was tantamount to cold-blooded murder. I may have raised my voice, I don't know. The army tends to get very itchy at words like murder, and this major was no exception. He told me to go to my quarters, relax, have a wash and a couple of drinks and he'd send for me. No doubt there'd be a full inquiry; a search party would go out first thing with trackers; jolly bad luck; did all I could; and so on. In the meantime, would I keep it to myself. Radici was in the outer office. We ignored each other.

"About an hour later the summons came. The CO was sitting in the company commander's chair and the major was dithering about the room like a jellied eel. I was five minutes into my spiel when there was a tap at the door. Radici entered, saluted, and handed the major a message, at the same time fixing me with the look I thought I should have been giving him. The major read it and passed it, wordlessly, to the CO, who read it and slowly rose from the chair. He looked, for all the world, like a hanging judge. 'Drunk,' he roared, glaring at me and fluttering the paper (later I realized his hand was shaking involuntarily). Did you *know* they were *drunk*, Lieutenant?' They were the first and last words he ever addressed to me.

"I was making a feeble stab at an answer when the major stepped forward. 'That will be all, for now, Smythe. Kindly confine yourself to your quarters.'

"There's nothing so fleet, they say, as bureaucracy threatened. And the army proved no exception. The very next day I was in Kuala Lumpur, and the day after that in Hong Kong, seconded to some Highland regiment I'd never heard of. I spent Christmas in British North Borneo where the regiment was immediately posted, and wiled away the final three months of my National Service in peaceful obscurity. Nine years passed before I discovered what was written on that piece of paper.

"I was teaching at a prep school in Wiltshire and had escorted the second eleven rugger team in an away match. It was February. The ground was hard as iron, water like a stone, and breath blended with the fog that lurked everywhere. About as far from a Malayan jungle as you could hope to get. I'd noticed this character charging up and down the touchline yelling into a bullhorn and he seemed vaguely familiar, but it wasn't till the final whistle blew and we were walking back to the locker room that I realized it was David Radici.

"His face had lost its sheen and his hair was greying. He was older than I, but not by much more than five years. I gathered, reading between the lines, that his army career had come to a grinding halt and he'd got out. The army, to me, had been a six-legged dog at a fair, an aberration, albeit unavoidable. To him it was life itself. He was obviously very bitter. While the boys wolfed their buns and cocoa, he took me off for something a little more fortifying, and pretty soon the talk turned to that far-off Saturday in Perak in the company commander's office, the last time we'd set eyes on each other. It was from that evening, I soon realized, that he charted his decline.

"The bare facts of the matter were these: sometime during the film in the New Village that night, six inebriated soldiers—a sergeant-major, a corporal and four privates—had wandered into the police compound and found their way to the house of the Chinese detective who had been our guide. They had left the village before the film ended and returned to barracks. When the film was over, someone, entering the detective's quarters, found his wife, his four children and two female relatives stabbed, hacked and bludgeoned to pulp. A canary, in a cage, had been strangled. Any noise they might have made was presumably covered by the film's sound-track.

"As soon as I walked out of the major's office, what Radici called the 'biggest damn cover-up of the whole bloody Emergency' was set in motion with himself in charge. From that moment—he realized in retrospect— his career was as good as over. An unfortunate family feud: that was the official line. Easy patrol was scattered to the four winds. The battalion decamped to Johore. Yes—in answer to my question—they'd returned to the ambush scene next morning; trackers, dogs, the works. They'd found where the cache had been dug up, followed fresh tracks deep into the jungle. No joy. Except that one of the scents the dogs picked up belonged to the Chinese guide. What did he have to gain? Damn all, as far as Radici could see. He had everything to lose. Radici couldn't sort it out to save his life. To crown it all, he huffed, that prick of a sergeant had insisted on getting married. Some Red Cross nurse. That episode by itself accounted for his grey hairs."

Cardew-Smythe got stiffly to his feet and held out a hand for Quint. "Quite possible, that's why Miller feels the way he does about the Chinese." He dusted himself off. "I don't know why I'm burdening you with it. Except, perhaps, because I'll never see you again."

"You hold yourself responsible? Is that it?" They walked back along the pier.

"How could I not?"

"And the Chinese guide/detective; he vanished? Did you ever know his name?"

Cardew-Smythe shook his head.

"And the name of the film—the one they showed that night—do you remember?"

"Darned if I do."

"It wasn't—by any chance—*Tarzan of the Apes*?"

Cardew-Smythe didn't respond. His mouth was set in a tight, schoolmasterish smile. Side by side, they climbed the steps to the Inn.

CHAPTER EIGHTEEN

"Yoo hoo! Mr. Quint. Yoo hoo!"

Ian Cardew-Smythe veered off towards his room to rouse his—with luck—still sleeping offspring. Quint continued on course to the terrace where the tables were set for breakfast and people were laying into papaya and toast and eggs and bacon.

"Mr. Quint, yoo hoo, come and sit down by me. We have business to discuss." Gwendy Jake flicked a napkin in his direction.

Quint raised his hat, bowed and sat down, and suddenly remembered his headache.

She leaned over and touched his arm, gesturing with her head at a table where the Frenchmen and the woman with the ash blonde hair were sitting. "It's the frogs you're after, ain't it?"

He looked at them, then back at Gwendy, assuming what he hoped was an expression that conveyed the infinite subtleties of the detective's calling.

Lady Jake cackled knowingly. "Frankie it was, put me onto that," she confided.

"Where is the noble knight?"

"Down the beach."

Quint wondered if she knew what was implicit in those three short words, and if, indeed, it was a daily fixture or a chance meeting on that one occasion. A waiter appeared offering tea and coffee, and filled his cup. Would they never remember the spiced milk? "You spoke of your thirtieth wedding anniversary the other day, Lady Jake. On what date exactly are congratulations due?"

"Very considerate of you, I'm sure. Actually we won't be here on the day, Mr. Quint, will we? We'll be at the E & O in George Town, over in Penang. Had our honeymoon there, Frankie and me, all them years ago. Quite the place to be seen, in the old days. Ever so posh." She sighed. "Nowadays, of course, they have all the luxury class hotels same as anywhere else. Still, it'll just be the two days, so we shouldn't suffer. Not overly."

"That won't be till next week, then?"

"Tuesday's the day. Engaged one day, married the next, and within the week back home having Christmas with my gran in Southend on Sea, showing off my sergeant-major. Some winter that was, too, let me tell you. Brrr."

"The proverbial whirlwind romance?"

"Once Sir Frankie makes up his mind, there's no stopping him." She observed Quint hungrily, then turned to glower at the French. "I'll bet it's the drugs, ain't it? A lot of trafficking in these parts, Frankie says. Oh, I'm all of a twitter. You will come with us to the plantation this morning, Mr. Quint. I do insist. All the time I was out here, I never did get to see one."

"Sadly, I must decline. Some phone calls." He pulled out his watch.

"Lucky if you get a line out. Nothing works anymore, does it? Still, I suppose you have something official you can wave at them." She looked at him shrewdly. "Do you, Mr. Quint, have something official?"

Quint managed a wink and borrowed a line from the captain. "No problem."

She lowered her voice. "Where do they *go* all day? Have you noticed? Between breakfast and dinner they disappear."

"Who, Lady Jake? Who disappears?"

"Come now, Mr. Quint. Our frog friends."

"I do wish you'd keep an eye on them," he said, absently.

She squealed with pleasure. "I was hoping you'd say that. If I hadn't been a nurse, I definitely would have joined the Force. I must confess, I'm a bit of a detective myself, Mr. Quint. Amateur, of course." Quint looked up in time to see a weary figure panting towards the pool. There was a faint splash. "You have to be, don't you?" She knows, he thought. "Always does his two laps, does Sir Frankie."

"You must be very proud of him."

"There I was in the ballroom of Buckingham Palace. I had to pinch myself. He was kneeling before Her Majesty. Her, on her dais, her throne behind her under its purple canopy. She held the sword in her right hand." Gwendy picked up a knife. "First on his left shoulder, then on his right. Then, 'Rise, Sir Frankie,' just like in the books. She switched the sword over and extended her hand. Gracious handshake, charming smile, pleased to meet you . . ."

A waiter approached—the one Quint had spoken to by the boathouse. "I fetch for captain, sir. Coming."

Quint stood up. "If you'll excuse me, Madame." She at-

171

tempted a gracious smile. He made his way inside, noticing that the Craddocks, all three, were ensconced in
stony silence at a corner table. None of the others were
down yet. Passing through the empty, shut-up bar, a faint
humming reached his ears. The noise grew: the helicopter on its morning rounds. Regular as clockwork. Vulture,
he thought. Devourer of dead fishermen. Today, he fervently hoped, it would go hungry, which put him in mind,
more urgently, of the call he had yet to make.

"I'm afraid there's a delay on calls to Penang this
morning, Mr. Quint, but if you wait in the lobby we'll let
you know the minute we get through." His friend was on
the desk, all brisk efficiency.

"At least you are getting through," he said, relieved.
"Any idea how long?"

"Five minutes, one hour. Impossible to say."

Quint hung about in the lobby, droopy tired. If only
someone would bring him his spiced milk, perhaps with a
little rum in it this morning. No, no, no; not rum. But he
didn't see any waiters or anyone else he might ask. He sat
down in one of the armchairs by the big plate-glass
window and watched the activity in the drive. A van
delivering, a man on a bicycle, two mean-looking dogs. A
taxi drove up and sat waiting. Quint wished it was Vellu's
Mercedes. He was worried about Vellu. There was something he needed to ask him; a question Vellu wouldn't
welcome. But no matter how much Vellu wriggled and
squirmed, Quint would hold him to an answer, because
there was only today and tomorrow and he'd wasted
enough time already.

Quint opened his eyes with a start and saw, through
the glass, the Inn bus. Its doors were open and it ap-

peared to have people sitting in it. From the other side of some potted plants, which screened his nook from the rest of the lobby, came voices, Sneed's castrato the most recognizable and the most persistent. Sneed, Quint concluded, had woken him up.

The kernel of Sneed's message involved a bed, an empty bed, an unslept-in bed, Miller's bed. Miller, Quint gathered, was in demand. Sitting in the van, Quint now saw, were Phoebe Cardew-Smythe, her three children, Peter Forbes, Leila and her silent Craddock guardian. Gwendy Jake and Briscoe were either getting out or getting in. Jake said: "The lad can't have vanished into thin air. Who saw him last, when?" He sounded exasperated.

"I rather think Quint saw him last," Cardew-Smythe said.

"Oh, no; not him. I don't want that one butting his nose in where it's not wanted. He's done enough damage already. Leave him out of this."

Quint, about to declare himself, changed his mind.

"I *suppose* Miller's all right," Cardew-Smythe seemed doubtful, "but should we just take off and leave him?"

Gwendy came in: "Couldn't have gone far, could he now? I'd leave a note at the desk telling him where his lunch is, if I were you."

"His lunch? Are you daft, woman? Who cares about his bloody lunch?" Sir Frankie roared. He was in a foul mood.

"All the same, I think I just might do that. No harm done, after all." Cardew-Smythe ran back to the desk while the others boarded the bus. A few moments later he joined them and the bus rattled off.

Quint sat up. He, too, wondered with some concern where Miller was. If only that confounded captain would show himself. He approached the desk.

"Your call went through half an hour ago, Mr. Quint."

Half an hour ago. Quint pointed at the armchair. "I was sitting over there." He was about to remonstrate but thought better of it, and, instead, apologized. According to his watch, he'd slept for an hour.

"I'll try it again. But it'll have to go on your bill, sir."

"Were they there, the Bauers?"

"*They* were there." She went to the far end of the desk, where the switchboard was, and sat down, her back to Quint. Two folded hotel message forms lay on the counter, inches from his fingers. The top one had Miller's room number on it. The second was addressed to a room he wasn't familiar with. He flipped it open. Just two words in hastily scrawled caps: MILLER MISSING.

The clerk was coming back. "Don't disappear again," she scolded, smiling, and pinged a bell on the counter. A porter came, picked up the messages, and left with them.

He waited ten minutes and took the call on a wall phone near the desk. Frau Bauer was puzzled but responsive, the more so when Quint lapsed into German. Ja, she remembered the postcard from the English lady in Langkawi. Ja, she had passed it on to the assistant manager here at the Eastern and Oriental Hotel in Penang. Ja, she knew the name of the Fraulein the card was addressed to, a Miss McCall from America, because the Fraulein had sought her and her husband out the next day to ask about Langkawi and the situation of her friend. But is anything the matter? Frau Bauer sounded worried. Is Fraulein McCall perhaps not well?

How would he know, Quint inquired politely, the state of the American Fraulein's health?

Ach, du liebe Gott, I knew it, I knew it, a so young girl traveling alone in such a wild country . . . It was a little while before Quint could get a word in to assure Frau Bauer that, as far as he knew, Fraulein McCall was fine. He definitely had not heard that she was not fine. The only thing he was wondering was, where was she? This unleashed a fresh flood of Teutonic anguish, during which Quint observed the entire squad of Chinese troop through the lobby, clamber into a bus, and drive off.

She left the E & O Hotel yesterday for *where*? For Langkawi? To see her friend? On the plane? Quint could scarcely believe his ears. In that case, Frau Bauer, she is here, undoubtedly, safe and sound. Yes, as soon as he found her he would let the worthy lady know. And, without a doubt, he *would* find her, if it meant looking under every palm tree on the island. No, no, a mere figure of speech, a turn of phrase. He returned the receiver to its cradle.

"Could you please tell me," he asked the desk clerk, "if a Miss McCall, an American, checked in yesterday?"

She consulted a list. "She did not, sir."

"Or is perhaps expected?"

The clerk shook her head.

Quint hurried across the lobby, and plunged into the heat and the sunlight. He felt almost normal again, ready to tackle the world. A taxi was pulled up on the far side of the drive. He'd seen it there earlier. He called out, waved, whistled, then crossed over and got in, slamming the door. The driver woke up and started the motor. As luck would have it, he was Indian.

"Take me to Vellu," Quint commanded.

CHAPTER NINETEEN

Vellu's brown Mercedes was parked in the main street, its bulbous rear end protruding rakishly. It was empty. Somehow Quint didn't believe that Vellu himself would have parked it like that. Perhaps he really was ill, as his nephew had said, not just hiding. The taxi pulled up behind the Mercedes and the driver jumped out, motioning Quint to stay put. He ducked under the tin-roofed arcade and through the darkened doorway of some sort of shop or eating place. Quint fanned himself with his hat. His shirt was already sticking to his back and he edged forward on the seat to let the air circulate. A bus trundled by, churning dust. It was far too hot to close the window.

In very short order the taxi driver returned, got in, slammed the door, pulled a U-turn and rambled back the way they'd come, all without a word or a look in Quint's direction. He made a left opposite the Chinese bicycle shop, then, almost at once, a right across a wide and bumpy expanse which could hardly be dignified by the name street. Up to the left sat—awkwardly, Quint thought, as though not sure of its status—what looked like a brand new building: long, low, raised on its own concrete plinth, painted orange. Turquoise pillars supported an arcade, behind which lurked a row of small shops. Its facade was set off by a row of concrete turrets rising, midway, to a crown-like elevation bearing the words, VELLUSAMY MANSIONS. Quint was suitably impressed.

The driver jumped out, again waving Quint down, and walked along the row of shops till he came to one at the door of which an old man bent over a sewing machine. As soon as he'd disappeared inside, Quint abandoned the taxi for the comparative cool of the arcade. Then, rather than subject himself to the gapes of a band of urchins that had gathered for that purpose, he began to walk. Soon he found himself alongside the old man who continued his rhythmic foot pedaling without glancing up. And from there it was just a couple of strides over the threshold into the shop itself.

It was cooler still in the shop and very dim. Quint, coming in from the light, could hardly see at all. He had an impression of bolts of cloth stacked all around, ascending into the gloom, and a pleasant smell of sandalwood. A woman, almost as broad as she was tall, wrapped in a sari of some phosphorescent hue, rose from behind a counter, like a full moon coming up over the ocean. Mrs. Vellu? he wondered. "May I help you?" Her voice was tiny and precise. She had a round red prayer mark on her forehead.

"Good morning. I came to offer my condolences to Mr. Vellu, who, I hear, is very ill. I hope I am not too late, " Quint added.

"Please," the woman said, smiling demurely. Then she turned to face the back of the shop and let fly with a string of what he assumed was Tamil—apart from 'condolences' and 'not too late,' that is. The result of this barrage of words was that the taxi driver burst from the gloom like a flushed partridge and was through the door

before Quint could even pay him off. Quint bowed gratefully to the woman and advanced down the length of the
shop.

Vellu was sitting on the ground in a small back room.
On a low table in front of him were spread papers in
sorted piles. Light filtered in from a barred window above
his head. He looked up not with surprise, or anger, or
embarrassment, but with resignation. His mustaches
drooped more than Quint remembered, but otherwise he
seemed his usual robust self. He started to rise, but
Quint quickly lowered himself onto a cushion, intoning: "*I
will arrange everything. I, Vellu, give you my word. Trust me.*"

Vellu hung his head. Finally, he said: "To think, Mr.
Quint, what a narrow escape you have had." He shook his
head. "And it is all my fault. That man, Mr. Quint, that
so-called driver who left here just now, he wants to
become official driver to Mr. Charles Quint. You know
how much he offered for position? Fifty dollars, Mr.
Quint. Fifty dollars Malaysian for you. Insult, is it not?
You see how fast I send him away? Why? Because he is at
all times asleep. You heard of 'sleep-walker,' Mr. Quint?
This man, he is called, 'sleep-driver.' I say to myself,
'Vellu, you are sick man, but you must go to Mr. Quint.
You must save Mr. Quint.' "

"I was sorry to hear how sick you were. Naturally, I
came at once."

Vellu laid a caressing hand on his heart. "Believe me,
at heart I am sick, Mr. Quint." The woman from the shop
entered with a tray. She poured two cups of thick, black
coffee and put the pot on the table between them along
with a plate of pink, yellow, and green cakes.

"Your wife?" Quint asked when she'd gone.

Vellu frowned. "Sister of wife," he whispered, glancing unhappily towards the curtain that screened them from the shop.

Quint sipped the coffee and nibbled a sweetmeat. He had intended to lay into Vellu with some tough questions, but now another approach seemed called for. The circumstances of their meeting had changed his mood. "This is your building?" he inquired.

"Not building; headache," Vellu waved a hand over the paperwork. "Seeing is not believing. No electricity, no telephone, no road, no hook-up whatsoever at all. Always taxes, taxes, taxes: for what? British, Japs, communists; so why not survive Malays also?" He shrugged.

Quint was intrigued: "You own buildings, shops, rubber trees. You must be a wealthy man. Why do you drive a taxi?"

"Taxi is hobby, Mr. Quint."

Quint could hardly imagine a more disagreeable diversion. "Each to his own, I suppose."

Vellu explained: "Englishman's home is his castle, is it not? Vellu's home is not castle." He cast a meaningful look at the curtain. "Vellu's home is lunatic asylum. Vellu's taxi is castle; also school. From teachers like yourself, eminent Mr. Quint, Vellu learns ways of world."

"I'm afraid I've been a poor teacher. But I mean to make up for it."

"From you I learn many things, Mr. Quint. Also, perhaps very soon, I learn embalming technique. Only lesson will be lost. Self-embalming is not possible, I think."

Quint sipped his coffee. A shrewd look had crept into the Indian's eyes. Quint had the feeling, without quite knowing why, that if he made the right move, it would all be plain sailing between him and Vellu. Accordingly he said nothing, which years of experience had taught him was often the best thing to say.

Vellu continued: "Leave well alone, Mr. Quint."

"Aha. It *was* you. I thought as much. Though I must say, Vellu, I'd hoped you were above sneaking into a man's room in his absence. Does it follow that you or one of your minions borrowed my book?"

Vellu looked deeply offended. "Sneak into room? Steal book? Who am I—thief? Nephew put small sign on door. That is all."

Quint apologized. After all, whoever returned the book could have seen the sign and stuck it between the pages. "*Because of you people is dying.* Strong stuff, Vellu. Perhaps you'd explain that."

"You do not listen, Mr. Quint. You do not take hint. After fisherman—" he drew his hand across his throat, "I tell you frankly, I am wondering who is next, Mr. Quint." He paused. "You know who is next?"—wagging a finger across the table—"I, Vellu, I am next."

A muffled cry came from the shop. Vellu rose and disappeared through the curtain. A moment later he came back. "I am too ill-mannered. I do not know how to address a gentleman, she says. You see what I mean?" He threw up his hands. "She likes you, Mr. Quint. You are married, yes, of course?"

"I was. So you've been threatened, Vellu. How, and by whom?"

"It comes on the wind, Mr. Quint. Who knows where it begins, or who starts it?"

"Then I'm afraid that by coming here I'm not helping."

"You are here. Let us talk. You concern me, Mr. Quint.

Last night, for example. Height of folly." He shook his head as over the transgressions of a child.

"Yet, as you say, I am here." Yes, he thought, it is a very small island. "Do you know of an American, Vellu, a Miss McCall? She was due yesterday on the plane. She's not at the Inn."

"Miss McCall? Please." He pushed a pen and paper towards Quint. Quint wrote the name and Vellu once more disappeared through the curtain. "And who is Miss McCall?" he inquired, coming back.

"A friend of that anthropologist." Vellu groaned and rocked his head in his hands. "Could I be very frank with *you* now, Vellu? I have had the feeling, ever since I arrived, that you think I'm someone I'm not. Perhaps some sort of American agent. I'm sorry if I've given that impression, but it couldn't be further from the truth. You seem to put this unfortunate anthropologist, who is not here to defend herself, in a similar category. Maybe you know something I don't, but if the winds that blow about me and the winds that blow about her are the same winds, then they blow false."

Vellu said: "Any American anthropologist in whole of southeast Asia would be suspect. This is unfortunate fact of life. But this is not ordinary run-of-mill American anthropologist, Mr. Quint. Or why was she killed, boatman killed, fisherman killed, all things she is writing, writing in a book destroyed? Why is body lying, even now, unclaimed?"

"This is what I'm doing my best to find out."

"There is a wind, Mr. Quint, a mighty wind over the islands. Innocent people, I fear, will be swept along in it. Such as yourself." He gave him a small despairing look.

The winds—the pilot had said, bouncing along the run-way—*Very gusty this time of year over the islands. Unpredictable.*

They sat for a while in silence. Vellu poured more coffee. Finally Quint said, "In two days, maybe three, I think the winds will die. Can you give me three days, Vellu? I leave on Sunday."

Again, the voice from the shop. Vellu went to investigate. He came back beaming. "You are in luck with your Miss McCall. She is very close by. New Asia Hotel, in fact."

Quint was on his feet, surprised. "Another hotel?"

"Very cheap. Actually fleabag. Not for gentleman."

"Can I walk?"

"One problem, Mr. Quint." Vellu hesitated. "Miss McCall is not now at hotel."

"Oh."

"She has gone to *kampong*—on bicycle." Did Quint detect a warning note?

"Then I must be after her. Incidentally, how did you know?"

"My cousin." Vellu cleared his throat apologetically. "Owns hotel."

"I, too, will go by bicycle," Quint declared, "to be as inconspicuous as possible."

Vellu regarded him with dismay. He was about to remonstrate, but, with a little sigh, changed his mind. Rather wearily, he said, "Do not worry, Mr. Quint. I will arrange everything. At any rate—" he had the grace to smile—"I will try." He contemplated the paper-laden table: "Taxes, hook-ups, drains." Sadly, he shook his head. "I survive so much, I survive you, Mr. Quint."

Vellu led the way through the shop, issuing orders in Tamil as he went. A youth appeared and ran off on an errand. Passing the counter, Quint remembered to bow to the sister-in-law who fluttered her eyelids in delight. Outside, the old man still pedalled his machine, clickety-clack. Shading his eyes against the glare, Quint saw the familiar Mercedes moored below the concrete bastion. A man appeared with a bicycle which he stuffed as far into the trunk as possible. Quint was ushered aboard with Vellu and the man up front. They bumped off. At the junction the car turned left in the direction of the Inn. Vellu pointed out a ramshackle building on the corner: "New Asia Hotel."

A mile down the road, past the mosque and the rest house, they turned left. Vellu pulled over under a shade tree near where a path led off among the palms alongside a seemingly abandoned construction site. "*Kampong*," he pointed. His man jumped out and readied the bicycle. Wobbling off along the path, Quint was conscious of three things: the heat, their watching eyes, and his own instability. Long ago, in the Resistance, he'd practically lived on two wheels.

Apart from two small boys, also on bicycles, who trailed him shouting wildly to each other but keeping their distance, Quint saw nobody. The path meandered, exhibiting no great sense of purpose. Quint looked for tire marks, but the ground was dust dry, and to his eyes, there were none. After a half mile or so the path joined up with another coming from the left, wide enough for vehicles. Emboldened, the boys zipped past him like hornets, then waited for him to catch up. By the short, anxious glances they threw each other, it was obvious they were nervous. Quint resolved to give them an even better story for their friends. As he came abreast, he stopped. "*Kampong*?" he inquired, pointing up the track. The boys, aghast at their own audacity, clutched their cycles, until, by superhuman effort, one squeezed out a nod. Quint thanked them, remounted and rode on; behind him the palm trees swayed to shrieks of triumph: they had talked to a white man with a beard on a bicycle and lived. They were heroes.

Quint felt less than heroic. Quite apart from the heat, it had finally occurred to him that white men did not usually ride bicycles into *kampongs*; white men came in cars, with cameras, if they came at all. He would be as inconspicuous as a goat in a bullring. It also dawned on him that a *kampong* is a spread-out, leafy sort of a place with no apparent focus like a temple or even a general store. Not an easy place to find a stranger in, even a white one. Gradually he realized he had arrived: wooden houses peeked through the foliage, with here and there in the green a splash of red or orange or purple. He passed a water buffalo, thankful it was tethered. No wonder Vellu had looked alarmed.

Basically, Quint thought, people broke down into two groups: those you could trust, more or less, and those you more or less couldn't. Vellu belonged to the former; as, he hoped, did he (though some might not agree). Two or three days, he'd promised Vellu; two or three days and the winds would die. He felt sure he was right. The Jakes' thirtieth wedding anniversary was on Tuesday; but before that there would be another anniversary—of a day on which seven women and children were brutally murdered during a film show. On that day—a Saturday, as it had been then—Easy patrol was scheduled to visit the Lake of the Pregnant Maiden.

The bicycle tires crackled over the *attap*-strewn surface of the track, crisscrossed now in every direction by sandy paths. Ahead of him, Quint sensed the land was opening: if he kept on he would come to the sea. Somewhere here had lived—for a short time—the woman whose last words had been *dayang bunting*, pregnant maiden. What part did that woman play in all this? She was, in Quint's mind, a misfit.

The tide was out. Quint stood—in a light that permitted no half-tones—at the edge of an expanse of mud: slate-flat, sprouting here and there with hard, dead, reed-like stumps. On either side of him curved the arms of a small bay. To his left, *perahus*—long, wooden native fishing boats—waited high and dry for the tide, and mangroves marched out from the shore in solid green profusion. To his right the land rose in a rocky, tangled ridge. Somewhere, he supposed, over that ridge or the next one lay the Inn. He kept hearing noises like lips smacking, disconcertingly close. But no matter how fast he turned, he saw nothing, as if a ghost was playing grandmother's footsteps. Anyone watching from a hut, a tree, a boat, would be having himself a good laugh at his expense.

He sought the shade of a tree and squatted down, and as he did so, his eye caught the glint of something shiny: a bicycle, lying on the ground behind the boats. He scanned the terrain for its owner. Eventually there was only one direction left to look in: out to sea. Between him and the horizon a few mangrove trees straggled across the shallows away from the main pack. As Quint studied the way the roots of one tree formed a sort of giant birdcage, he became puzzled.

Though Quint didn't move, the tree did, as if something was uncoiling itself from its lower branches.

CHAPTER TWENTY

The sun hovered, with blanching directness piercing the chinks between the leaves above Quint's head. Being neither mad dog nor Englishman—though some might dispute the difference—he had no excuse for not having brought his own shade, except that he had had no idea he'd find himself sitting on a log, in fetid mud, on the edge of a mangrove swamp, at high noon, watching a tree. It was still now, the tree, in its own dark pool of shadow. He screwed up his eyes. Had he really seen movement there?

Plop! This time the sound was right in front of him. He had only to lower his eyes to see the bubble of gas ooze from the mud which closed untraceably behind it. For a moment he speculated on the phenomenon, then raised his eyes to the tree. Quint had heard his share of tales of thirsty, heat-crazed soldiers seeing visionary women standing before them in the desert. He had campaigned himself in the sandy wastes of Africa. But he was quite unprepared for what he saw now.

Coming towards him over the mud—floating might better describe it—was an apparition: a dark figure whose head was rimmed with fire. He sensed an echo of his own voice: *Thank you, Vellu. I shall avoid the man-*

grove swamps. It was not his voice. It was a woman's voice: "Hi, there!"

Quint opened his mouth to speak. A croak came out. Tentatively, he raised a hand.

"For a second I thought you were deaf or something."

"The sunlight," Quint said feebly. "It plays strange tricks."

"Incredible, isn't it? I can't get over the—well, the sheer purity of it." She held something up. "Been taking pictures." It was a camera.

"Ah, yes," Quint said. In her other hand dangled a pair of shoes. On her head was a straw hat. The sun, shining though the brim, gave the illusion of fire. Strange tricks indeed. "My name's Quint. Is yours, by any chance, McCall?" From her accent she could be an American; but not exactly the American he had—for some reason—envisioned; her skin was a deep, natural brown.

"Yes, I am," she answered, surprise showing on her small, expressive face. She put her head on one side, trying to place him. "You live around here?"

"No. I came looking for you."

Her eyes grew wide. "You must be a friend of Gail's." Then she frowned. "But she wasn't expecting me. It was kind of a last minute thing."

Gail. "How did you know where to find her?"

"This island? Well, I knew she was somewhere around this part of the world, and she knew I'd be in Penang, and a couple of days ago I got a card."

"Saying she was here?"

"Yeah. Well, not exactly *here*." She looked around. "But when I said '*kampong*,' they pointed in this direction. I guess there are others though." She looked puzzled. "Is anything wrong?"

"I think we had better sit down." They did—on the log.

She stuck out her legs. Her jeans were rolled to the knees. "How the heck am I going to get cleaned up enough to put my shoes on? Ow!" She jumped up. "Ants."

Quint got up, too. The log was seething with them. He brushed himself off. No other shady place presented itself. With a little laugh, she said, "Can you imagine *living* in a place like this?"

"Were you—are you close friends, with—er—Gail, Miss McCall?"

"We were roommates for two years in college. You go through a lot. And we've kept in touch. That's the real test, I guess."

"You are also an anthropologist?"

She laughed and dug a toe into the sand. "That's a touchy question. There comes a time in the life of every anthropologist when one has to earn a living. The short answer is, no. I'm not. I don't know how much you know about Gail, but her thesis caused quite a stir after it was published. She became what we call 'weaned.' That's when you go from mother's milk to bottles. In other words, she got grant money. Did she tell you about her book?"

Quint scratched his beard which had developed an annoying itch. "We never spoke at all. I'm afraid, Miss McCall, your friend is dead."

There was a silence, broken only by the plopping of gas bubbles in the mud; then came a sort of gentle moan which ended abruptly as the woman put a hand to her mouth. A moment or two later she withdrew it—gradually—and appealed to Quint: "Why . . . How . . . I mean . . . how do you know?"

"The way I heard it, she was in a boat." He pointed at the *perahus* nearby. "Like those, I suppose. It was at night. The night before I got here. An accident, they say. They took her body to Penang on the plane. Strangely, it has not been claimed. The boatman died, too."

She stared blankly at the boats. "That explains it."

"What?"

"Oh, people. I've been desperately trying to find her, asking everyone I could where she lived, and so on. All I got was some sort of fear: head shaking, doors closing. It was weird. Because Gail had said that everyone was so nice to her."

"In letters?"

She nodded. "A postcard. *Dead*. I can't believe it."

"I think we should go back to your hotel." She went for her bicycle. Quint picked up his. "There's a bit of a stream over there." He pointed. "If you want to wash."

"Good, the sand's sure cooking my feet."

She washed them and put on her sandals. They rode slowly back through the *kampong*. On the way in, Quint had noticed a house different from the others in that it had rattan furniture spilling out and propped against it. Now he saw three men standing outside. One of them waved. Quint waved back, curious. One of the boat crew, perhaps, from yesterday? An Inn employee? He dismounted, and, approaching, saw that the place was, in fact, a small furniture factory. Headboards of intricately twisted fibre, a couple of rockers, a mirror framed in plaited cane were set out on display. The man greeted him warmly at the door in halting English. His colleagues smiled. Miss McCall came up and Quint introduced her. They shook hands all round. He still couldn't place the man. "Boat? " he queried, pointing back and forth.

The man shook his head and made a drinking motion. He pointed at Quint. Then his head slumped forward onto his chest and his friends roared with laughter. Quint joined in, somewhat weakly. Embarrassed, he turned to Miss McCall and tried to explain. "A surprisingly potent brew, they make here; but it seems it made me a friend."

"Do you think he could show us where Gail lived?"

With sign language and the few words of English the man knew, Quint managed to make himself understood. Leaving their bicycles, they followed him through the trees, past wooden houses in neat compounds, some with laundry hanging out to dry and water buffaloes tethered nearby. On the edge of a little clearing he stopped and pointed. There, framed by leaning grey-stemmed palms, stood a house smaller than any of the ones they'd seen, yet in every respect similar—from its *attap*-thatched roof to the hand-hewn wooden supporting posts, to the lean-to at the back for livestock. Bright red flowers cascaded from hanging planters, and a hammock looped from post to post. The back wheel of a bicycle protruded from a dark corner. It might have been someone's dream cottage. The windows were shuttered tight.

Miss McCall stepped forward, but their guide, with a word and a raised hand, restrained her. She seemed to accept this, and stood for two minutes, quite still. It was clear to Quint she was saying goodbye to her friend. Then she held her camera to her eye, clicked the shutter, and turned away. They trooped back, shook hands again with their new friends, and pedaled on.

Not only was Quint hot and sticky, his legs and back were sore. By thinking from one bend to the next, and trying to fool himself about the overall length of the journey, he somehow kept the wheels turning. His companion, in much better shape, was already only glimpsed at intervals on the straighter stretches, flitting among the trees. She seemed to have forgotten about him. They had left the *kampong* but were still on the wider track when, looking up through sweat-splattered glasses, Quint saw the Inn bus approaching. As usual the driver had his foot down—fast was the only speed he knew—and Quint prudently pulled over and dismounted. He didn't have the energy to wave. A blur of squashed, moist Anglo-Saxon flesh and they were past.

As Quint prepared to coax a leg over the saddle, he heard behind him the squeal of brakes, and, looking back through a dust curtain, saw the bus door open. He waited. After a short interval the head and shoulders of Ian Cardew-Smythe emerged. "I say, Quint, you've no idea where Miller could have got to, don't suppose?"

"No idea."

"But he was with you last night?"

"Yes."

"And you returned to the Inn together?"

"We went our separate ways."

Cardew-Smythe would have persevered, Quint had a feeling, had not his fellow passengers restrained him with howls of protest. He waved feebly and the bus took off, leaving Quint with a mouthful of grit to add to his woes.

Miss McCall was waiting for him at the New Asia. She

had had time to get cleaned up and change into a blouse and skirt, and was sitting at one of three tables in a tiny eating area across from the desk. A tall glass in front of her held the remnants of a drink. Quint leaned his bicycle against the wall and collapsed onto a chair. "The food here's pretty good," she said.

A young Indian woman came out from behind the desk. "Two more of those, please." She vanished through a green plastic curtain at the back. Quint downed his drink as soon as it came, and asked for another. "What is it?"

"Mango and pineapple." They ordered curry of the day from a blackboard. "Why wouldn't he let us near the house?"

"You're the anthropologist."

"Kind of taboo, do you mean?"

Quint shrugged. "Very likely."

"What happened to her things, I wonder. All her notes. Do you think they're all still in there?"

"Whatever there was went with her, I'm told." No point in elaborating. "She was writing a book, you mentioned?"

"Expanding her thesis on the Sea Gypsies of the Malacca Straits. Everyone thought they had died out, more or less. B.G. Before Gail."

"She rediscovered them, so to speak?"

"She lived with them for a year, moved with them up and down the coast. That was the basis for her thesis."

"What do you know about them, Miss McCall—these Sea Gypsies—from her writings?"

"They live on boats, I gather. They look down on the Malays as an inferior race. They make temporary settlements on land, particularly, these days, on so-called 'uninhabited islands.' Officially they don't exist any more, except in a controlled environment—as a tourist attraction, mainly in Thailand. They've been given pretty much the short end of the stick by all the authorities, which is why they lie low. I think Gail saw herself as a sort of tribal mother figure—a voice to the outside world type of thing. She was very involved. She wouldn't even tell people where she was at any given time—even her parents—in case it compromised her work. The postcard kind of surprised me."

"And yet you came?"

"She didn't say *not* to. And—I don't know—I just had this feeling."

The curry was excellent: chicken in a rich coconut sauce. Quint ordered beer. "That's interesting. Do you still have that postcard, Miss McCall?"

"Yes, I have. Right here." She produced it from a canvas hold-all slung over the back of her chair. The picture was of a sandy beach dotted with brightly quartered sunshades and semi-naked white tourists, palm fronds in close-up and a couple of islands, shaped like chefs' hats, floating in an azure sea in the background. In yellow script along the bottom were the words: 'Greetings from James Bond Beach, Phuket.' "Typical Gail. Probably the most ghastly card she could find."

"Funny. I left there only last week," Quint said. "It's in Thailand." He turned it over, noting the uncanceled Malaysian stamp. "May I?"

"Go ahead. It's not her writing, by the way, which was kind of spooky at first."

'Dear E,' the card read, in a prim, schoolgirlish hand, 'Surprise, surprise. Am just a hop across the water from you—Langkawi. 99 islands, mostly empty. Living in *kampong*. People v. helpful. Have neat boatman to take me round for a song. Verification etc. Many OL legends originated around here: white rats etc. V. exciting. Something more in your department, too. Would rather not get involved myself. Sprained wrist yesterday, stupid me, but nice English lady took pity, in case you are wondering why you can read this. Wanted to get it off today. G.' The address was, Edie McCall, c/o E & O Hotel, George Town, Penang.

"OL?" he queried.

"*Orang Laut*. A Malay name for the Sea Gypsies."

"And what do you think she means, 'in your department?' "

"I kind of wondered myself."

"What *is* your department?"

"Social studies. I teach. You know: if you can't do it, teach it."

Quint knew precisely. "Some day I will read her thesis," he declared. "I don't even know her name."

"Gail Sonnenberg."

"Gail Sonnenberg," he repeated thoughtfully. "Could you describe her, Miss McCall? Was she tall, short, blonde, brunette?"

"Oh, tall. Taller than me. Hair brownish; she could never do anything with it, which always bothered her." She smiled. "Gail was an extremely precise person. One reason she was such a very good anthropologist. Trained observer and all that."

"Precise, you say," Quint scratched his beard. "I find that interesting."

"Her writing was the only messy thing about her. She had kind of a long, thin, serious face. But a terrific sense

197

of humor. Her father is a rabbi. Somewhere near Boston. Her parents just doted on her, which I think she sometimes, well, tried to push away, you know. Gail was an only child."

"I'm not sure how to say this," Quint groped for the right words, "but in some parts of the world the American anthropologist has acquired an unfortunate image, I am told, almost as if he was, by definition, an extension of his government's intelligence network . . . "

She laughed. "Don't worry. If Gail was here she'd say it for you. And rather more succinctly. You should have heard her last fall at the AAA Convention. Fairly laid into them on the subject. She was determined to keep her Sea Gypsies out of politics: the ass-kiss of death, she called it, typically. I can see her now . . . That was the last time I did see her." She leaned her face in her hands and cried.

Quint waited. He had one more question to ask. When she removed her hands and wiped her eyes, he said, "Do those words *white rats* mean anything to you? Anything at all?"

Edie McCall thought. She thought for a long time. "Yes. It's coming. It wasn't just rats. Other things, too. They were white because they lived all their lives in caves. And the Sea Gypsies knew the caves. That's where they would hide. A recurring theme in their songs and legends."

"White crocodiles, too, perhaps?"

"I used to kid her that they must be racist, those Sea Gypsies."

A small crowd had gathered on the street corner, watching the visitors eat. When the brown Mercedes pulled up, Vellu, from behind the wheel, admonished

them, and they drifted away. Before leaving, Quint asked
Edie McCall what her plans were. "I guess I'll take off as
soon as there's a seat on the plane. But I wish I could be
sure about her notes."

"I'll do my best," Quint promised. "If there's any problem, I'm at the Inn." They shook hands. The last he saw
of her was through the rear window of Vellu's car. A for-
lorn figure wheeling a bicycle.

CHAPTER TWENTY-ONE

"You know more Langkawi legends than anyone, Vellu. Do any of them tell of white rats?"

"White crocodile, Mr. Quint, you already know. White rat?" Vellu frowned, then brightened. "But all things can be arranged."

They drove towards the Inn.

Quint explained Miss McCall. "It is as I feared," he concluded, "the American anthropologist stumbled onto something and was killed, along with the boatman and the man who tried to rescue her. As you yourself pointed out in a perceptive moment, Vellu, the crocodiles are not out in force any more; on the island, it is common knowledge. Yet this woman, who was nobody's fool, had the last word—two words, to be precise. And she was, Vellu, according to her friend Miss McCall, a most precise person."

The car rolled into the driveway of the Inn, turned a half circle and stopped by the front door.

"There *is* one thing perhaps you could arrange. A space on the next plane. Miss McCall would—wisely—like to leave as soon as possible. And Vellu, perhaps a little sightseeing, so she does not wander off alone."

Vellu bowed assent over the wheel. "I am also, only this afternoon, hearing of incident at airstrip, Mr. Quint.

Unauthorized person is trying to board today's plane, offering pilot much money. One of the English."

"Miller," Quint said.

"Same person who accompanied you last night." Vellu's voice dripped disapproval. I told you so, it said.

"Well, what happened?"

"Without proper booking it is impossible to board. Plane is chockablock. Man is desperate, Mr. Quint. Wants to climb in with baggage even. Did not come in bus or taxi, but crawled out of bushes."

So Miller had roughed it for the night. "Where is he now?"

Vellu shrugged. "And you, Mr. Quint, what will you do now?"

"First, a brief siesta, or I, too, will be crawling out of bushes. Then," he tapped his head, "I must think. We are in the third act of a tragedy, Vellu. We are almost on the stage ourselves. It is in our power, if not to fashion a happy ending, at least to bring about a less unhappy one."

"*Our* power, Mr. Quint?"

"Yours and mine, Vellu." He patted the dash. "We are both learning, are we not, the ways of the world?" He got out. The Mercedes glided away. The absence of the Inn bus indicated that Easy patrol had not yet returned from the excursion.

Quint didn't stop at the desk. His key was in his pocket, and he hurried straight to his room. Turning the key in the lock, he pushed open the door. Then quickly closed it. Cautiously, he reopened the door. The curtains were drawn, and in the half-light he made out the shape of a body stretched out on his bed.

Leaving the door wide open—Quint didn't believe in

unnecessary risks—he tiptoed towards the bed. It was
Miller. He was lying on his back, half clothed, with two
day's worth of hair on his face. He appeared to be asleep.
Quint went back and shut and locked the door. He was
about to open the drapes as a prelude to waking Miller,
when something he saw stayed his hand: on the floor, on
the window side of the bed, was the little green airline
bag Miller had had with him the night before. He scooped
it up and carried it into the bathroom.

Sitting in the spot where, as the French say, 'the king
goes alone,' Quint unzipped the bag, which bore the im-
print *Nigerian Airways*, and looked inside. On top were
some papers. He pulled out an airline ticket, made out
to Miller: Lagos—Abu Dhabi—Bombay—Bangkok—
Penang, and back. A second ticket, Penang—Langkawi—
Penang, showed Sunday as the return date. A British
passport, well-thumbed, was made out in Miller's name.
Quint examined it curiously. Birthplace: Bermondsey.
Occupation: oilrigger. A change of clothes—slacks and a
shirt—was all that was left in the bag. Yet its weight
suggested more. Quint felt around: something solid
wrapped in the slacks. He carefully unfolded them, and
soon was staring down at a sizable revolver. He probed
the shirt. Something there, too. A box—he opened it—of
slugs. He examined these, wrapped everything back up
and repacked the bag. Then he switched off the bathroom light, opened the door, and peered out.

Miller still lay prone. Quint kept an eye on him as he
circumvented the bed, replaced the bag, and doubled
back. Quietly, he let himself out, and stood in the hall, ear
to the door, listening. Satisfied, he proceeded to reenter
the room as noisily as possible. He switched on the light,

banged the door, shouted, "What is the meaning of this?" and exhorted Miller to wake up.

At last Miller stirred. He groaned, blinked, swore, twitched, subsided. "Miller!" Quint roared, and the strength of his voice surprised him. "Miller!" He thwacked the bed with a handy umbrella, raising dust.

Miller sat up like a jack-in-the-box. "No," he screamed at the ceiling, holding his arms out rigidly to ward off the expected blow. "Get away from me!"

"I'm over here," Quint said. His voice was very measured. "And I want to know what you're doing on my bed. Wrong floor, old chap. Yours is upstairs." He pointed with the umbrella.

Miller cringed. He looked not at Quint, not at the ceiling, but down at the floor, where his bag lay, and Quint knew he was back to normal. "Blimey. Must have dozed off." He slid off the bed, picked up the bag, and looked at Quint: "Mind if I use the back?" He pointed. "The bathroom."

Quint eyed the bag. "Yes, I do. You've a perfectly good one of your own. State the purpose of your visit, then kindly leave. Unless you've come to pay me what you owe. In which case, do that and leave."

Miller felt around in his pockets. "Bloody leeches," he cursed. "Suck you bloody dry."

"Spent it all on the pilot, did you?"

He grinned ruefully. "Got around, has it? Mind if I sit down?"

"Oh, go ahead. Break in, sleep in my bed, make yourself at home. How *did* you get in, anyway?"

Miller jerked a thumb at the balcony door. "Piece of cake." He sat in the armchair. Cool customer, Quint thought, if a limited repertoire: the precocious brat and the craven bully. "Yes, well now that I'm here," Miller settled himself comfortably, "reckon we have some unfinished business, you and me."

"You intrigue me. Go on."

"If I have something you're after, and you have something I'm after, seems a pity not to do a swap."

"Go on."

"Information," Miller began.

"In exchange for?"

"Protection?"

"Depends on what you've got."

"Red hot." Miller rubbed his hands.

"Meaning?"

"I told you last night: he's here."

"Come, come, Miller. You've got to do better than that."

"How about, if I win the reward, it splits two ways."

Quint smiled his most pitying smile. If Miller imagined he was some sort of spook, as Peter had put it, he would play the part to the hilt. Some stray words of Vellu's came to mind. "Do you know what C.O.D. means?"

Miller cursed. Suddenly he looked like an out-of-shape boxer sagging against the ropes, gooseberry eyes dull with the introspection of defeat.

Encouraged, Quint ventured further. "If you want protection, what are you afraid of?"

"Friggin' Chinks, that's what. Too damn many of 'em for Milly's liking hereabouts."

Quint decided to push his luck. "How do you know he's here?"

Miller said nothing for a while. He stared at the wall. "It's him all right."

"But how do you know?"

"Who else would go to all the trouble?" He got to his feet, swaying dangerously. "Come out yer damn yeller bastard." He jabbed left and right into the air. "Come out and fight like a man."

Quint stared dispassionately at a picture of a very fat woman engaged in bestiality with a monkey pricked out in purple on Miller's stomach. He was thinking. Would Miller have ever known, let alone still remember, the name of that Chinese guide/detective who'd led the patrol into the ambush thirty years ago? Would he know about Ah Sook, the wanted bandit of today? "If I'm to be of any use to you, I need an answer. How do you know it's him?"

"It's 'im."

"Have you seen him?"

"Nah," Miller shook his head.

"Do you know his whereabouts?"

"Nah." He rubbed his perspiring face with the inside of an arm.

"Perhaps your conscience is playing tricks on you. You see, I know what happened."

Miller bristled. "Meaning?"

Quint ignored him. "What I don't understand is why you accepted Sir Frankie's invitation in the first place. Did you find him, or did he find you?"

"Me find him?" Miller laughed. "What would I want with him?"

"He's a wealthy man."

"Should be. Got a few grand of mine tucked away for his rainy day, and Sneedy and me stony as Gibraltar. About time he coughed up a round or two."

"Yet here you are trying to run away?"

Miller bridled. "Who said run away? I'm just going to claim what's mine, that's all."

"A little prematurely, perhaps, since you've yet to find your man."

"The island's small enough. He's here."

"Where does Sneed come in? You've been friends for a long time."

Miller considered this. "We have our ups and our downs. He's Paddington, see, born and bred. I'm Bermondsey. Larked around a bit in the forces; then, when the boot came, we landed on the same stinkin' dungheap. Two's better than one—as they say—and we've looked out for each other ever since. On and off. Oil rigs and such. From the Java Sea to the Gulf of Guinea. Thirty years." Miller slumped back into the chair. "But there comes a time . . . Between you and me—bit of a twerp, ain't he? Milly may be all by his lonesome on this one."

"I suggest you go to your room, shave, get some rest, and, for the next day or so, stay close to your friends here. Charging off on your own makes you an easy target."

Reluctantly, Miller moved towards the door. "Come on up with me, guv'ner," he bleated, clutching Quint's arm. "I'd feel ever so much safer."

The first thing Quint did, after shaking off Miller, was open his balcony door to let in fresh air. The man had picked the lock efficiently without breaking it. Part oil rigger, part petty thief. Whatever he was, Miller alone had sensed the menace hanging over the group and tried to do something, however inept and self-serving. Quint lay down on the bed and closed his eyes. His mind whirred away like the works of a clock. Someone was moving around overhead. After a few minutes he reached for his book and read. 'Those who have a better understanding of the Oriental mind tell me that among the uneducated Chinese, personal pique can reach such limits that a man will be quite prepared to kill himself—let alone sell himself—if he thinks that it will cause sufficient harm to his rival.'

Quint snapped the book shut. Everything was conspiring to keep him awake. In that case, he wouldn't fight it.

In Fort Wayne, at the home of a friend, he had once assisted in the laying of wall-to-wall carpeting. And this humble domestic activity had appealed to his sense of the way things should be done. The room was a certain shape; the carpet must lie in a certain way. Starting at one wall, pulling and kicking the carpet to fit the idiosyncrasies of the room, proved counterproductive: while conforming in one spot, it would be out in others and develop unseemly bumps and wrinkles. No. First the room must be cleared and the carpet arranged the way it wanted to lie. Carpets, like people, Quint had noticed, have minds of their own. Once the carpet was at peace with the entire floor, then it could be cut to shape painlessly, a perfect fit, and tacked down. The room—cleared—was the mystery. The fitted carpet was the solution.

As the impedimenta was removed, bit by bit, the shape of the room—the shape of the mystery—clarified. The solution was allowed to embrace the mystery in the most natural way. Most mysteries, in Quint's experience, inhabited the minds and emotions of people. The measure of a person would be the measure of the mystery. Now, at last, the measure was emerging with all its nooks and angles. Quint had a feeling it already stared him in the face, in all its simplicity and humanity.

CHAPTER TWENTY-TWO

In the words of that little-known savant, Hegesippe Simon, whose misfortune it was not to have lived in the era of wall-to-wall carpeting, 'Everything falls naturally into place, given a sporting chance.' Lying on his back, on his bed, Charles Quint attested to this. And despite bodily lassitude, his mind was busy. It was putting together the composite of what at first had seemed just a presence, but now was taking on the semblance of a man.

A man of patience: he had waited thirty years. A precise and secret man, with a head for detail and organization: to have gathered so many antipathetic people under one roof. A confident man: to have imposed no restraints on them. Yet ruthless: three people dead. A man at home with the symbolic: timing, place, numbers—seven victims, seven vanquished—the film show, even the plantation tour. A rich man: it must have cost a pretty penny. A cat among mice: who knew intimately the prey he was playing with; and here Quint was nonplussed, because that Chinese guide/detective, as far as he knew, had only spoken with Cardew-Smythe in the cab of the truck, and sparsely, above the din of the engine, nor was there anything to indicate that the others knew him from Adam. Radici—the intelligence officer—had been his only contact.

From all this Quint drew one further conclusion: the man must have an accomplice, someone on the inside, a Judas perhaps, who—for whatever reasons—was prepared to deliver up erstwhile mates and colleagues to the day of judgment, which was to be—Quint was convinced—the day after tomorrow. Saturday. The night the New Village held its film show. Would it be at night, he wondered; if so, where? And how? Would they all answer, or just the seven men? Had one man—or woman—been granted immunity? Who was this person? This, Quint knew, was what he had to find out; his chance to intervene in the third act.

Quint closed his eyes. He summoned up the faces of the condemned—yes, the condemned—in ghostly lineup. Which was different; the face of the white rat? Young Peter he dismissed at once. Merely the stand-in for his dead father; the child—as he himself had said—of a man who had eaten a sour grape. Beyond his old man's vague allusions, he knew little of Easy patrol, though perhaps more than he admitted. Padinki, alias Briscoe: a man much changed, apparently, from his soldier-boy days, even to his name, and hardly for the better. What had caused this? What was his game? Why had he not arrived by plane like everyone else? Quint would have to probe more deeply here.

Miller and Sneed. Tweedledum and Tweedledee. Were they in it together? Why did Sneed not show the same fear that Miller did? Why had Miller tried to escape alone? While both men struck him as opportunists, the type who are in constant need of cash, neither seemed to have the requisite intelligence. Craddock. A bully of a man, separated from his soul, like curds from whey.

Quint could see him making a deal, in cold blood; drawing up a contract, specifying a sum, killing with a shrug. *Had* Gwendy Jake called him a murderer? Then there was Cardew-Smythe: an interesting case. Preoccupied, solicitous, jumpy, he too, by his own admission, in need of cash. Overly sensitive for the role? Or so guilt-ridden— a conscientious officer haunted by his failure to meet his responsibility—that he saw this as a form of retribution? And he remembered the Chinese guide.

Quint in his mental checklist had left the Jakes to last because they seemed in all but one respect the obvious choices. Sir Frankie was footing the bill. The invitations had gone out under his name, travel arrangements were handled by his office. It was the Jakes' anniversary; to all intents and purposes their idea. Yet Sir Frankie was rich, successful, a brand new knight with a respectable retirement to look forward to. It didn't make sense. It had made sense—briefly—when Quint had perceived Gwendy to be the power behind the throne, seeking to revenge a lost love. Indeed, he still did not rule out a capacity for foul play in that department. But he had come to the conclusion that Gwendy was neither more nor less than she seemed: a fussy, chattering, bewigged remnant of a once-flirtatious, golden-haired Red Cross nurse. Except in one respect: under her sugary crust seethed something close to hatred for the man who called her Lady Luck, his little fortune cookie.

A sunbeam, playing on his eyelids, worried Quint awake: the late afternoon sun was slanting through a chink in the curtain. He got up, showered and changed. All was quiet in the room above. The hall was deserted. Quint passed the housekeeper's trolley laden with towels and linen, cleaning articles, water decanters, and saw, through an open door, the floor-maid making up a room. People came and went, but some people just stayed, he thought, oblivious of danger. He had set himself the task of saving them; and had little more than a day to do it in. As he turned to climb the stairs to the floor above, he saw that a few people were gathered on the terrace, probably for cocktails or early supper. It was that time of day. Easy patrol would soon be filtering down, rested from the exigencies of the *kampong* tour.

Quint crossed the upstairs lounge and tapped on the door of a room not facing the sea. He waited, hoping as before, that Craddock would not charge out of his room further down the hall. The door opened a crack, then wider, then all the way. "Why, if it ain't Charlie Quint; it's a pleasure." They might have been in Purley. Briscoe closed the door, locked it and stood rubbing his hands in a 'Mine Host' attitude. He seemed to be alone. "Name your poison." He advanced towards the dressing table on which were arrayed an assortment of bottles and some glasses.

The bed was unmade. Articles of clothing—mostly women's—were flung around, a sweetish smell hung in the air, and the steady drumming from the bathroom indicated that the shower was on. Quint gestured towards the noise. "Have I come at an inconvenient moment?"

Briscoe's baby face registered surprise. "Inconvenient moment?" he repeated. "What's an inconvenient moment? There's only two sorts of moments known to Nicholas Briscoe of 2, The Warren, Purley: convenient and even more convenient. And you, sir, our quintessential Mr. Quint, have chosen the latter. But then I always said, didn't I, as soon as I saw him," he moved some clothes from a chair, addressing them, "this one has breeding, didn't I? This one is a cut above." He offered Quint the chair. "Now when she makes her entrance, do me a favor: jot down on this pad—here's a pencil—the first figure that pops into your head. That's all you have to do." He bustled over to the drinks and picked out a bottle. "Can I interest you in . . . ?"

Quint waved it away. "I'd like to talk," he said. "Either here, or," he glanced towards the bathroom, "elsewhere."

Briscoe sat down on the bed and spread his arms in a welcoming gesture. "Fire away." He seemed to adjust quickly to the turn of events. "Take your time now. All the time in the world." Though his smile did seem a trifle forced, Quint noted, ascribing it to the investigative reputation he had so shamelessly cultivated with the help of Gwendy Jake.

"Since your time is obviously valuable, I'll be brief. Does the name, Ah Sook, mean anything to you?"

Briscoe shook his head and shifted the gum he was chewing from one cheek to the other. "Nah." He seemed surprised by this apparent deniability, so much so that Quint believed him.

"Thirty years ago you were an army private doing your National Service here in Malaya. Am I right?"

"On the nose."

"You went out with Easy patrol under Lieutenant Cardew-Smythe, as he then was. The patrol was ambushed?"

"Right."

"Where were you in line of march?"

"Right behind Miller. I had the legs of the Bren."

"I wonder if you could recall just what happened?"

"It was darkish in there, in the jungle. All of a sudden they was blastin' away at us. I dropped right where I was and crawled into the bushes. I thought I felt blood, you see; that I was hit. Turned out I was one of the lucky ones. My water bottle got it. Bloke behind me died." He added, with a touch of pride: "I still got that bottle."

"In Purley?"

After a second's missed connection, "Yeah, yeah, Purley," he said. "2, The Warren, Purley."

"Yet you volunteered to go back in with Craddock and Jake to look for the missing guide. Why?"

"Here was my water bottle, and three blokes dead, and I hadn't even fired a shot. I could have been dead and never knew what hit me. I'm telling you, if I'd found the son of a bitch I'd have done him in for what he almost done to me. Fuckin' Chinks. Stab you in the back soon as look at you. Anyway, we settled his hash good and proper. And I'll tell you this, Mr. Q," he leaned forward and tapped Quint on the knee, "that was a red letter day for Stinki Padinki. Never again did he take it without giving it back with interest. I suppose," something struck him, "come to think of it, that was the day old Stinki died." Briscoe roared with laughter. "I'd do it again today." The next thing Quint knew he was leaping around the room, lunging and jabbing with an imaginary dagger, as though possessed by a fiend.

"And the canary," Quint asked when Briscoe sank back onto the bed, a happy smile on his flushed face, "was that your work, killing that?"

Briscoe dismissed the canary. "Sneed done that. I saw

him." He added in belated self-defense, "Had it coming to him, didn't he?"

"Did he? Because of the ambush?"

"And other things." He chewed his gum defiantly.

"Such as?"

"Diddled us, didn't he? It wasn't just me. Not a man among us wouldn't agree. Highway robbery. Come to think of it," he snapped his fingers and his face took on a remembering glow, "that's what we called him. Yeah. The Highwayman."

A small portion of Quint's mind registered that the shower had stopped running. His faculties were intent on this new bit of information, casually tossed out: the Chinese guide/detective was no stranger to Easy patrol.

"Did you know his real name?"

Briscoe waved a limp wrist in the air as if swiping half-heartedly at a fly. "Some Chinese shit. Who knows. From that day to this, who cares?"

Quint waited, eyeing the bathroom door. He knew somebody cared. He wasn't sure whether it was Briscoe. "This—er—diddling; what was that about?"

With a dismissive growl Briscoe was back on his feet. He seemed to find it hard to keep still for very long. A pink bubble of gum escaped from between his lips. "What's it matter; what the hell's it matter?"

It mattered very much at the time, Quint reflected; but he didn't pursue it. Briscoe was getting jittery. Instead he asked, "By the way, how were you ticketed here? Originally, I mean."

The pink bubble flashed and, this time, popped. "London—Bangkok—Penang—Langkawi."

217

"In actual fact you skipped Penang and came by boat from the mainland. Any special reason?"

"Business, as I think I mentioned. I came under my own steam from Bangkok."

"Business, and, perhaps, pleasure?" Quint glanced towards the bathroom. "Sir Frankie raised no objection?"

"Not when he inspected the goods. For a man of his years to run a mile for his little piece of fun—tempting fate, isn't it? So much more convenient just to step up to Nicky's place. And Nicky is ever so discreet." He winked. "Convenience: a very saleable commodity, by and large."

A sound which seemed to come from just outside the window distracted Quint: something between a yawn and a train whistle. He got up and moved aside the curtain. Laid out, corpse-like, on the concrete balcony was Sneed. As Quint looked, Sneed's mouth opened and the sound came again.

"One of my best customers," Briscoe cracked his knuckles. "Course, I don't ask what I should. There are other ways of seeking your reward on earth, as you yourself well know, I'm sure. Take Miller, for instance. I brought him in here, him and Sneed, and I said, 'Gents, be seated,' I said. Then the door opens, and in she comes, just like I taught her." Briscoe wiggled his hips suggestively. "You could have heard Miller's jaw drop over in Perlis. So I says, 'That's your teaset by Tupperware. Looky, looky, but no touchy, touchy.' Then she withdraws like I told her, and I say to Miller, 'Sneed stays. You go.' I swear if I'd have pricked him with a pin he'd have burst. The look on that face: fury. Worth gold to me."

Which, Quint remembered from the day before, was hardly an exaggeration.

Sneed stood braced in the doorway, trying to focus on Quint. "Must have dozed off," he murmured pleasantly.

Briscoe nudged Quint: "Ask him. Ask old Sneedy about The Highwayman. Tell him, Sneedy. But don't tell him here. The Happy Hour is over." He had them both by the elbows and propelled them towards the door. "Company coming. And by the by," he whispered on gummy breath into Quint's ear, "*should* you ever want to do business, I may have something of interest."

The door was open. They were leaving. Quint said: "Who's in the room opposite, do you know?"

"Some of our yellow friends." Even as Briscoe spoke, his words were confirmed: two Chinese filed out, locking the door behind them. Without so much as a glance at the three watching, they disappeared downstairs. To Quint, they looked very young. Why in the world, he wondered, would Cardew-Smythe want to send them a message?

"Miller's back," Quint told Sneed, "in case you hadn't heard."

Sneed hadn't; nor did he seem particularly concerned. "Comes and goes, that one. Like breakfast, tea and dinner." He shook his head philosophically.

They were ensconced among potted palms by the silver screen in the upstairs lounge. Sneed was still in a state bordering on trance.

"He's suffering from what he thinks may be a terminal case of sinophobia," Quint continued.

Sneed smiled his pleasant smile and closed his eyes. "Got the jitters, has he? Same as in Haadyai. Came over him something frightful."

"Haadyai?"

"Don't tell him I told you or he'll kill me, but we

stopped the night there between Bangkok and Penang, Milly and me. Bit of a lark. R and R."

"This place—Haadyai?—is in Thailand?"

"Just across the Malay border. Regular joy town."

So Miller and Sneed had made an unscheduled stop in Thailand between Bangkok and Penang. Interesting. "Does the name, Ah Sook, mean anything to you?"

Sneed shook his head. "Who's that?"

"Briscoe tells me you knew a man you used to call The Highwayman. What was his real name?"

"The Highwayman? That Chinky tec. Nasty customer. Led us into that ambush, he did. Cost the lives of three good men to my certain knowledge. We paid him back though, in our own way. Even Steven. Best thing we did all war, though you'd hardly have thought it, the way they hustled us to kingdom come as if we were lepers."

A slight figure in a sweat suit appeared at the far door and stood for a moment, as if sniffing the wind. An old fox, Quint thought, who has turned the hunt into a game, going through the motions after real fear has fled. Sir Frankie, satisfying himself that the coast was clear, advanced softly into the room on rubber-soled running shoes. Then he saw them. Raising a hand, half in salute, half to quell verbal communication, he walked on, his face a mask.

"V.I.P." Sneed sniffed. "Ask *him*."

"Ask him what?"

"About that Chinky tec."

"Why ask him?"

Sneed held up two yellowed fingers. "Like this they were." He rubbed them together. "Thick as thieves."

CHAPTER TWENTY-THREE

Old fox that he was, Sir Frankie Jake would not easily let himself get caught. Of this, Quint was sure. But once cornered, Quint was reasonably certain he would talk. Sneed had told him enough about Sergeant-major Jake, British Armed Forces Malaya, to persuade him of that.

According to Sneed, Frankie Jake and the man they called The Highwayman, or the Chinky tec, formed two legs of a flourishing partnership. An extraordinary alliance that fattened itself in the seamy interface between two warring worlds, one British and one Chinese. It was the sort of operation that lent itself to a nasty backwater of a war that the world by and large ignored. The sergeant brought to the business a knowledge of the workings of British army bureaucracy; he knew the rules and how to bend them. The Chinese detective added to this the cunning of a seasoned guerrilla: trained by the British to harry the Japanese occupation forces; fighting with the so-called communist terrorists against the British; finally leaving the jungle to assist the British against the CTs. As Sneed put it, "Quite an act." Their combined expertise served them well.

The meat and potatoes of the operation, Sneed explained, was the cash reward system administered by the authorities. As Quint had learned earlier from Cardew-

Smythe, amounts ranging into the tens of thousands were paid out, depending on the rank of the fingered communist and his or her status on the wanted list. If the big fry were few and far between, even an ordinary CT could fetch a respectable $2,500 Malay, a year's normal working wage. The detective had the knack of pulling them out of the jungle; and since everybody looked good when a CT gave himself up, not too many questions were asked. CT food dumps and hide outs were, similarly, highly convertible.

Jake specialized in arms and ammo, also profitable as every recovered enemy weapon was paid for. A cache could net a fortune. As Sneed said, "Jake knew where every gun and bullet in Perak was, from the Portuguese musket in the Ipoh museum to the latest Yankee submachine gun, and had dug the holes to prove it." Well, not personally, of course. The tec arranged that. And Jake couldn't collect the take; Chinky did that, too. The men called their sergeant-major The Undertaker, but if he overheard, he'd dock you three days pay and make you back marker; so, in Sneed's words, "it passed into history."

Jake brought his own flair to the partnership, running a lucrative 'sweepstakes on death,' where soldiers going out on patrol bet on their own or their comrades' chances of 'copping it.' The dead won big; the wounded did not do badly. For some, Sneed said, it made the prospect of the next world easier to bear, though he'd never gone for it himself, not having any loved ones at home to benefit.

Another profitable sideline of the partnership was servicing the Tommy in his off hours. 'Safe' prostitutes were arranged for in 'safe' coffee shops; supposedly in all respects contamination free. For which, naturally, a percentage was skimmed. The 'cloak and dagger brigade,' as Sneed called the base intelligence unit, haunted by the fear of spy penetration, looked with a certain favor on this arrangement: an effective means of minimizing risks.

Yes, there *had* been an incident, Sneed recalled, where Padinki—as he then was—caught something. He'd sworn it was from the girl. The Highwayman had sworn she was clean. The problem was that this was the first girl Padinki had ever gone with, and when he finally had to admit it, he became the laughing stock of the platoon with The Highwayman right there, laughing along with the rest, which Padinki hadn't appreciated. Jake, Sneed went on, must have made a mint in his few years in Malaya. "How he got it out is the poser, but he must have, mustn't he? It takes money to make money. We all know that."

Sneed's pencil mustache arched and fell to his words which seemed designed to paint his former sergeant and present host in the worst possible light. Conceivably he was under the impression that Quint's mission was to investigate Sir Frankie Jake, and laid it on with malice born of envy.

Quint did nothing to correct his assumption. He asked if it were true that Sir Frankie had used his influence to get Sneed released from jail so that he could join the Easy patrol reunion.

While affirming that someone had 'lubed the tube' and advising Quint to stay out of Lagos jails ("the worst in the world, not that I'm any judge"), Sneed declared that he was in only on a minor charge and would have got out anyway in a matter of days. Sir Frankie, he avowed—if indeed it was Sir Frankie—had done it for some convoluted reason of his own. Which was fine by Sneed; he wasn't complaining. Sir Frankie was constitutionally incapable of an unselfish act; was, indeed, the prototype for Sneed's Second Law of Survival: 'Do unto others what they would do unto you if they could.'

Quint mused aloud that Sir Frankie's generosity was indeed interesting in that he had brought them to this beautiful island, all expenses paid. To which Sneed's only comment was a sniff.

Quint had observed that Sir Frankie liked some last laps in the pool before the light faded. He had used this knowledge earlier to ensure his time for conversation with Gwendy. Now he would put it to use again to catch her husband. He stationed himself on the terrace with *The Jungle is Neutral* and a tall drink, maintaining a detached air lest anyone take it into his head to join him.

Sir Frankie appeared on schedule through the gloaming, still in his sweat suit, from the direction of the tennis court. On leaving Briscoe's, he must have skirted round past the air conditioning plant to appear—to one particular pair of watchful eyes—to be returning from a harmless jog on the beach. Appearances, Quint thought, still mattered to shrewd Sir Frankie Jake. He strolled with his drink towards the pool.

"Yoo hoo!" Quint had barely had time to arrange himself on a chaise longue strategically placed near the little heap that was Sir Frankie's sweat suit, when the dread chirp of the Gwendyfowl—as Peter Forbes had once put it—sounded at hand. He lay back and closed his eyes. Perhaps it chirped not for him. "Mr. Quint, Mr. Quint."

He opened his eyes. Gwendy Jake was bending over him like an examining physician. Her eyes were tiny lights at the bottom of dark wells. Her headdress glowed a brighter orange in the sun's last burst. "I did it," she whispered.

"What?"

"What you said. And guess what?" Quint tried to recall what he'd said. Gwendy Jake sat down on the edge of the chair reserved by Quint for her husband. "They meet in a specially provided room. The manager's probably in on it."

"Our French friends?" he at last remembered.

"They write things on a blackboard. Stuff and nonsense. Code. Mark my words, that's what they are: code crackers. Knock me down with a feather, you could have." She watched his face intently.

"Well, indeed!" The figure in the water was slowly breast stroking his way to the deep end. Sir Frankie wasn't good for many more laps. One, perhaps. Quint wished Gwendy would fly away. Then, in one of those bizarre mental leaps that turn annoying interruptions into heaven-sent opportunities, inspiration came. "My dear Lady Jake," he said in a voice as low and urgent as he could make it, "you have the makings of a first-class international spy. So listen carefully. This is a memory test. Cast your mind back thirty years. You are married. You are leaving Malaya with your husband to return to England. You are boarding the plane. You did go by plane, did you not?"

"From Butterworth, the R.A.F. base. Just across from Penang. First time for me, on a plane. We'd spent our honeymoon, see—if you can call two days a honeymoon—at the E & O on the island . . . "

Quint held up a hand. "You are walking out to the plane, you are mounting the steps, and you are carrying in your hand," he leaned towards her confidentially, "*what?* What are you carrying in your hand?"

"I am carrying in my hand . . . Let's see now. Frankie has my left arm in his." She pushed out her left elbow. "And in my right hand I am carrying—my blue silk purse to match my going-away outfit, which was . . . "

"Quite so," Quint interrupted. "Very good, very good. I should have realized. And Sir Frankie, in *his* left hand, what is he carrying?"

She thought for a second. Sir Frankie, streaming wet, was pulling himself onto the concrete. "Our wedding cake! The one the chef at the E & O made special. Ever such a surprise, it was; weighed a ton. Frankie insisted we take it with us to show the people at home."

"After tasting it yourselves, of course?"

"Oh no; cutting it would have ruined the icing. 'Gwen and Frank,' it said, with two hearts entwined, and silver wedding bells." How ingenious, Quint thought, a wedding cake. A number of things slipped neatly into place.

Sir Frankie padded towards them. He did not look pleased. "Excellent," Quint congratulated Gwendy. In truth, it was himself he was proud of. It was one thing for fate to throw morsels in a man's way, quite another to concoct a meal of them. "Great memory you have. I wonder if you can get what's on that blackboard. Quickly, before they rub it off." Gwendy scampered away, just as her husband came up.

Quint watched Sir Frankie step into his sweat suit and zipper up. "I'll thank you not to fill her head with absurdities, Mr. Quint. She's a simple lassie, highly suggestible at that." It was supposed to be a parting shot. Sir Frankie turned to go after his wife.

"Would you rather I told the truth?"

"Truth?" Sir Frankie rounded on him as if he'd been spat at.

"Oh, not about your little assignations. That, after all, is your own affair."

"What the bloody hell are you on about?"

Quint saw two spots of color mount in Sir Frankie's cheeks. He knew he had hooked something. "I suggest you sit down. It won't take long."

"It better not." Sir Frankie sat.

"Happy anniversary, by the way. Or, as I believe you say, many happy returns of the day, which, I gather, is Tuesday."

"Mr. Quint, I did not come here to be insulted by a complete stranger and a fool at that."

"Insulted? I merely wished you . . . "

"It is sufficiently trying being in this place at all, without your wishes. And now, if you'll excuse me." He stood up.

"Then why do you stay?"

"As I told you before, *I pay my debts*." He hammered in each word.

Quint gestured at the empty chair, as if Sir Frankie was still in it. "Ah yes, your debts. Which brings me to my point."

"There is one, is there?"

"Do you know the name Ah Sook?"

"Never heard of it."

"It's Chinese." Quint watched closely. The sun had set and the lights not yet come on around the pool. Sir Frankie's face was shadowy. "But you do recall your one-

227

time business associate? Arms, you were in then, I believe. And other things."

Sir Frankie's face betrayed not a glimmer of feeling. He
eyed his interlocutor squarely. At length, very conclusively, he said: "He's dead."

"Aha? In the ambush, was it—you were close behind
him—or later perhaps, when you went back to search?"

"He was a double-crossing son of a bitch, and he's
dead. Shall we leave it at that? Whatever you're playing
at, Quint, it's not going to work."

"Suppose I told you that next morning the dogs picked
up his tracks, fresh tracks, leading into the jungle?"

"He was a turned CT. They didn't turn two ways. Too
much blood on his hands. If you knew anything, you'd
know that." A pause. "You're in over your head, Quint.
Take my advice. Get out."

"What was his name—in those days?"

Frankie Jake laughed; mechanically, like a tractor
starting up; mere noise, without conviction, without reso-
nance. "He's dead and gone. If he's not—show me."

"I'm not a betting man, but you're on." Quint stared up
at the smattering of early stars. "Why have you gathered
them here? Why are you doing all this?"

Sir Frankie stood up. "As I told you: I pay my debts."
He walked away. Quint closed his eyes. He heard light
feet pattering on the tiles. A good epitaph, he thought:
He paid his debts. Something like despair was plucking
at him, the hand that creeps across the face of a harp.
Then he heard the steps coming back, and Sir Frankie's
voice nearby saying, "You're barking up the wrong tree,
lad. You know what they say, don't you: ask an officer."

After the footsteps had mingled with the clink and

chatter from the terrace, Quint went on sitting. The cicadas, the frogs and the other night voices kept him company. Collaboration with the dead is impossible. And Sir Frankie, Quint leaned to the conclusion, thought the man was dead. Unless he wanted so badly to believe it that he'd convinced himself.

When the pool lights popped on, Quint rose and hurried towards the Inn. After all, he thought, there's more than one way to silence a pig.

CHAPTER TWENTY-FOUR

Dinner was well under way by the time Quint reached his ringside seat on the terrace. A wind was getting up and giant rattan awnings had been rolled down on his side. They banged and rustled like restless sails. *Are you sure, Mr. Quint, that only the winds will die?* It was not a good omen. And, like the proverbial bad penny, the captain had turned up. He bustled over as soon as he saw Quint, gold teeth flashing. "Hey, Mister, you're welcome." He bent to light the candle on his table in its little red jar. "So you like our native *arak*, eh? Heh, heh. I trust you are operative after some shut-eye. I myself had the pleasure of tucking you up."

Quint wondered dimly how much this extra service had cost him. "And Miller, what did you do with him?"

"That crazy guy." The captain scowled. "Nothing but problem, problem, problem. He passed the night in the airport lounge. No kidding."

The airport lounge, Quint recalled, was a shed with a thatched roof at the end of the landing strip. "I see he's back now at the heart of things." Miller was indeed dining with the rest of Easy patrol, though, from the look on his face, he wished he was anywhere but.

"Lousy no good British tour group," the captain muttered darkly, following Quint's gaze. "See that golden oldie with the red top. That one is forbidding me near her table. Me, captain." He thumped his badge of office. Quint wished he had Gwendy's nerve. "Well, tough shit. Because the moon will drop into the bay before a British leaves one single percent over ten. I am speaking of tips, you understand." He summoned a waiter, who was already standing beside him, to take Quint's order and stalked off to glower at Gwendy Jake from a safe distance. Quint looked at the waiter to see if his captain's performance ignited any spark of amusement in his eyes. Not a glimmer. He gave his order.

If Miller looked glum, Cardew-Smythe looked ill. His thin face had about it the pallor of the grave. Yet he struggled to show interest, concern, amusement or whatever mask the farce in progress seemed to demand. Quint had the feeling he was watching some intricate classical mime. He had a sudden urge to clap, but suppressed it.

Ask an officer. Sitting at dusk by the empty pool, thoughts of Ian Cardew-Smythe, husband, father, schoolmaster, one-time conscripted officer, had floated in Quint's mind. What, besides rank, had distinguished him from the others? In the eyes of the Chinese guide, surely one overarching factor: he had not participated in the bloodletting, had wielded neither knife, bayonet, *parang* nor blade of any kind. Nor, of course, among present company, had Peter Forbes. But Peter's father had. And—in the mind Quint was seeking to know—wouldn't father and son be one? As he supped, Quint watched Cardew-Smythe with a nagging fascination.

He was still watching when a stir in the far corner of the terrace nearest the kitchen caused the assembled heads to turn. Even the French paused in their deliberations.

Quint saw a white cake, aflame with candles, held high by a waiter who zig zagged towards the center of the room. The cake reached the Jakes' table amid a smattering of applause and much neck-craning. 'Gwen and Frank,' it proclaimed, with two hearts entwined, and silver wedding bells. Quint didn't need to look. He looked, instead, at the lookers.

Emotions, from delight on the part of Gwendy Jake to stony anger on the part of Sir Frankie, flitted across the faces at the table. Phoebe Cardew-Smythe appeared mildly amused. Her husband, on the other hand, looked relieved, as if the burden of appearances had been temporarily transferred to the cake, which had been placed not in front of Gwendy, as might have been expected, but at Sir Frankie's end of the table.

Gwendy had jumped up and joined her husband, and those at her end—Sneed, Briscoe, Leila and the elder Cardew-Smythe girl—had followed. Only Cardew-Smythe himself, who'd been sitting on Gwendy's right, hung back. He appeared to drop something, and as he bent on one knee to pick it up, rested an elbow a trifle awkwardly on the table. To cheers and bravos Gwendy blew out the candles.

As people went back to their places, the waiter cut the cake and passed it, and Cardew-Smythe stood dutifully to propose a toast, or several toasts. Quint couldn't hear the words, but three times glasses were raised to lips. The Queen, most likely, then the loving couple, and finally— Easy patrol, the future, long life and happiness—Quint could only guess. Then, suddenly, confusion. People running, crowding together, some shouting, a woman's scream. Standing, Quint saw that Leila Craddock had collapsed, face down, over the table. He saw Craddock and Peter leap towards her. The Turk screamed. Phoebe Cardew-Smythe bent solicitously over. Ian shouted for a doctor.

A hush spread across the terrace as faces once more turned to stare, alarmed, inquisitive, anxious. Here and there people stood to see better. Several approached the table; others restrained their children from doing so. Someone, nearby, said "Food poisoning." Quint had once seen a man poisoned in Italy, where you could never be too careful. The victim had jerked backwards, tearing at his neck, and been dead in seconds. Leila's symptoms were different, though she looked deathly ill. Then, as sometimes occurs in an emergency, someone stepped forward out of the blue and took charge: the elegant woman with ash blonde hair from the French table, the silent one with the piercing eyes. At her approach people stepped back, yielding place. Definitely a doctor. Even Gwendy the nurse, fussing ineffectually on the periphery, fell silent.

The Frenchwoman knelt beside Leila as Phoebe, under direction, raised the limp body gently from the table. The doctor felt her pulse, her forehead, peered into her eyes, and, looking round, dipped a finger into Leila's glass and licked it. Frowning, she repeated the process, and glanced at Phoebe with a question which was answered to her apparent satisfaction. She gave some incisive commands, and Leila's body was gathered into Craddock's arms and, with Peter rather superfluously holding up the legs, whisked off through the curious crowd. The wailing of the Turk rose in frightful dissonance with the bleating of the electric organ which chose that moment to start up.

The French doctor followed, but not before picking up Leila's glass, which she took with her. Sir Frankie, making a show of comforting his wife, stood for a moment glowering at the table, before he, too, swept out, Gwendy on his arm.

Quint pushed aside his half-eaten dinner, sat for an interval, then wandered towards the cleared table, empty now save for half a cake: one silver bell and the word 'Gwen.' He stood behind Gwendy's chair. To her right had been Cardew-Smythe, next to him his daughter, and beyond her, Leila. Quint proceeded to a point between the daughter's chair and Leila's, dropped down on one knee and, pretending to pick something up, examined the floor. When he looked up it was into the suspicious eyes of Gwendy Jake.

"Did you ever see such a thing?" She put her hands on her hips.

"How is she?"

"How would I know! That woman," Gwendy hissed, gesturing with her thumb at the table where the French group sat, "has got her. Barged in without so much as a by-your-leave. Won't let anybody near."

"I presume she's a doctor."

"Of what, I'd like to know." Gwendy picked up the remains of the cake. "Ain't that something," she looked lovingly at it, "and what a coincidence after what I was telling you. Only this time I'm going to be sure and have some."

"This time?"

"Didn't I tell you? After nursing it all the way home in the plane like a baby, he goes and leaves it in the blooming train. How do you like that? Thought he'd have clean forgotten, I did. Full of surprises is my Frankie. Such a lovely evening—spoilt." She wandered off clutching her trophy, pleasantly tipsy. Quint went back to his table.

As soon as the French doctor rejoined her party Quint approached, bowed, and introduced himself. He spoke French adequately. What was the prognosis, he wondered, in respect of the young woman who had been taken ill? He only presumed to interfere because he was engaged in reviewing the establishment for an influential travel guide, and, in the event of food-poisoning . . . At this the woman gave vent to a contemptuous snort. Food poisoning! Nothing of the kind. Simply a case of induced vomiting. Quint raised an eyebrow. The beer in the glass, explained the doctor, contained a large dose of an emetic, a common enough substance, widely utilized in the medical profession. The sample, of course, had not been chemically tested, but she would go on oath . . . How or why it had found its way into the glass was anybody's guess. She shrugged expressively.

So there was no real danger? Quint wanted to be certain. A little discomfort, that was all, replied the doctor. She seemed healthy enough otherwise. Bed rest for twenty-four hours, yogurt, and yes—in answer to another question—the effect would have been more or less instantaneous. The doctor introduced her colleagues: distinguished mycologists on their way to an international symposium in Bangkok. Each man delivered himself gravely on the improvements he would make to the hotel, until Quint, at last, managed to back away, nodding and gesticulating. He left them enmeshed in the pros and cons of mosquito netting over screens.

For an instant Quint wished he *was* writing a travel

guide. The organ, now blaring "White Christmas," would be the first thing to go. The captain was running after him: "Mr. Quint, there is an Indian guy from town waiting to bother you. Shall I tell him to get lost?"

A brisk moonlight walk around the side of the Inn helped restore Quint's equilibrium. Vellu was sitting alone in the Mercedes on the far side of the driveway. He climbed in beside him.

"News, Mr. Quint." Quint could tell it wasn't good. "That young man who is coming to the car, when fisherman is here, who wanted very much to become drunk, who later cut his foot?"

"Peter Forbes. What about him?"

"Today, in *kampong*, he is trying to find boatman to take himself and one other tomorrow, crack of dawn, to Perlis on mainland."

"Peter and Leila!" Quint exclaimed. "I can hardly believe it."

"You are right not to believe," Vellu said. "Next forty-eight hours no boat may leave island with any tourist. By order."

"Whose order?"

A tired smile puckered the Indian's cheeks. He shrugged.

"I see," Quint said. "Well, no matter. They wouldn't have got far." He recounted what had happened at dinner. The lambs who stray from togetherness must be coerced. What had Phoebe said? *I think in some previous incarnation he must have been a sheepdog.* "Incidentally, how long would a fast boat take to reach Perlis?"

"Maybe forty minutes," Vellu said, "maybe one hour."

Nevertheless, Quint felt bad that his little experiment with the cake had furnished such a timely diversion.

CHAPTER TWENTY-FIVE

He was standing, this morning, at the very end of the jetty, leaning on the wooden rail, looking down. Quint chose a spot a few feet away and leaned over, too. A shoal of tiny fish wheeled this way and that, their bodies shimmering in the clear water. Ian Cardew-Smythe showed no signs of noticing him. He was intent on the fish. Then, in a soft, clear voice, he said, "I think I should like to die like Albine, in a supreme hiccup of flowers."

Quint was surprised, glimpsing in those words a whole other person, like a chink of blue heaven through a clogged and cloudy sky. He said nothing. As much as he'd thought about it, he hadn't come up with an opening. Cardew-Smythe had seemed a reasonable man; and it was to his reason, not to his emotions, that Quint wanted to appeal. As he stared into the deep, he fancied the water-logged features of Cardew-Smythe were already down there, looking up at him. They seemed to smile. He glanced to his right. He *was* smiling; faintly.

"A penny for your thoughts," the Englishman offered lamely.

The tables were turned. "To be honest, I was thinking of you. I noticed you at the dinner party last night. You seemed preoccupied."

"Never good at that sort of thing."

"At slipping potions into glasses?" A long pause. Quint kept his eyes steadfastly on the fish.

At last the other man spoke: "What are you going to do?"

"I must know the truth, all of it, before I answer that." He added, "I'm trying to save lives."

"I, too." Cardew-Smythe's voice was tone-dry. "Does that surprise you?"

"Not entirely."

"To make any sense I'd have to go back a few months. I'd also have to ask you for an undertaking. You see," a pleading note crept into Cardew-Smythe's voice, "it's come so far. In a few hours it will all be over. You must not intervene."

A doubt stole into Quint's mind. The wonder was it hadn't done so before: was this man sane? "Tell me," he said.

"Then I suggest we sit. Less visible." He looked towards the Inn. "No, this is absurd. It's too late, anyway." But he slipped down, his back to one of the pilings. Quint also. "It's quite simple really—brutally simple. A year and four months ago I took a high school teaching post in Singapore, a decision I've come to regret bitterly. My subjects were—well, are, I suppose I should say—literature, history, that sort of thing. I also coached the senior debating team. One day, last June, one of my best debaters told me his father would very much like to meet me. I was gratified. I'd hardly met any of my boys' parents and on the whole I felt rather cut off from the Chinese community, although I wanted to be friendly and to know them better. On the appointed day I was picked up at school by a limousine. The chauffeur ushered me into the front seat and we drove off. I was surprised the boy didn't get in, too. When I looked round, he'd gone.

"We drove in silence, and it wasn't till we were crossing the viaduct on the East Coast Expressway that I began to wonder where we were heading. It seemed strange that a man who could afford this sort of transport would live in one of the high-rise flats near the airport, so I questioned the chauffeur. When he didn't respond, I tried out my Mandarin, which is rudimentary to say the least. You can imagine my pique when the man started chuckling, and went on chuckling.

"We were almost at Changi before, in good English, he said: 'Do you not remember our last little trip together, Mr. Ian Cardew-Smythe?' Of course I'd no idea what he was talking about. Then he said, 'Conversation was restricted by noise. Those army lorries were rattletraps. You had the kindness to inquire after my wife and children. Had you delayed your inquiry a matter of four hours, I would have furnished a very different answer.' He took off his sunglasses and chauffeur's cap and laid them on the seat.

"At the airport he didn't stop, just circled back towards town. We spent the next two hours driving around Singapore: Jurong, Bukit Timah, the Race Course—it was all a blur to me as I sat listening to this hungry ghost. Even minus the cap and glasses I wouldn't have recognized in his hard, lined face with its grey, bushy eyebrows, the young, rather soft features of the guide of thirty years ago. At the end he dropped me at my house—he knew exactly where it was—saying that, in future, all communication would be through his son. 'I am here at

some risk,' he explained. I haven't seen him since."
Cardew-Smythe stretched out his legs and settled himself more comfortably.

"But you were sure it was the same man?" Quint had
followed intently.

"Absolutely," Cardew-Smythe insisted. "He recalled
details no one else could possibly have known."

"He had married again, I take it?"

"Yes. He'd obviously made a new life for himself. But
he didn't go into that."

"Did he talk about the ambush?"

Cardew-Smythe nodded. "As if it happened the night
before." He seemed to sink into a kind of reverie. Quint
noted that, this morning, he hadn't brought his book.
"They took him alive, the CTs. That was the plan. They
knew he'd be coming; they knew when, they knew where.
And he made it quite clear to me that he wasn't the one
who told them. They planned to torture him. For every
one of their comrades betrayed to the British since he
had left, they proposed cutting off a member. They
started, that night, with an ear; his left. He showed me.
Then, he said, he had an idea. He admitted his sins. He
agreed to die the most excruciating death they could de-
vise. But first he would lead them to the arms cache."

"Surely," Quint interjected, "it was their cache?"

"That's what we thought. But war does what it does.
He told me candidly that he himself had buried those
arms so he could claim the whopping great reward that
was offered for bringing such stuff in. Anyway, the CTs
hurried back so as to be well on their way before dawn,
knowing that soldiers and trackers would be out in force
at first light. They were delighted with the haul. Each

man staggered off, laden, and of course their prisoner had to shoulder his share, though they were careful not to give him ammo. While they were trekking back through the jungle, he escaped anyway. They chased him for a while, but in the end the arms seemed more important and they returned to where they'd dropped them. Our friend made his way north by jungle trails into Thailand."

"If he was blameless, why not return to the village?"

"He was afraid. He knew what people would think. He didn't stand a chance. He was right: he wouldn't have. And he heard what had happened to his family."

"So all these years he's been waiting?"

"For a sign, he said. It came when Phoebe and I moved to Singapore. One of his sons was at school there. Immediately, he had him transferred to my school."

"How did he know . . . ?" Quint didn't need to finish.

"He knew precisely where every member of the patrol was, and what they were doing; dates, places, finances, personal lives. He reeled it off like a school text, without recourse to a single note. He didn't say how he knew. He just knew. His request to me was, as I say, simple: Easy patrol to foregather here on this island for one week in December, money no object. A holiday; everything paid for. It was either this, or, he was sorry, but each member of the patrol would die a separate death.

" 'So,' I remarked somewhat facetiously—I suppose by then I'd got used to him—'We die separately, or we die together. What difference does it make?'

" 'Not you,' he said. 'You are the exception.' And of the others, only one would suffer, not a hair of the other's heads would he touch.

" 'Why only one?' I asked, cynically.

243

"Because, he said, only one man besides himself knew in advance about the buried cache. 'He alone will die. But before he dies, he will confess in front of all of you that because of him three British soldiers died, because of him seven innocent Chinese were slaughtered. The proof of guilt will then be irrefutable.'

"What could I say? He was talking about his own wife and children, and though it had happened so long ago, it was obviously as fresh in his mind as the face of the son he'd just seen. Besides, I had a responsibility for what had happened. It had haunted me. This was my chance to exorcize it. I told him that such an opulent invitation, out of the blue, from a penniless schoolmaster, would only arouse suspicion and disbelief; that it would never work.

" 'But you were their officer,' he insisted.

"I'm afraid I laughed. It seemed so pathetic. The man had gone to incredible lengths, at goodness knows what cost, emotional and otherwise, yet he'd misjudged on such a simple point. And then I thought of Frankie Jake. Of all of them, his was the one name I'd come across in all those years. And a couple of days before, it had turned up again in the paper—in the Birthday Honors. Sir Frankie—as he was about to become—owed me a favor; and a quick calculation disclosed that his thirtieth wedding anniversary was coming up. An invitation at this time from the sergeant who made a name for himself would be much harder to turn down than one from me. Besides, he could afford to fund the whole thing himself. It might even appeal to his ego. And, of course, his office could take care of the arrangements. Much simpler.

"When I mentioned the idea to our friend, he was immensely tickled; the thought of Sir Frankie footing the bill particularly appealed. 'You ask him,' he said, 'and I will make it hard for him to refuse.' I asked him what he meant. 'He is not a Sir, yet,' was all he would say."

"It must have been quite some favor," said Quint.

"I saved the man's life. Sounds a bit melodramatic; in fact, it was frightfully mundane. To cut a long story short, a lorry was backing over him and I stopped it."

"And Jake's Betting Parlours sprang up all over England."

"A life is a life."

"And the life that will be lost—tomorrow?"

"Retribution is retribution."

"And 'our friend,' as you call him, where is he?"

"I don't know—physically. But I must say I sense his presence."

Quint murmured a room number.

Cardew-Smythe was clearly surprised. "Yes, that's the son. Here with a number of friends, though none from school, I might add. He is still my only contact. My job is simply to keep our group together. Phoebe—who knows none of this, by the way—would point out that I was eminently qualified. She's fond of telling people that 'sheepdog' is my middle name. However, I have my work cut out. One has to resort to the most bizarre methods at times. *Vide* last night. They were trying to run off on their own, you know. And, I must say, you haven't been too helpful." He shot a sideways glance at Quint. "What is your interest in all this, may one ask?"

"Tell me the name of our friend."

"I know this sounds ridiculous," Cardew-Smythe was embarrassed, "but I don't know. At school the son is registered under the name of an aunt, his guardian. I myself only met our friend once before—in the lorry—and if I heard the name then I have forgotten it. Radici, the IntO, seemed a likely source, so I wrote off to him, but the only address I had was that school in Wiltshire. After a couple of months the letter came back. It had been forwarded from one place to another and was returned, postage due, with a note in a shaky hand saying that the poor chap had passed on. Reading between the lines, one rather deduced it was by his own hand."

As Cardew-Smythe spoke, Quint began to feel vibrations. Solid as it seemed, the pier was tingling. He leaned forward and saw a phalanx of Chinese advancing towards them. "We have company."

His companion seemed unconcerned. "Oh, it's the fire brigade. Ignore them and they'll go away." Quint recognized the Chinese from the Inn. Faces here and there were beginning to stand out. They milled around on the pier, admired the sunrise, exclaimed over the fish, and all the while, with studied zeal, avoided noticing the two men sprawled against the pilings a few feet away. After a while they drifted off and the pier ceased to tingle. "They gather at potential trouble spots, like red corpuscles. Probably wanted to make sure I was all right. You are developing a reputation, it seems."

"A word from you, and they'd have torn me limb from limb?"

"I'm not sure what they'd do. It's never come up, and, touch wood, never will. The worst they've done so far is 'borrow' a book from you. Apologies. I made them put it back."

"And fiddled with my fountain pen, perhaps?"

"Your arrival caused a bit of a flap," Cardew-Smythe

confessed. "Nobody knew who you were. In the world we live in, innocent things like pens become lethal weapons, it seems. I trust yours passed muster."

"I've given up weapons," Quint said. "Dangerous to one's health." He wondered if Miller's pistol had also been cleared. "Tell me, does the name Ah Sook mean anything to you?"

"Ah Sook. Well, *Ah* is a prefix denoting a certain amount of respect or perhaps even affection. I rather think *Sook* is Cantonese for uncle on the father's side."

"And this helicopter that comes around," Quint asked, "what's that all about?"

"There's been a lot in the *Straits Times* about bandits and smuggling and so on north of here. I think they're cracking down. They have a joint border patrol, which would account for its Thai markings."

"How do your Chinese see it?"

"The helicopter?" He thought for a moment. "They don't particularly like it."

"I ask because the man known as Ah Sook happens to be one of these bandits. The kingpin, quite likely; with a price on his head, I'm told. It's rumored in the town that he's hiding out round here. Do you suppose 'our friend' and Ah Sook are one and the same person?"

"He didn't strike me as the bandit type," Cardew-Smythe began cautiously. "More chamber of commerce. Still, it would explain a few things . . . " He relapsed into troubled silence.

Quint scrambled to his feet. He leaned on the railing. At this hour of the morning the place was at its best, before the heat of the day set in. Puffy white clouds, tinged golden pink, flecked the sky. "Were you aware

that the night before we arrived two people were killed
here?"

"On the island?" From the look on Cardew-Smythe's
face Quint inferred ignorance.

"A young American anthropologist and a local Malay
boatman she'd hired to ferry her around. Seems they
were abducted from the *kampong* where she was living,
taken out to sea in the man's own boat, hacked about a
bit and left for the crocodiles. An 'accident.' However, as
any local could tell you, crocodiles are scarce hereabouts
these days. The bodies were washed up almost whole, the
man dead, the woman barely alive. Her last words, in Malay, were 'pregnant maiden.' "

"Good God." Cardew-Smythe was clearly appalled.
"Who would want to do a thing like that?"

"All her notebooks are missing. I assume she saw
something she wasn't supposed to. A couple of days later,
the man who found her—and told me about it—was also
washed up, dead."

"So that's your interest here." Cardew-Smythe stood
up and began to pace. He walked along the jetty, then
back, hands thrust into pockets. "But what's it got to do
with—us?"

Quint answered with a question. "Where do you all go
tomorrow?"

Cardew-Smythe stared out across the bay. Far over to
the right the dark lump of an island stretched into the
distance. "Pregnant maiden," he said at last. "What
could she have meant?"

"She was a most precise person." Quint stood behind
him. "Seven of his family were butchered. There are sev-

en of you—from the patrol. When he has you in his power, why would he stop at one?"

A pair of hands clenched the jetty railing. "Oh, God," Cardew-Smythe cried out. He leaned his head on the wood and sobbed. Quint laid a steadying arm along his back, but Cardew-Smythe moved away. "Sorry," he muttered. "Let's get back. I'm not supposed to crack up. Besides, I promised Phoebe breakfast in bed."

CHAPTER TWENTY-SIX

As they approached the Inn, two of the Chinese came running down the path. They seemed agitated. Making no pretense this time, they buttonholed Cardew-Smythe. Quint, tactfully, walked on, but not before he'd heard a word or two: "attacked," "very bad," "disappear." On the terrace a few early birds were breakfasting, and all was serenity and decorum. He walked through the closed, empty bar towards the lobby. Here, too, nothing seemed amiss. There were very few people about. Miller, he decided, had done something foolish.

He climbed the stairs, passed the TV and the pool table and looked through the door giving onto the passage in Miller's wing. A radio blared from somewhere, voices, a woman came out of a room and walked towards him—no one he knew. He tried the other wing. Here a maid was swabbing the tiled floor, squeezing a mop into a bucket. The floor was wet and shiny. It seemed early to be washing the halls. A door at the far end opened and a head peered out. It was Craddock. On seeing Quint, Craddock withdrew. Then Briscoe's door opened and—surprise—the French doctor emerged followed by a man. But really, Quint thought, he shouldn't be surprised; every time he passed this door, something happened.

"Bonjour, Madame le Docteur."

251

"*Bonjour, Monsieur l'Ecrivain.*"

"Is everything all right?"

"He will live."

"May I?" Quint stepped past them into a pool of water.

"But nobody is allowed in," the man, who seemed to be an official of the Inn, protested. Behind him, Quint heard the doctor say, "But he's writing a hotel guide," and this seemed to settle the matter. He closed the door. Yes, a decidedly good cover; it generated respect, at least in hotels. He must remember.

Gwendy Jake was sitting at the bedside in a robe. She hurried forward. "Oh, Mr. Quint," she whispered hoarsely, peering round him at the door, "those French spies; they haven't half got the wind up."

"The what?"

"They're leaving. I heard her say so. Doctor, my foot. Quacks like a duck, is a duck."

Quint bent over the inert form on the bed. It was Briscoe. The only visible part of him was his face, and that was deathly pale. He seemed hardly to be breathing. "What happened?"

"Him?" Gwendy glanced at the body. "A disgrace, that's what. Getting himself into a fight when he's someone's guest. No consideration, that's what some people have. Word gets around and it comes back on us, don't it? Frankie and me. Very unsavory, I say. That's gratitude for you. You'd expect it with some of the others," she sniffed, "but he was always a quiet one. Never rowdy like the rest, not back then. Ah well," she sighed and shook her head, "that's life. Gets us all in the end."

"But what happened? Is he badly hurt?"

"Enough to learn his lesson," Gwendy said, close-mouthed.

Quint started for the door.

"It was all that water in the passage," she went on hastily. "Somebody saw it. He was lying on the floor all bashed up." She pointed to a spot near the door. "Left for dead, if you ask me, and the sink running over."

"When was this?"

"About half an hour ago. That's when they come knocking on my door. Said he was dead, the boy did. And Sir Frankie off down the beach and all. Gave me quite a turn, I don't mind tellin' you."

"It must have been a shock." I was right about Miller, Quint thought. "And the, er, wife?"

"Wife, my barnacles," Gwendy snorted. "Good riddance, mark my words. That's what all the fuss was about."

The white veil that had draped Briscoe's mysterious companion when Quint had seen her in the lobby lay on the floor. He picked it up. It seemed the only trace of her left. "I think I know where to find her," he said.

Instead of going to Miller and Sneed's room, Quint went downstairs towards his own, meeting Cardew-Smythe hurrying in off the terrace. He looked questioningly at Quint, almost beseechingly. "Upstairs on his bed," Quint pointed. "Sedated. Doctor says he'll live."

Cardew-Smythe hurried on, muttering. Quint caught the word, "Phoebe." The man seemed on the verge of a breakdown.

In his room, Quint listened for signs of life from above, and hearing none, drew back the curtains and stared out of the window at the brightening day. The ferry from Perlis was due soon. Perhaps Miller would try to sneak a ride on that. If so, he'd need a good disguise. Quint bundled the veil into a drawer and went along to breakfast.

Sitting on the terrace, tucking into eggs and bacon, were Miller and Sneed. They looked their usual bleary-eyed selves. Cut lips? Puffy eyes? Torn clothes? Neither one of them seemed fresh from a knock-down battle with Briscoe. While Quint was scrutinizing them, Sneed looked up and pointed with his fork to a spare place. Miller, through a mouthful, lodged a protest, but Quint sat down anyway. At last Miller made room in his mouth for words: "Reckon ol' Stinki'll be needing that." He eyed Quint suspiciously.

Quint remained seated. "Has there been a reconciliation, gentlemen?"

Sneed giggled.

"Well," Miller said sourly, his fingers bursting with chips, "Stinki's not a bad sort. Screw loose, but . . . "

" . . . when all is said and done . . . " Sneed took it up, "mostly done." He giggled again. "Old Milly obtained visiting privileges last night," he explained. "Right old time was had by all, ay, Mill?"

"All three of you?"

"Four," Sneed said. "Don't forget the Mrs."

"When did you leave?"

"Half one, was it, Milly?"

"I take it Briscoe and the, er, Mrs. stayed on and you went to your room."

"Slept like new born babes," Sneed affirmed.

"What is this, an interrogation?" Miller growled through a mouthful of potato.

"Chitchat, small talk, call it what you will," Quint said. A waiter set a cup down in front of him. It looked like spiced milk. A minor triumph, he thought; my next to last day.

"Stinki'll be along. You better clear off," Miller said.

"Unlikely," Quint stirred his milk. "Not in his state. He's out cold."

"He's what?" They looked at him, then at each other. "You mean he's copped it?" Sneed asked.

"Not quite copped," Quint admitted, extending his vocabulary.

With a speed he'd thought them incapable of, his breakfast companions disappeared in the direction of Briscoe's room. Quint sipped his milk. Over by the edge of the terrace he could see Peter Forbes. He was sitting alone, staring at the hibiscus in very much the same dreamy manner as on that first morning. Poor Peter. How would he fare in the drama that would be played out tomorrow? Of all of them, Quint pitied him the most.

Miller and Sneed returned puffed and cursing. "Bloody gladiator they've put on the door there."

"What about *her*?" Sneed wanted to know.

Quint said, "I was hoping you'd tell me."

"Done a flit, has she?" Miller sounded disappointed. "You don't suppose . . . ?" He looked questioningly at Sneed. "Stinki wasn't any Charles Atlas, was he?" Fists clenched, Sneed executed a couple of boxing feints and they both roared with laughter. Quint excused himself.

He stood at the edge of the terrace, cradling his cup in his hands. So he'd been wrong about Miller. The Perlis ferry was rounding the point beyond the rocks. It skittered across the proscenium of his vision on a calm sea and vanished in the direction of the town. She had come on the ferry. She would likely leave on it. Probably Briscoe had picked her up in Perlis. But the white veil . . . Why had she taken what little was hers, and left that? Then it came to him: without the veil, no one would know her.

The helicopter passed over, like the ferry going from left to right; the morning direction, the example set by the sun. Quint stepped forward, holding up his hat against the glare, studying the dark, khaki-clad figure squatting in its belly with more than passing interest, wondering if he was always the same man. The soldier held binoculars to his eyes, searching perhaps for an elderly Chinaman with one ear. If they knew for sure he was here they'd bring in reinforcements, Quint surmised. So they still only suspect. Reinforcements. The word jumped out at him. Decisions must, alas, be made. And now. He couldn't count on Cardew-Smythe; that was clear. How he disliked the finality of decisions, always postponing them to the last possible moment. Because the longer he waited, the more he had to go on, and the better his judgment.

"A learned professor of government
Vacationing out in the Orient
Stared at the sun
Each morning: for fun?
Or to check up on which way the bugger went?"

The voice was close behind him. Quint was indeed still staring at the heavens, shading his eyes with his hat, with the helicopter a dull rumble beyond the point. He put the hat on his head and turned to confront the wry grin of Peter Forbes.

"If you'd stood there much longer, you'd have turned into one of those Greek statues of discus throwers."

"Except that I'm clothed. Or is the Fool saying, in so many words, that the Emperor is naked?"

"I'm afraid I'm far too preoccupied with the tattered state of my own garments to worry about anyone else's," Peter lamented. "The truth is," he blurted out, "I've a perfectly good fiancée back in England. And I don't have the guts to tell Leila."

"A somewhat academic problem at this point. How is she, by the way?"

"Under twenty-four hour armed surveillance. Craddock's convinced someone's gunning for him and is using her. He sees murderous Chinese behind every potted palm. He packs a gun, you know, in a shoulder holster. I saw it last night when we carried Leila out."

A waiter came up: "Someone to see you in the lobby, sir."

Quint handed him his cup. "Where's the captain today?"

"Captain?" The man glanced quickly around. "Day off."

"Again?" Quint frowned. The waiter excused himself. "I'll see you later," he said to Peter. "Off to the beach with the rest?"

Peter shrugged, "Last chance for a tan. Might as well take something home with me."

Vellu was waiting in the car. He handed Quint a folded piece of paper.

'Dear Mr. Quint,' he read, 'I won't sleep until I tell you the whole truth, but please, *please* don't pass it on. You asked what Gail meant by "more in your department."

True, I was in social studies. I work now for the D.E.A. out of Washington (Drug Enforcement Administration). Gail knew. She knew why I was here. That postcard must have cost her—possibly her life. Obviously she saw something. Smuggling maybe—they're always looking for ways to get the stuff out. Nice meeting you, and good luck. Edie McCall. P.S.: if you still have Gail's card, I'd kind of like to hang onto it. For old times sake. Here's my address in D.C.' Quint looked at Vellu. "Has anyone else read this?"

"Even I myself have not."

He pulled the card out of his shirt pocket: 'Many OL legends originated around here: white rats etc. V. exciting. Something more in your department, too. Would rather not get involved myself.' "*White rats!*" He almost shouted the words, so that Vellu jumped. "Legends, white rats, caves. What a blind fool I've been."

"I beg your pardon, Mr. Quint."

"That's why she was silenced. That's why the boatman was killed. Yes, they saw something all right. *In a cave.* In one of the old Sea Gypsy caves. Not smuggling, as she assumed, but I'll bet I know what. Brilliant." He felt an irrational surge of admiration for the mind he was up against. "All the helicopters in the world could drone around forever and not spot it." He handed Vellu the postcard.

"But famous last words—Lake of Pregnant Maiden?"

"Not lake Vellu. She didn't say lake. Is there perhaps a cave on the island *near* the lake?"

"Not one, many."

"Does any one come to mind?"

"Cave of Banshee," Vellu volunteered hesitantly. "I tried to show you."

"The Banshee! It's not on the schedule, but then of course it wouldn't be. But it's in the right direction. Easy patrol will likely stop there on the way back, as we almost did. I should have listened to you, Vellu. You must hire a boat. We will go out and have a look. But we must be very circumspect."

"Only one problem, Mr. Quint," Vellu said mournfully. "Boat impossible. No one will rent. Not for you. The others, they have already failed."

"But they'd rent to you, Vellu. And of course, I'd pay double."

"Even ten times, they will not rent, Mr. Quint."

Quint stroked his beard. "There's the Inn launch. We'll take that. It's faster and I can run it myself."

Vellu pulled a long face. "May I ask, have you ever driven speedboat, Mr. Quint?"

"It shouldn't be hard. I can drive a car."

Any qualms Vellu may have had about riding the waves with Quint at the helm were soon suppressed. In the boathouse they found the launch. Its engine had been extracted, and was sitting on a bench in several piles. As they contemplated it—Quint in dismay, Vellu with relief—a Malay in greasy overalls entered and joined the silent vigil. At length Vellu addressed him: "No good, eh?"

The man launched into speech. Quint caught 'spare parts,' 'mainland' and 'one week.' Vellu explained: the boat had been in good shape only yesterday; someone overnight had wrecked it; spare parts would have to come from mainland and would take one week. "Or one month," Vellu commented.

"Sabotage," Quint said, as they walked away. "But

there must be someone on this island who will lend me a boat." A man was lounging at the entrance to the employees' wing. "Where is the captain today?" Quint asked him.

"Captain? Captain wife come back." He gave Quint a knowing look.

"Just now, you mean, on the ferry?" The man nodded. Quint turned to Vellu. "There's only one thing for it."

"No, no, please." Vellu held up both hands as if to ward off fate, and all but fell to his knees.

"Get some tourists, get a boat, and tour the Cave of the Banshee."

The Indian quailed. "Oh, my God." His face turned grey; he clutched his stomach.

"Blame yourself—for living on an island," Quint said heartlessly.

"No man can choose place of birth, Mr. Quint. And how can I find tourists? Out of thin air?"

"Anyone will do, as long as they don't have white faces. At my expense. Your wife's sister, for instance. No, no, I insist."

Vellu's anguish erupted. Tears came to his eyes. His whole body went limp. "Believe me, Mr. Quint, after this she will definitely marry you." Quint knew that he'd won.

"I promise, Vellu, I will not turn her down."

"But what am I to look for?"

"Act the guide, recite the legends, but keep your eyes open. Take a flashlight. Peer into every cranny. And Vellu—later we will telephone your wife's cousin with the Penang police."

"If line is not down."

Quint, watching him drive away, felt a pang of empathy. If Vellu hated the sea, he, Quint, could not abide rodents—of whatever hue. He took out Gail Sonnenberg's postcard and pressed it to his lips. A moment later, two of the young Chinese emerged from the lobby, jumped onto Vespas, and sputtered off towards town.

CHAPTER TWENTY-SEVEN

T he sign read: Tanjong Rhu 22½ Km. The cream bus
with the Langkawi Inn logo on the side turned right. It
was the road that went to Seven Falls; only the beach at
Tanjong was beyond, on the island's northern shore.
Quint sat up front beside the driver. He had his bathing
suit on under his pants; the first time, he noted ruefully,
that he'd worn it. Doubtless his travel agent would be
amused. Behind him sat all five Cardew-Smythes, the
two Jakes, Craddock, Miller, Sneed and Peter. Only
Leila, her guardian Turk, and the savaged Briscoe were
absent. Quint hadn't exactly asked to go along. It seemed
to be the driver's idea. Since the cockfight Quint had at-
tained celebrity status among a certain segment of the
Malay population. The driver, it turned out, was a fan.

Gwendy Jake marathoned on about garden parties,
Honolulu, first aid, and whatever popped into her versa-
tile mind; Sir Frankie snoozed; and the youngest Cardew-
Smythe kept up a barrage of questions all beginning with
'why,' none of which anyone made any attempt to answer.
Sneed sang snatches of a song about a dubious wench
called O'Reilly's daughter, and Miller kept telling him to
shut his gob. Craddock maintained iron-clad reserve,
beefy forearms crossed on hairy chest. No one except the
driver seemed happy to have Quint along.

The sight of the beach marginally cheered them. The tide was out, revealing, through clustered casuarinas, acres of golden sand, a travel agent's dream. Indeed, the driver proudly informed Quint that a brand new luxury hotel was planned for this precise spot. Quint thought of Vellu attempting to land at the Cave of the Banshee—if, indeed, he'd got that far. In vain he watched for signs of the Chinese. There were few people on the beach, activity being centered under the trees where open air foodstalls were set up. Quint left his clothes in a neat pile on the sand and waded out to sea.

He splashed around in water that barely reached his chest, and watched Phoebe Cardew-Smythe swimming strongly towards a little off-shore island on which a few trees leaned precariously. The way her arms arced with keen grace like glistening wheels of water made him long for simplicity, straightforwardness, joy—the silver note on the organ—instead of this web of deceit and innuendo pulling at him everywhere he turned. For a while he floated on his back, eyes closed, tracing the patterns on the inverted red bowls of his eyelids, even hoping they might tell him what he wanted to know. Then he waded back towards the beach.

A small figure raced along the firm sand at the water's edge: the littlest Cardew-Smythe. When she reached the point past which Quint would walk, she waited, and held something out to him in cupped hands. "Look what I've found." He bent to see. It was a bit of shell, and as he looked a tiny creature poked its head out. Holding the shell carefully, she trotted up the beach to where her father sat in his floppy hat, a towel draped over his shoulders. "A hermit crab. Very nice." He dutifully examined it, but his mind was elsewhere. "How bad is Briscoe?" he asked Quint. "They wouldn't let me in."

"From the little I saw, not good."

"They can't blame me for this," Cardew-Smythe said petulantly. "They'll just have to go ahead without him."

"Assuming he's not the star turn." Quint sat down.

"Him?" Cardew-Smythe sounded incredulous. "Well, I wouldn't have thought so."

"Why?"

"He's an innocent . . . " He stopped. "I suppose the real reason is, I rather suspect I know who it was. It's almost embarrassingly obvious." He looked out miserably from under the brim of his hat. "I shouldn't be telling you this, should I?"

Quint shrugged. "It's all the same to me. I still dispute the logic of sacrificing six men—to punish a seventh."

"Sacrificing?" Cardew-Smythe bridled. "You don't for a moment think I'd have . . . I'm sorry," he swallowed hard. "I'm just not myself."

Quint said, "You have your problems and I have mine."

"I say," the other man sounded anxious, "you're not going to do anything silly, are you? Tomorrow, I mean."

Quint lay back on the warm sand. *Silly?* He turned the word over in his mind. "You and the rest of Easy patrol are walking into an ambush, just as surely as you walked into one that day thirty years ago. Having said that, I intend merely to sit back and watch—from as near as your Chinese fire brigade will let me. I don't see them about today."

Cardew-Smythe glanced around, "It does seem strangely empty." Something in him had relaxed, just a little.

"Yoo-hoo!" Gwendy Jake was picking her way across

the sand in a pair of flip-flops. Her swimsuit, a sickening chartreuse, rendered her body curiously compact. Over her red wig—wig, not hat, Quint had finally decided—was drawn a tight pink rubber bathing cap. A fringe of bright orange escaped around the edge. "Your wife is out there," she pointed, addressing Cardew-Smythe, "and the tide's turning. Serve her right if she gets stranded." She flip-flopped on without stopping.

"She and Phoebe haven't hit it off, I'm afraid." Cardew-Smythe watched the retreating figure. Unexpectedly, he smiled: "One can't help noticing a certain resemblance to a clown."

"She's not a clown, Daddy," piped up an indignant six-year-old.

"No, darling, of course not."

"She's a lady in a bathing cap."

Touché, Quint thought. Clowns are serious business. Things are what they seem. It depends on your point of view. He got up to fetch his hat and shirt, then took off briskly along the beach towards a distant point. Ahead, in the towering sky, a bird was soaring and gliding.

The walk did him good. He returned to find Easy patrol, less Phoebe Cardew-Smythe, gathered around Gwendy Jake who was distributing food like a monarch on Maundy Thursday. Exercise had made everybody hungry. When she saw Quint coming, she said in a loud enough voice for him to hear, "Dearie me, an extra mouth and nothing to put in it." The others turned to look. "Oh, *here's* a sandwich. I wonder whose it could be . . . "

But Quint wasn't listening to Gwendy Jake. He had seen something that stopped him in his tracks. He stared briefly, then forced his eyes away. Yes, he thought, things are what they seem; they are exactly what we say they are: depending on the point of view. "Thanks," he called out to Gwendy, "but I have to get back." He was already walking purposefully towards the trees.

The Inn bus was not due till later, but a dilapidated public bus was just pulling away. Quint banged on the side, and it stopped. "Town?" The driver nodded. Quint climbed aboard. Every few hundred yards someone stepped into the road and, wheezing and sighing, gears grinding, the bus stopped for a new passenger and baggage. By the time they reached town, the aisle was jammed and Quint had a basket of chickens on his lap. This might have been fine had he not left his pants behind on the beach. As it was, at every jolt, claws pressed into his flesh. He tried to think of Briscoe. Briscoe, the innocent; Briscoe, maimed and drugged on the bed; Briscoe, the one man who might tell him what he needed to know, if . . . "Ouch!" He smiled bravely at the chicken woman who was standing in the aisle beside him. Could he do what he had to do in time, he wondered. In the town he found a taxi, and—somewhat self-conscious in his semi-nakedness—entered the Inn.

He picked up his key and, in his room, pulled on fresh pants, all the while wondering how to elude the guard posted at Briscoe's door. The sight of his black leather traveling bag sparked an idea. Grabbing the bag, he took the stairs two at a time. "Doctor," he announced, breathlessly.

The guard, who turned out to be the ancient, rifle-toting night watchman, pointed wordlessly at the bag, and it dawned on Quint that it was empty. With fumbling fingers he snapped open the catches and the guard peered in, nodded approvingly, and opened the door. Guards, Quint realized, love empty bags. "Doctor, sir," the old man announced, like a major-domo.

Briscoe was sitting up in bed. He raised a fat, green bottle waveringly towards Quint: "Got all the doctor I need, old sport."

Quint sat down on the bed aware that the guard was watching him to see what he, the doctor, would do. At this very moment he should be feeling in his bag for his stethoscope or some other identifiable tool of the trade. But he knew, and the guard knew, that the bag of tricks was empty. "Coffee," he ordered. "Bring coffee, now."

Obediently, the guard left.

"Name your poison," Briscoe held out the bottle. Dom Perignon. Quint placed it on the table. "Am I under arrest?" Briscoe asked.

Quint considered the question. It seemed to have been posed in a genuine spirit of inquiry; and as with all questions based on hidden assumptions called for prevarication. "What makes you think that?"

Briscoe laughed sourly. "That's a bloody great gun he had."

"Have no fear." Quint sat down again. "I will see to it that no harm comes to you—provided," he smiled, "you follow doctor's orders. This doctor's. How do you feel, by the way?"

" 'Orrible. That bloody great lout would have done for me, if it hadn't been for . . . Christmas, pass the pain-killer." He groped about with one hand, clutching his head with the other.

Quint shoved the hand firmly under the covers. He was

developing a passable bedside manner. "If it hadn't been for . . . ?"

"If it hadn't been for the dame. 'Course, I treated her right. You saw for yourself. Nothing for her to gripe about. Three meals a day, little perks I bought her, a nice clientele. How did I know she was hitched? How did I know he'd come bustin' in after her? Just a little bit of fun, no harm to no one . . . " Tears of self pity welled in his eyes.

So the captain's wife *had* come back on the ferry from Perlis. But not today's ferry. On the ferry with Briscoe. Briscoe was lucky to have kept his fingers, let alone other parts of his anatomy.

There was a tap on the door and a waiter entered with coffee. He looked with unfeigned curiosity at the figure on the bed. Quint took the tray and tipped him, then poured a cup and forced Briscoe to drink. "How long were you in Perlis?"

"Matter of hours."

"You were two days late getting here. That's two days between Bangkok and Perlis. What were you doing?"

"Business."

"Where?"

"Place called Haadyai, over the Thai border. Non-stop action they got there. The traveling salesman's mecca." The memory seemed to revive Briscoe; or maybe it was the coffee.

"How far is this salesman's mecca from Perlis?"

"Couple of hours by taxi."

"Haadyai is in Thailand. Perlis is Malaysia. Am I right?"

"So?"

"Your passport was stamped at the border?"

" 'Course it was."

Quint held out a hand. Briscoe leaned over, dragged a suitcase from under the bed, opened it and produced a passport. He found the entry and held it up. Quint took the document. Both Thai departure stamp and Malaysia entry stamp bore out Briscoe's story. He closed it and handed it back. The name on the front was S. Padinki.

"Did anyone see you in Haadyai?"

"Sneed." He added a little less confidently, "I saw him. Whether he saw me's another matter."

"Meaning?"

"He was drunk as a lord."

"What about Miller?"

Briscoe shrugged. "I didn't see Miller."

So far, so good. Quint refilled the coffee cup. "I want you to think back thirty years. After the man you called The Highwayman humiliated you over the business of the girl . . . "

Briscoe swore, spilling the coffee. "Who said that? Just let me get my hands on them."

Quint continued: "After that, did you go out with Miller and Sneed to an establishment called Rose's Milk Bar and, shall we say, try again?"

"Rose's Milk Bar," Briscoe cooed delightedly, like a baby. "Talk about a classy lay. Oh, ho ho." (Miller and Sneed had seen it differently, Quint recalled: *Come and get it! I can see old Mill saying it now. And Stinki standin' there like a bloomin' statue.*) " 'Course, it was the jitterbugging at Rose's I was partial to," he went on. "I was a famous jitterbugger in them days, no mistake about it. Jitterbug for hours, I could."

"Sir Frankie, was he seen much at Rose's?"

"Go on wiv yer. Enemy territory as far as he was concerned. Strictly the Sunshine for him. You'd have thought he owned the place, the way he carried on. Every bloke what went in there, Frankie got a percentage. Between him and The Highwayman, they had it all sewed up."

"So it annoyed him when you switched to Rose's?"

"Annoyed? The guy was livid. See, it wasn't just us. A whole mob came over. There was talk about putting him out of business, making deals with The Highwayman behind his back. Oh, he was hoppin' mad, was Frankie."

"And The Highwayman, *did* he make deals behind Sir Frankie's back?"

" 'Course he did," Briscoe flared in anger. "That one would sell his gran twice over."

"So Sir Frankie's little empire was crumbling, you might say?"

"Did well enough for himself, didn't he?" Briscoe said enviously. "Sometimes I think to myself, it's not fair, life, I mean."

"Redress may be coming," Quint said. "Meanwhile, stay away from the Dom Perignon. Doctor's orders. You'll need your wits about you, and at their sharpest."

Briscoe sat up. "Cor," he said, "You're not serious?"

As Quint closed the door behind him, he had a feeling that he and Briscoe had different things in mind.

He returned to the lobby and was glad to see, through the plate glass window, Vellu's Mercedes in its usual spot. But as he strode towards it something struck him as odd. The man at the wheel was a stranger. Of Vellu himself, not a sign.

CHAPTER TWENTY-EIGHT

The man at the wheel of Vellu's Mercedes jumped out and held the rear door open for Quint. He was young, Indian, and wore dark glasses. "Where is Vellu?" Quint asked.

"Mr. Vellu indisposed," the man answered. "He is sending me to fetch you, sir."

"Are you his son?"

"Myself, I am henchman only."

Further conversation seemed pointless. To Quint's relief, the self-proclaimed henchman drove past the turnoff to Vellusamy Mansions. He had no wish to encounter the sister-in-law just now. They continued a hundred yards down the main road and stopped in a squeal of rubber outside the dingy eatery. The driver got out smartly and held Quint's door, leaving the car jutting rakishly into the road. One could tell a lot, Quint concluded, from a parked car.

Quint followed his guide into the shop, blindly after the white street glare. He had a dim impression of a counter with foodstuffs crammed under glass, of tables and chairs sparsely occupied, and advertisements tacked onto walls. A milky, rather sickly smell assailed his nostrils. The henchman waited, holding aside a curtain. They passed through into a narrow unlit passage with doors off either

side and rough, wooden planking underfoot. At the far
end of the passage Quint saw daylight and heard an un-
mistakable lap-lapping sound. As they continued, he realized that the passage was indeed built out over water,
becoming a sort of private pier: the town backed onto a
lagoon, he remembered, protected from the sea by a reef.
His guide opened a door to the right and ushered Quint
through. He himself remained outside.

"Congratulations, Mr. Quint." Vellu was seated at a
table laden, as before, with paperwork. He rose and
stretched out a hand. "On happy event."

"Event?" Vellu, Quint was relieved to see, looked fine.

"State of marital bliss you are about to enter."

"You went?"

"And I am returning."

"Your man said you were indisposed. I was worried."

"Sit down, Mr. Quint. I am not indisposed. I am dis-
posed." Vellu sighed and shook his head. "His English is
not up to snuff. No matter, it is not his fault. So-called
English teacher here in Langkawi school is teaching me,
is teaching my son, is teaching my son's son, is leading
whole of Langkawi down garden path. Hopeless situation,
you understand?"

Dumb waiters, Quint thought sympathetically. "I'm
afraid I sent you on a wild goose chase," he said.

Vellu nodded. "And because I am not chasing two wild
geese in one day, I am sending car in advance; because
frankly, Mr. Quint, you are being spotted running in town
half-naked under midday sun."

"I was trying to stop a taxi."

"Not to worry," Vellu held up a hand. "You have
lunched?"

"No. You see, we haven't much time . . . " Vellu shouted something in Tamil at the top of his lungs. "It wasn't till after you'd left—in fact not till I was at Tanjong Rhu—that, as the English say, the penny dropped. Which is why, incidentally, I forgot my trousers. The clue I'd been hoping for, searching for, was staring me in the face all along, and I hadn't seen it. Why? Because Vellu, I no longer have the eyes of a six-year-old. I say to myself, 'Things are *not* what they seem,' because I am clever, an adult, sophisticated. And wrong."

"And what has this very-interesting-to-be-sure observation to do with Cave of Banshee, which contains only bats, not even white?"

"It means, Vellu, that every single cave on these islands is now suspect, those on the Isle of the Pregnant Maiden no more and no less than all the others. And since, as you say, there are many caves capable of hiding whole fleets of war canoes, and we cannot visit them all by tomorrow, we shall have to narrow the field by other means. In the words of the immortal Hegesippe, 'Not by looking, but by thinking are things found.' But first, we have a phone call to make."

"But last words . . . ?" Vellu protested.

"I was misled. I blame myself entirely. Do you have a phone?"

Vellu searched under the papers and found one. He stood up, gesturing to Quint to take his place. "Please."

"No, no." Quint motioned him down. "You must speak to your wife's cousin in Penang and get an urgent message through to the police."

"No, no, no, no." Vellu, who had sat down, stood up again. "Much better you telephone Penang police direct.

Deliver urgent message personally." The henchman had entered noiselessly with a tray of food. He cleared a space on the desk between them and—after setting down a number of dishes—backed out of the room. Neither man paid any attention.

"And what will happen when a complete stranger, a foreigner, a mere tourist, telephones with a request he says is urgent? I know perfectly well what would happen where I come from."

"Same thing as will happen when I, Vellu, telephone wife's cousin's daughter's boyfriend to pass message. Nothing." The two glared at each other across the steaming tray of food. "Whole point, Mr. Quint, is this: no one, in whole world, can put baksheesh through such an instrument." He fixed the phone with a look of scorn. "Besides, wife's cousin's daughter's boyfriend is humble clerk only. Who will listen to humble clerk?"

Quint leaned forward: "When he has passed on this message, he'll be well on his way to promotion. What are marriages for, Vellu? To further the interests of the family. Think of the advantages of a high-ranking police connection. Besides, your name, the name of an outstanding taxpayer and citizen of Langkawi, cannot be so easily ignored."

"But cousin will die of stroke," Vellu wailed, looking at the phone. "He will think Vellu's wife is very ill. Before, it is only time I phone when wife is at death's door."

Quint sat down: "The message is as follows. The police must come immediately with a warrant to arrest the murderer of the American woman whose body was shipped by plane last Monday. If they don't come today, it will be too late." He looked at his watch. "There's still time to catch the plane, if they don't have one of their own. Instructions will await them at the Langkawi Inn."

Vellu slumped into his chair. He looked at Quint. He looked at the phone. He leaned back and shouted something at the ceiling. A woman's voice answered, reciting, in English, a number. The whole town is listening, Quint thought bleakly. Vellu picked up the phone, pushing the tray towards Quint. "Eat. Even if line is not down," he said gloomily, "maybe landlord's shop where phone is, is shut; maybe landlord himself is dying, already very old man, by the way; maybe phone is cut off from non-payment; maybe wife's cousin is in Malacca with sister; maybe marriage is taking place and honeymoon is starting already in Singapore; maybe . . ."The woman's voice interjected hotly. "No, no," Vellu amended, "she is right. Invitation has not come. Hello? Operator? Vellu here. Penang line is down, is it not?"

The line was not down. It took only ten minutes to raise Penang. Quint chomped his way through lunch while Vellu, an ear to the receiver, sifted half-heartedly through the paperwork. "Supposing you are wrong, Mr. Quint. Supposing this is not the culprit. Then I, Vellu, am left behind with blame, isn't it? You have evidence, yes? Watertight, perhaps?"

The evidence Quint had was circumstantial, except for a couple of words that might be ruled hearsay. But he felt reasonably sure that the presence of an arresting officer would produce the desired result. And the arrest of a man who was, Quint was sure, destined to play a star role in the forthcoming production would surely make it pointless to carry on. No stand-in could take this part. "Those Chinese students from the Inn, Vellu—did you see them at all while you were out?"

"They followed me, Mr. Quint. Whole boatload. I thought last hour had come. Mercifully, when we are turning, making for Cave of Banshee, they are going on. That was last I saw."

"On where?"

"How do I know on where?"

"It's important, Vellu, because the next thing we have to do is find our cave. And maybe that's where they were heading."

"Same direction as we are going before."

"Towards the lake?"

"Exactly." The number in Penang was ringing. They waited, hardly breathing. At last someone picked up. Vellu unleashed a long string of Tamil. Watching the usually tell tale face, Quint found he had not the least idea what was happening. Finally Vellu put his hand over the receiver. "Landlord's wife." He made a face. "She has gone to find cousin upstairs. Landlord very ill, she says; telephone make him worse. I say, please; life and death matter." This last plea, though true, had been a mistake Quint realized, as soon as the next voice—presumably the cousin's—came on. Anguished words spewed from the earpiece like wasps from a disturbed nest. Vellu battled manfully with explanations, and eventually the woman beyond the wall added her say.

Suddenly, in a lull, Vellu yelled in English: "Please listen. She is speaking to you now. How can she be speaking if she is already dead. Is she speaking from next life, you imagine?" He held up the phone to catch the woman's words, all the while looking daggers at Quint as if to say, I told you so. Equanimity restored, Vellu again covered the mouthpiece: "He is now fetching daughter. No, no," he barked into the telephone, "please, operator, we are by no means finishing. Intermission only."

The daughter sounded to be a different proposition entirely. Vellu relayed the message word for word, in English, and she repeated it, in English. "She is going now, this minute, in person, to police headquarters," he said proudly, putting down the receiver. "Penang-educated. This is difference." There was the feeling of a battle fought and won; exhausted camaraderie.

"Vellu," Quint whispered. He didn't want what he had to say to get all over town. "In case, as you point out, nothing happens, and the police do not come, we must be prepared. For this reason, I am going into the *kampong* tonight to search the hut where the anthropologist lived. No," he put up his hands to forestall a new outburst, "I am not asking you to come. I am merely saying, if anything happens, that's where I am going."

"But, Mr. Quint, it is very dangerous for you, a stranger. Even I myself would not venture after dark to *kampong*. Only wild beasts in search of tasty buffalo or chicken move around there then. Bang, bang. Shoot first, ask later."

"I need a clue, Vellu. The Cave of the White Rats. Maybe she left something."

"That is very good." Vellu smiled in spite of himself. "Cave of White Rats." He turned it over on his tongue. "That will make very handsome new Langkawi legend."

Quint stood up. "I have a feeling your grandchildren will thrive on it. For the present, I must go back and wait, hoping the police will come. The next twenty-four hours promise to be full of surprises." They shook hands. "Thank you, Vellu."

"Take care, Mr. Quint. Remember—mangrove swamps."

Back at the Inn, Quint found the Tanjong Rhu party had not returned. Nor, apparently, had the Chinese. So much the better. Lunch service was over, so he walked down the hill to the boathouse. A woman was pinning clothes on a line. Quint waited in the shade while she went to fetch the captain. When, at length, he emerged, Quint was surprised at his battered state. Scratch marks across one cheek, a swollen lower lip, not a glint of a gold tooth. Briscoe had acquitted himself well.

"They tell me your wife came back."

"Sure." A hand went up and stroked the torn cheek.

"A stormy reunion."

"A guy fights for what's his."

"And suffers the consequences." The captain stared with studied blankness. His eyes were red and dangerous. "The Penang police are on their way. They will arrest you, no doubt, for assault. Whatever the provocation, I imagine, in your profession, a police record is no help. Perhaps this is not the first time; perhaps this is why you left your last job; but that's not my affair. What is my affair is this: a few words from me can help to clear you completely. In return for which, you will accompany me tonight in a secret visit—hush-hush, understand—to the nearby *kampong*. Do we have a deal?"

The captain's face cleared. "You're on, partner. No problem."

Quint spent the balance of the afternoon in an armchair in the lobby apparently deep in his book. He saw off the French mycologists, who added last minute suggestions for his travel guide. (Though the question of mosquito nets was still unsettled.) When, an hour later, the bus returned from the airstrip, no policemen were on board. The driver swore that none had been on the plane. He drove off to pick up the beach party, leaving Quint to fret. But, beyond this, and thinking, he did nothing: there was nothing to do. Suppose they didn't come, or came too late? A number of scenarios began to form themselves out of the nebula of his mind, floating freely, allowing him to view them from different aspects. Some he sent packing into the void, others he looked more favorably on, storing and remembering.

Somewhere along the way, Quint dozed off. He woke up when a shadow seemed to pass between himself and the light. Opening his eyes, he found he was staring at a familiar pair of free-floating trousers.

"The Emperor's old clothes."

The trousers fell into his lap, and Quint turned around to see Peter bowing deeply, backing away.

Easy patrol was pushing through the door into the lobby, a rabble of whining kids and tired adults. Quint eyed them with fresh interest. What, it occurred to him, is Cardew-Smythe going to do with his family? As if responding to some telepathic signal, Cardew-Smythe extricated himself from his brood and hurried over.

"How's Briscoe?"

"Well enough to fix himself a drink," Quint replied.

"Thank God." He started away.

"I see Phoebe got safely off the rock," Quint called after him. "About tomorrow: what happens to your family?"

Cardew-Smythe turned briefly. "All taken care of, thanks." He might have been answering a query about a baby-sitter. In a way, he was.

The light was fading by the time the Chinese trooped through the lobby. Not a single one—Quint counted twenty-two—so much as glanced at the figure sitting quietly by the window. They seemed tired and disheveled, and Quint drew his own conclusions. But he wanted them to see him, to see how harmless he was, a man in a straw hat with a greying beard in a rattan armchair. His hopes that the police would come in time faded with the light.

Sleep—he needed sleep. Would anyone try to follow him into the night? He wondered.

Nobody did. Were they that confident, so certain of the success of their plan? If so, it boded good and bad, Quint thought. Tomorrow, perhaps, it would blind them to his real intentions; tonight, it probably meant there was nothing to worry about—in the hut, or anywhere else.

The captain brought food to his room and a flashlight, and shortly after eight they set out, openly, in the captain's friend's decrepit car, on the premise that an observed obvious exit would arouse less suspicion than an observed secret one. The car dropped them near an unused quarry, whence a path led to the *kampong*, shorter and narrower than the one Quint had bicycled over. Along this path they walked, single file, in the bright moonlight.

After some fifteen minutes, Quint sensed that they were nearing the inlet where he first had seen Miss McCall. They were approaching from the right, more or less at a tangent to the other path. Soon he became aware of houses—taut, boxy shapes amid the silvery curving foliage. In some, pencil lines of light still rimmed the shutters. The rattan furniture shop would be over to the left, and beyond it, the house that Miss McCall had photographed. The captain seemed to know the way. Quint followed.

The house and its clearing looked even smaller than Quint remembered, perhaps just because of the absence of color. Dark patches in the surrounding jungle suggested lurking danger. And not unreasonably; it was there, a week ago, that danger would have crouched before the final assault. He wondered whether they had slashed her there, or waited till later, in the boat?

The stars, prickly in their clarity, twinkled above the tiny clearing. Quint looked for Canopus, the star of the dead, a candle shining forever in her memory. Carefully they climbed the bamboo rungs—one, two, three, four, five, six—and paused, listening, on the little platform outside the closed door. Above them, in the *attap*, something rustled—a mouse perhaps or a lizard. In the stillness, it sounded like the crackle of gunfire. The captain pushed the door. It opened onto darkness. They stepped in, closed it, listened again. Quint switched on his flashlight.

There was only the one small room; a single bunk bed in one corner, a low table, two matching rattan stools, a few boards fixed to the wood walls serving as shelves, a red and white enamel basin with a well-used bar of soap in it. A small mirror hung from a nail at Quint's eye level and a kerosene lamp from another. On the shelves were folded garments—sarongs, blouses, underwear; a toothbrush and other toiletries, a pair of sunglasses, some pens of different colors, two jade bracelets, and a round plastic spool wound with gut for fishing. A pair of leather thong sandals sat neatly side-by-side on the board floor, which was partly covered with some sort of matting.

Nowhere could Quint see papers of any description or even books. There were no signs of a frantic search, the illusion of an accident at sea carefully maintained. Beside one of the two shuttered windows a birdcage hung from a rattan chain fastened to a beam in the roof. At first, shining the light around the room, he thought it was empty. On closer inspection, he saw he was wrong: a little hump of yellow feathers lay at the bottom. Poor thing, it must have died of hunger and thirst. Then he noticed that the cage was open. Does a bird fly back to its cage to die? He poked at it with one of the pens. The head was limp: the bird's neck broken. *Sneed done that. I saw him.* He shone the light over the thatch of the ceiling which seemed the most likely hiding place for paper. It revealed nothing.

"Psst." Quint turned. The captain was standing by the door, leaning forward, intently listening. He signaled to Quint to douse the light. Very gently he pulled the door open a crack, and peered through. Quint tiptoed up behind him. The door swung wider and wider. Outside it seemed as bright as day. Quint leaned forward. What had so riveted the captain's attention? Motionless, beyond the overhang, staring up at them, skin in the moonlight the color of burnished pewter, were not two or three but ten or a dozen men. And each, in his hand, held a drawn weapon: the sinuous *kris*, the Malay killing dagger. The captain spoke, his voice soft yet urgent. After a long pause, came an answer. "They want to know," the captain said without turning, "are you that white man who came before at night?"

CHAPTER TWENTY-NINE

Charles Quint rubbed his fingers up into his beard and thanked his stars for it, itchy as the heat made it. From the safety of his balcony he wondered what would have happened had he been taken for the man who had climbed the steps to that *kampong* dwelling a week before. From the look of those blades and the looks on those faces, he'd have been cut into bite-sized chunks and fought over by scavenging dogs. But the man who had come had not—he knew, and, mercifully, they knew—worn a beard.

Quint was pleased with his night's work. Unintentionally, the anthropologist had provided him with a clue: a plastic fishing spool. He had rechecked the Easy patrol schedule Peter had given him and, sure enough, after the visit to the lake came the single word, "Fishing." A harmless enough pursuit, unless you happened to be a fish. Quint saw in his mind's eye the Chinese crowding the sides of their boat, intent on the sea beneath them, hardly moving. He recalled how there had seemed to be fewer of them than were previously at the lake. What was a puzzle to him then bore out his hunch.

It was now a little after six. Across the island people would be stirring, the work of the day beginning. Quint had hardly slept. At one point he left his room and roamed the corridors, encountering no one, going over and over in his mind all that the day might bring. Thoughts of the person who, for thirty years, had lived and schemed for this moment kept recurring: all that effort, all that pain. Didn't things balance out in the end? Should he interfere? An eye for an eye, a tooth for a tooth—till there were no more eyes and no more teeth? And no more Quint. Because he knew he couldn't stand by and do nothing and expect to survive as a man in his own estimation.

Unless the police arrived before Easy patrol left for the lake, he hoped now they wouldn't come at all. They would be outnumbered; there might be shooting; people might be killed. Ah Sook would not be one to take chances, not at this stage of the game. The chances would have to be taken by Quint. Whatever was going to happen, wherever it was going to happen, he would be there. He, too, was going fishing; he had brought along Gail Sonnenberg's plastic spool.

The Chinese left at seven from the Inn jetty. A boat came from the direction of town and picked them up. Quint counted at least twenty, although it was hard to be accurate. He watched them sail away to the west, like Argonauts. Rosy-fingered dawn colored them pink. Another fine day, by the looks of it.

Quint ate early and substantially, not sure when he'd get another chance. The captain sidled up to his table, whispering that the manager was in a towering rage because someone had stolen the night guard's rifle. Rooms were being searched, employees and guests alike. The manager had been trying to raise the police for an hour, but the line to Penang was down. Quint smiled grimly.

Cardew-Smythe came down and sat alone. Quint went and stood behind him: "I'm told that in the old days Sir Frankie took bets on a man's chances before a patrol went out. They say it helped morale."

"Phoebe insists on coming," Cardew-Smythe said leadenly. "She has been looking forward all this time to sketching the lake, she says. No talking her out of it. Goodness knows what the children will get up to; drown, I imagine."

"So the plan is to leave the women and children at the lake, while the men go fishing? I'm surprised 'our friend' hasn't laid on day-care; he seems to have thought of everything else." Quint raised his hat and retreated, leaving Cardew-Smythe to his misery, which was, he reckoned, richly deserved.

Back in his room, Quint moved fast. He stuffed a pillowcase with a number of items, selected the largest towel he could find, and, checking as far as possible that no one was watching, climbed over his balcony. He pushed through the hibiscus to where he'd hidden the night guard's gun, wrapped it in the towel, and sauntered towards the boathouse.

The motor was laid out along the bench just as before, but this time all Quint needed was a dressing room for the quick change act he was about to perform and had rehearsed a number of times that night in front of the mirror in his room. First, he wedged the gun down his backside so that his belt held it secure. Then he wrapped a hotel sheet about his middle so that it barely touched the ground, pinning it securely under his armpits. Lastly, he slipped the white veil left behind by the captain's wife over his head and shoulders so that only his fingertips showed. The towel and his straw hat he put into a pillowcase, and, thus accoutred, shuffled off along the beach. He'd allowed himself about twenty minutes.

The Inn, up to Quint's left, was out of sight of that part of the beach that ran below it. He kept to the dry sand so as not to leave man-sized shoeprints. For as far as he could see, the beach was empty, but approaching the point where the steps came down from the terrace, he heard voices. Trees and bushes obscured the end of the path, so that when, ten yards ahead of him, a near-naked couple dropped, like Tarzan and Jane, into the sand, the surprise was mutual.

The man shouted excitedly in German to the woman to quick get a picture. The woman yelled at Quint, also in German, please to wait. She fiddled with her equipment saying good day, how are you, we have come from Hamburg to your beautiful country, we are your friends. New arrivals; Quint had seen them getting off the bus the day before. Quint struggled on up the beach, the woman dancing and crouching with her camera, shooting wildly, circling him as though in some weird mating ritual, the man bellowing instructions from behind. Quint resisted the temptation to reply with some choice German phrases he happened to know, and at last the couple withdrew, congratulating themselves on their amazing good fortune.

Ahead was the rocky point, and beyond the point, out of sight, the little bay with the mangrove swamp at its far end. The bay was Quint's objective. If Ah Sook had spies out, surely they had not seen Charles Quint heading east along the beach, only some bulky Moslem woman. But relief was short-lived. Splashing around the point, in an uncanny replay of a scene still fresh in Quint's memory, came Frankie Jake. This, he hadn't reckoned on. With the break-up of Briscoe's love-nest, Sir Frankie seemed to have lost no time in reestablishing former contacts. But what if he hadn't? What if the noble knight's appetite for a maiden a day was unquenched? Quint's disguise might prove embarrassingly effective.

The prospect appalled him. And his predicament was compounded by a choice that had to be made: to splash around the point in foot-deep water leaving tracks in the wet sand, or to clamber over the rocks which—with the rifle—would be like climbing in a suit of armor. As it was, he didn't have to choose. Sir Frankie was coming straight for him. Quint sprinted for the rocks, gaining their comparative shelter in the nick of time. "Whoa there, my little filly," Sir Frankie gasped, as Quint squeezed his far from lissome frame through a crevice and looked around for a missile to help cool the knightly ardor. "Playing hard to get, are we? Well, well, don't I know the cure for that, heh, heh. Never fails, heh, heh." He waved what looked like a fistful of bills above his head. "Me rich tuan." He really believes money can buy anything, Quint thought. Sir Frankie ducked as a piece of driftwood skimmed his head. It was like a morality play gone berserk, where the beautiful maiden resists the noble knight and turns into a swineherd. The low drag and hiss of the sea on the sand were the guffaws of a medieval audience. Quint kept an anxious ear open for another sound. Sir Frankie, with a few choice parting epithets, jogged reluctantly away.

It seemed to Quint an age before he managed to extricate himself from that jagged pile of black lava. The sheet was a write-off, which was the least of his problems.

It would still serve its purpose. The bay was deserted. He picked a spot midway on its sandy yellow curve between the rocks and the mangroves and extracted the rifle from the hiding place where it pressed painfully on his back. It wasn't loaded. Even if it had been, he doubted that it would fire. It was not for this that he'd brought it. He looked at his watch. Shouldn't be long. Yes, there was the Perlis ferry, chugging across the bay. He positioned the rifle on the sand and stretched himself out full length some three yards off. The scramble over the rocks had shaken him. Not so much the exertion as the encounter with Sir Frankie. Stupid. The one thing he hadn't thought of. Now there was nothing to do but wait, and hope, and listen.

At first it was just another wave, but it kept on coming. Then it was a hornet, angry, and Quint turned his head. Through the veil he could see the line of the mangroves running out to sea, dark bushy green against the pale blue sky. Rearing over the trees came the helicopter, this morning as every morning. Quint lay still, watching, wondering what it was going to do. A body on a beach was one thing—though it had landed before to pick up bodies—but a body on a beach with a gun beside it, surely this was irresistible. A woman's body, at that.

The helicopter whirred low over the water. If they couldn't see him they must be blind. The opening where the gunner usually sat appeared to Quint as a black hole because the sun was in his eyes. It wasn't stopping. It was pressing on beyond the point, towards the Inn. No, it was circling, coming back. Quint felt the tremor pass under him as the skids thumped the wet sand some yards away.

Still he didn't move. The air was acrid with fumes. A wind tugged at his costume and the noise was deafening.

Footsteps, now, from behind, going first for the gun; then a small brown face appeared above him framed against the sky, dark glasses staring down, bare arms protruding from tightly rolled khaki. From the right shoulder a mean looking weapon was slung, its business end directed at Quint's head, the slight swaying motion putting him in mind of an aroused cobra. The man slowly circled Quint's body till he reached the feet. With a flick of the vintage rifle, grasped in his left hand, he uncovered a pair of large, brown, rubber-soled shoes. From the shoes, he glanced back at the head, perplexed; then, laying the rifle down, he bent over and drew back the veil. For lack of anything more profound, Quint said, "Good morning."

The man seemed torn between dying of fright on the spot or running away and then dying. In the moment it took for him to make up his mind, Quint added, "Are you looking for Ah Sook? Ah Sook," he shouted above the din.

At last the man responded: "Ah Sook?" He pointed incredulously at Quint, who shook his head vigorously.

"I will take you to Ah Sook." Quint pointed to himself, to the soldier, to the helicopter, up into the sky, then gave a pantomime of looking down at something. At last the man smiled. He gestured towards the helicopter. Quint picked up his pillow case, pulled off his veil, and together they ducked under the still-whirling blades. Soon all that remained behind were mystifying patterns in the sand.

Strange, to be suddenly seeing it all from the other side of the mirror, so to speak: the breakfasters on the terrace, the waiters, the bright hibiscus, the very Inn itself—a microcosm of unreality in contrast to the great beyond to which the helicopter was an adjunct. The crew of three were Thai airmen, operating as part of a joint border patrol from a temporary base on a Thai island just north of the Langkawi archipelago. None of them spoke much of anything except Thai, but they managed to raise a major at the base who knew English, with a drawly Texan bias. While Quint talked over the radio and listened on the earphones, the helicopter continued its routine patrol.

He was looking into the recent murder of an American anthropologist, Quint explained, and had come to believe that the murderer was a white man who was in cahoots, for whatever reason, with Ah Sook; the murder had been ordered because the American, in the course of her field work, had stumbled on Ah Sook's hideout. They had received a tip, the major said, that Ah Sook was on the island, but so far nothing had come of it. Other witnesses had him further up the coast.

Some three hours from now, Quint went on, a meeting would take place at which both Ah Sook and this white man, who was British, would be present. He was ninety percent certain where the meeting would be held, and one hundred percent sure that the place would be inaccessible from the air. The only way to it was by sea, but the entrance would be closely guarded. A cave? Yes, it was a cave on a small island, an island with no beach on which to land, rising straight out of the sea like a chef's hat. But other people would be present, who must not be harmed. He, Quint, would undertake to enter the cave and safeguard those lives. How enter the cave? Was he a

frogman? No, he had something else in mind. Quint out-
lined his plan.

The helicopter swung south in a wide arc over the several smaller islands that dotted the entrance to the broad
straits dividing the main island of Langkawi from the Isle
of the Pregnant Maiden. Quint began to adjust to the
free-swinging motion of the vehicle. The noise, he could
never get used to.

Through binoculars he could see that the Chinese boat
had already anchored in the lee of the tiny island and that
a number of the young Chinese were resolutely applying
themselves to catching fish. As before, there seemed
fewer of them on board than he'd seen set out earlier that
morning. What would the stage set be like, he wondered,
and had the impresario himself arrived—or had he been
there all along, living among the white rats, in his command post? If not, how would he come? In what guise?

They were heading now over the Isle of the Pregnant
Maiden. Behind them the sea stretched away, losing itself in a thin haze in the direction of Sumatra. The helicopter climbed to clear the green mass of a tree-covered
hill and banked left, revealing, through the open hatch, a
silver mirror set in a frame of green: the Lake of the Pregnant Maiden. A few minutes later Quint again saw the
Chinese boat, anchored well under the rocky overhang.
Then the bulk of the tiny island intervened, and it was
lost to sight. The helicopter hovered over the spiny back-
bone of the islet like a dragonfly over a porcupine. Something fell from it, dangling clear of the trees: a ladder.
And down the ladder climbed, with exceeding caution, a
man.

CHAPTER THIRTY

Quint dived for the protection of the nearest tree as the ladder came crashing down behind him, followed, with a thud, by the pillow case. Crouching in a space between two rocks, he heard the helicopter throbbing its way down the coast, a long muttered complaint. Easy patrol would be on its way by now; no doubt some of the party would look up, see the great whirling bird, and say to themselves, 'There it goes again.' Others wouldn't bother to look. How often are the agents of salvation—or doom—masked by the camouflage of familiarity. Hegesippe? He couldn't remember.

It was unlikely anyone had seen him drop from the sky, since the Chinese fishing below were out of sight. But with a couple of hours to kill, Quint decided to lie doggo. There was always Chance. Ironic that Ah Sook, the man who left nothing to chance, was up against a man whose belief in chance was implicit. Chance was all around, all the time, constantly available, constantly shunned, evaded, battled, ignored, thwarted, feared, wooed, wept over. The skill lay in how to use it, and, like any skill, was honed through use.

The islet Quint was on was hardly bigger than the tennis court at the Inn. It boasted—Quint counted them—eight trees. They seemed to grow out of the rock. Their roots burrowed into thin crevices, searching for the last drop of moisture; their trunks leaned with the prevailing wind; their spiny branches clawed the air, attempting to hang on to what little greenery was left to them. Quint rolled up the ladder and set about anchoring one end to the trunk of a tree with a length of rope that his Thai accomplices had put in the pillow case. He had refused the pistol and grenades they wanted to wrap in the sheet. No guns, no explosives. The sheet he took. In his predicament, a sheet had it over a gun any day. The sun was scorching, but since his hat wouldn't have stayed on his head—and a straw hat floating out over the boatload of Chinese might have caused comment—a handkerchief served instead, knotted at the corners.

Some twenty minutes later a boat hove into view round the point coming from the direction of town, the type of local fishing boat Quint was used to. He watched it crawl through choppy water, painfully slow, belching smoke, passing below him almost in hailing distance, going doggedly on its way. First stop, the lake. Even without binoculars, he could see that the boat had a full quota on board. Easy patrol was out in force. He checked them off, one by one; even Leila, sitting alone in the prow, letting the wind and spray and smoke swirl around her. Was there a one-eared man watching too, Quint wondered, bending over a reel, perhaps, peering from under a hat? For thirty years to the day, he had been hauling in this line. What would he feel? Triumph, contempt, hate? No, if he was the man Quint took him for, he wouldn't allow himself to feel—not yet. Not until they were absolutely in his power. Then he would feel. And what if Cardew-

Smythe were right, and Ah Sook, at the end, exhibited mercy?

Quint lost sight of the boat around another small islet. He checked his watch. They would probably lunch at the lake after splashing about by the bamboo jetty, Gwendy meting out sandwiches, Sneed fussing over beer. He imagined Phoebe calmly striking out for the far shore, pooh-poohing tales of the white crocodile, while her husband, strung out, at the breaking point, looked at his watch and wondered feverishly how to keep the children from drowning themselves and how to separate the men from the women and children so that the men could go fishing.

Quint, for his part, intended to fish, and had brought along the reel with line and weight. By then Cardew-Smythe would have handed over, like the conscientious officer he was, to his CO. In the meantime Quint lay on his back, waiting, looking at the sky in which white clouds were drifting, seemingly as unaffected by the wind as he was in his rock-walled trench. He had already selected the tree from which to fly his purple bedsheet banner when the time came. From his first sighting of the returning boat, he would have perhaps ten minutes to do what had to be done. If he hoisted the flag too soon, they would see it. And if he waited too long, well, he would miss the boat.

Morning drowsed towards noon and only some gulls and a lizard took any interest in Charles Quint. Birds of prey must have realized he wasn't carrion, though he moved parts of himself now and then in case a myopic vulture happened by. Gradually he became aware of a monotonous droning sound coming from the south, from the direction of Penang. A mere mosquito of a plane was heading straight towards him. It was too soon for the regular daily flight. Were the police acting at last on his message? Unlikely. Vellu's scepticism had proved well-founded. Police here didn't charge around in planes arresting people. A private plane, more like, yellow, single engine, coming in low over the water. Ah Sook? Surely not like this, openly, in broad daylight. He watched the plane drone on, undeviating, knowing precisely what it was about. Then it began to circle, once more just a speck, and disappeared behind the land mass of the main island. Yes, Quint thought, the airstrip would be just about there. Probably tourists for the Inn, doing it in style.

Ship ahoy! From his crow's nest, Quint saw that his moment had come. He crept to the end of the islet furthest from the cave mouth and tied his sheet firmly to the appointed tree, where it fluttered as bravely as any standard over a captured fort. This was the signal. Now for the part he least relished: getting down.

Quint had several things going for him: there'd be no wind to battle once he was over the edge; the Chinese would be watching the approaching boat, not the cliff above, and if they did look up, the overhang would hide him to the last moment. Even if he was spotted, he doubted that Ah Sook would permit any rough stuff outside the cave. It would spoil the entertainment within. The thing Quint feared—and there was nothing he could do about it now that he was on the rope ladder—was that it wouldn't reach beyond the overhang. It was hard enough climbing down with the rungs jammed up against the scratchy rock; climbing up would be impossible.

The ladder reached. Quint dropped the last ten feet, onto something soft and indignant. There was to be no fishing. Instead, the boat plunged on into blackness, bearing its surplus passenger like a sack of coal heaved aboard in an unexpected moment. Quint's precipitous arrival was instantly, as it were, eclipsed by this headlong dash into what, seconds earlier, half those on board had thought was the rock face of a cliff. Cries—of warning, fear, outrage—danced raucously in whatever rockbound space the boat had entered. From blinding light to blinding darkness. Quint lay still. Near him someone cursed. He had landed on Sir Frankie Jake.

The boat halted. The sounds gradually died down. They were becalmed in clammy darkness. Though the engine had been cut, its acrid fumes made Quint's eyes smart. Someone retched. A voice—Sneed's—ventured a timid, "That you, Milly?", to which was vouchsafed a strangled, "Yeah." Cardew-Smythe said tautly, "Stay as still as possible, everyone."

"With bloody acrobats raining down," Jake growled. "Get it over with and get us out of here."

"Get what over?" Craddock sounded belligerent.

"Don't ask me," Sir Frankie snapped. "Ask an officer."

Sneed said, apropos of nothing, "tunnel of love."

"Quint, is that you?" It was Peter, from the stern, by the sound of it.

Quint said nothing. He had a strong feeling they were being watched by eyes grown accustomed to the dark. He looked for the light that should have marked their point of entry; but saw none. A few feet away a match hissed and flared, and, for an instant, Craddock's face hung above it like a jinni, till someone—one of the crew?—dashed it from his hand. A simple act, with savage implications. Craddock was silent. A sense of waiting for what would happen next, as against fretting about what had already happened, took control. The cool, welcome at first, seemed to Quint suddenly oppressive: the difference between sitting in an air-conditioned room and a meat cooler.

Peter Forbes said: "Has anyone caught anything yet?" As an attempt at levity, it failed.

No roll of drums prepared them for the drama that was about to unfold, no flourish of trumpets, not even a spotlight. Just a small, somewhat high-pitched voice of indeterminate age, ancestry Chinese, speaking three English words: "Many happy returns."

It was enough for Sir Frankie. Quint heard a hoarse gasp. One man, at least, had caught on. The next moment Quint was aware of quick hands patting him under the armpits, down his sides, urging him to his feet, frisking him. His fishing reel was confiscated, but not his watch.

The voice—Quint saw what Cardew-Smythe had meant by chamber of commerce—continued: "Welcome, Easy Patrol Reunion. I would like to make special welcome to Mr. Peter Forbes and say to him very sorry his late father, Private Timmy Forbes, is not with us today. Also same to Second Lieutenant C.S. Reid, Corporal B.T.R. Jenkins and Private T.S. O'Rourke, murdered on this day, thirty years ago at 16:30 PM in line of duty. May their hungry ghosts rest, after today."

"Of all the . . . " Sir Frankie was too choked up to continue.

Quint sensed a change all around him in the boat, as if a magnetic force had come into play. Whatever he expected, Sir Frankie, clearly, had been caught by surprise. Nobody else said anything.

The voice continued: "Also, it is my duty to welcome guest who, I see, has come here of his own free will. I will ask him to join me this side. Perhaps, after all, it is not a bad thing to have with us an independent witness. Please, Mr. Charles Quint."

Quint felt hands behind him, propelling him forward, coaxing him over the edge of the boat. To his surprise, his foot made contact with a hard surface down which he was walked for some ten paces. From this he stepped onto a rough-feeling floor with a slight give to it. Hands pressed him into a soft canvas chair. All at once came the dull rumble of a generator, and as the cave burst into light, Quint closed his eyes.

When he opened them, he was looking at Easy patrol. They stood, lined up and blinking, in the glare of two spots mounted somewhere behind Quint, like a hungover, losing rowing crew; dazed, sweaty, an odd and pitiable assortment. White rats, indeed. This, surely, was the moment of power. He was on a sort of anchored raft. A dozen paces to his right, in a folding chair, sat a man in a silk business suit and an open-necked white shirt. The man leaned forward intently, his sandaled feet inches from the black, oil-still water. Because the light was not directly on him Quint couldn't be sure, but the man's left ear seemed to be missing.

"I have brought you here for a small history lesson."
The man in the silk suit sounded like a teacher who had
kept his class after school. He seemed to eye each captive
in turn.

Behind each Englishman on the boat was a young Chinese. One or two of them Quint recognized. The generator, the lights, the floating platform, whatever blocked
the entrance to the cave—the rigging of it all must have
kept these men busy for days. What exactly had Gail
Sonnenberg seen, he wondered, when she blundered in
with her boatman looking for legends. And who knew
what the darkness beyond held, whence came the rumble
of the generator. Ah Sook might have been living here for
some time.

"It has been said," the close-cropped man in the suit
continued, "and Second Lieutenant Ian Cardew-Smythe
will correct me if I'm wrong, that history is written by the
victor. Today, perhaps some of you will say, we have a
new victor, and therefore a new bias. In order to avoid
such confusion, I myself am not going to teach history. I
am going to listen like a model pupil—like my son, who is
also here to learn. You gentlemen are going to teach history. Please proceed." He settled back in his chair, ex-
pectantly.

Quint looked along the line of silent faces: glowering,
resistant, in Peter's case, bemused.

"Well?" Sir Frankie at last threw out, bending to glare
at Cardew-Smythe. "Get on with it. I haven't got all day."

All eyes now turned on Cardew-Smythe who looked as
though he'd swallowed deadly poison and was waiting for
it to work. "I, I . . . " he began feebly. Then, peering directly into the light, he appealed to the man in the chair

opposite: "You can't expect . . . I mean, he's not going to simply . . . "

Quint saw Craddock's hand steal to his shoulder and emerge from his starched, sweat-splotched safari jacket wrapped round something small and hard which he pointed into the light like a marksman, trying to approximate a target he couldn't see. No one grabbed him; no one cried out. The gun fired. Quint ducked. The sound ricocheted round the cave. Again it fired, and again. Six times. The reports bounced crazily, cackling their way to oblivion in distant recesses. Sweat glistened on Craddock's beetroot face. His whole body shook and would have fallen, had not two of the Chinese made a move to support it.

The man in the chair was unmoved. "So you see, Lieutenant Ian Cardew-Smythe, you need have no fear. Little if anything is left to chance by Ah Sook."

Sir Frankie now faced the light, shading his eyes. "Thought you'd copped it, Chinky." His tone was almost chummy. "Honest. Glad I was wrong. You should have been in touch. So how much? Tell me what I owe. Name a figure, it's yours. That's what it's all about, isn't it, lad?"

They waited, hanging on the silence.

"I didn't do nothing," Sneed blurted. "It wasn't me. It was them. All I did in was the bird. Swear to God, Chinky. Ask any of 'em. You can't nab me for that; not for a friggin' budgie."

Briscoe took up the cry, only not to beg for mercy: "Eye for an eye, ain't it, Chinky? Ain't that it? You good as did for us, the lot of us. What do you expect? We're men, flesh an' blood. Same as you. You get what's coming." He waited. "Murderer!" he shrieked, his cherub's face contorted with rage.

As the echo of Briscoe's words died away, Quint looked at Cardew-Smythe. An English idiom came to mind: he hung his head. Cardew-Smythe had done exactly that, on a convenient post. The post happened to be his body.

Some people kill in the fury of passion, some to get even or to further a cause they believe in, some in self-defense, some to bury something they are afraid of, and some simply because they are told to. If killings had grades for degrees of bestiality, then he, Quint, would rank this last category most bestial. He was looking now at such a man, at the indelible brand that proclaimed him a murderer. The mark of the pregnant maiden.

He was looking at it from considerably further away than Gail Sonnenberg must have seen it on that moonlit night in the boat when its bearer wielded—so clumsily as it turned out—the murderous parang. As Quint had realized the day before at the beach, and cursed himself for his blindness, she could hardly have been more precise. Not a lake, nothing to do with legend, just a fat lady pricked out at the point of a tattooer's needle.

CHAPTER THIRTY-ONE

"**R**ose's Milk Bar, that's where we met up," Miller began truculently. The guards had isolated him from the others, who looked on, bitter and subdued. "New, she was, and me on sick parade with the whole place to myself. Not a uniform in sight, not even an M.P., and them coolies—pardon me—them Chinamen all bowing and scraping and giving credit like it was Christmas; which it was gettin' on to be. King of the coop, I was; and pissed as a parson on brandy and ginger and not yet had my lunch."

The history lesson had begun. "So, like I said, it was just me an' her when the time come to go out back. 'You very big *tuan*, make plenty dollars, plenty credit.' She kept on and on at me." Miller warmed to his account. "Well, I knew what the bint was getting at, didn't I?"— here he couldn't resist a smirk—"I says, 'Me very small Tommy, no dollars.' She says, 'Make no dollars, how you pay? How you pay me whole time?' She was good, the best yet. I wanted her all to myself and I figured I got the jump on all the other guys 'cause, like I said, she was new in town, not the shopworn article we was used to.

"So I tells her, I says, 'Come Saturday I'll be rich tuan.' Because me and him," he jerked his head in the direction of Ah Sook, who sat rigid, listening, "had a deal going. We was sick and tired of the sergeant-major here ripping everybody off. Fancied some gravy ourselves, we did."

Quint looked at Frankie Jake, but the sergeant-major's face was stony.

"The bint said she didn't believe a word. Strung me along right proper, she did. I ended up hinting at," Miller faltered, "—well, more than I should have." He peered into the light like a hound whose master has inexplicably kicked it.

"In other words," Ah Sook intervened sharply, "you told this communist whore about our buried arms, so that on that particular Saturday her friends knew enough to organize a reception committee for us."

Miller grunted assent.

Ah Sook leaned forward, "Speak up."

"Yeah," Miller addressed his feet.

"You stupid greedy scum." Ah Sook spat out the words, half rising from his chair. For the first time a chink of feeling showed through his armor.

The others, at first frozen in their own fears, were waking up to the meaning of Miller's words. It was Briscoe who acted. He lunged towards Miller, teeth bared as if to rip his throat. It took two of the Chinese to hold him. The boat swayed.

Ah Sook resumed his former restraint. "Tell us what you did a week ago, on our little night boat trip?"

"I . . . ," Miller's throat worked violently. He looked as though he was going to throw up. "I killed someone."

"A woman," Ah Sook reminded him. "You killed a woman. Repeat after me, 'I killed an innocent, white woman.' "

"He made me," Miller cried out, appealing to the others as to a jury.

"Say it," Ah Sook commanded.

Miller began to sob. He seemed to surrender control of his body so that the Chinese, pressed tightly round him, propped him up. His sagging belly, protruding from his gaudy shirt, heaved and quivered, and Quint, even from where he sat, saw the pricked-out woman twitch and jerk as if in a dance of ecstasy. The words, when they came, came in a rush. "I killed an innocent white woman."

"And the bird," Ah Sook said relentlessly, "what did you do with the bird?"

"Broke its bloody neck," Miller blurted.

"What did I tell you at Haadyai a week ago?"

"You'd let me go." Miller's voice came in a hoarse, pleading whisper.

"And so I will," Ah Sook said, matter-of-factly. "Go. May the winds carry you out of my sight forever." A white speedboat glided in from the wings, as if on cue, paddled by one of the Chinese. A scene from Swan Lake. "You see," Ah Sook turned towards Quint, "I am a man of my word."

But something in the way he said it left Quint unconvinced.

Relief played across Cardew-Smythe's thin face when at last he looked up. Surprised, initially, that it was Miller, now he seemed to think the worst was over. With a rattle and a bang the outboard started and Miller was helped on board. His Nigerian Airlines bag was chucked in after him. The motor revved, the water churned and the boat moved slowly away, turning a ghostly grey before disappearing altogether. Miller didn't look back.

The lights dimmed. Was it over? A tang of black depression and despair hung in the air, like hate unconsummated. Or was it just engine oil Quint smelled. He peered anxiously at his watch.

Ah Sook's voice sounded through the gloom. "You see, Mr. Quint, you need not have worried so much." He was clearly pleased with the show so far. "All is for the best." He indicated the boat where the men stood, stone-faced. "Do you think they are wishing they had not acted so foolishly?"

"I think," Quint said, approaching his host's chair, "they are not the only ones to have committed foolish acts. Gail Sonnenberg was innocent. You said so. Yet you killed her. Why?"

"But I did not kill her. Miller killed her."

"Miller was the knife in your hand. Your act is as despicable as his."

Ah Sook sighed sadly. "I admit this was a last minute improvisation. She had seen too much, you see. But it was the chance not only to punish Miller most appropriately, but also to insure his presence here. He was my star. There is a price on my head. This murder made it less tempting for him to go to the authorities. Shall we say her death was his Sword of Damocles."

"You spirited him away from Haadyai that night, leaving Sneed alone, and drunk as a lord."

"A round trip of a few hours. You are well-informed, Mr. Quint."

"And the boatman, and the fisherman?"

"At least they died swiftly—at the hands of experts. It is almost amusing now to think that Miller, in his clumsiness, came close to sabotaging the careful work of years; thanks to your intervention."

"I blame my slowness in the uptake for what will, no doubt, happen next." From where he stood, Quint watched the remnants of Easy patrol submitting to handcuffs.

"Not a hair of their heads, I said. I assure you, Mr. Quint, I am a man of my word."

"Only one man will die, you told Cardew-Smythe."

"You are impatient, Mr. Quint."

Around them preparations for departure were under way. Boxes and crates were being stacked. Ah Sook excused himself. Quint was asked by one of the Chinese to surrender his chair.

"Excuse me for taking book," the man mumbled shyly.

"If you'd asked, I'd have given it to you," Quint told him. "Are you at school in Singapore?"

The man shook his head, frightened, backing away. A ridiculously out of place conversation.

Grey limestone walls rose straight from the liquid black, the reason, presumably, they had had to build the platform Quint stood on. Some words, crudely sprayed in yellow above the high watermark, caught his attention: BRUCE LEE LIVES. The hum of the generator slowed. The lights went out. The hum ceased. Quint squatted. Was there, perhaps, an air vent? He craned his neck, but no telltale glow shone from above. Torchlight flashed to and fro like shooting stars in a firmament that stretched forever, as darkness dissolved the walls. Nobody talked. Evidently Ah Sook's people were well drilled. Quint let guiding hands maneuver him into the boat, which pushed off, feeling its way into the tunnel.

Where seconds before had been total darkness, Quint saw light, as if a door had been opened in the rock. But as they passed from cold night into broiling day, he saw no sign of any barrier, so cleverly was it concealed. The fishing was still in progress. Quint looked for Ah Sook, but did not see him. Nor was there any sign of Easy patrol, though both boats had emerged from the cave. Calmly, the crew began dumping crates over the side. Destroying the evidence, Quint assumed. For as far as he could see, in sea or sky, not a thing moved bigger than a bird. Again, he looked at his watch.

Several minutes passed. The boats, their motors cut, drifted in calm waters clear of the rock, still in the island's lee. One or two of the Chinese began pointing, and before long everyone was staring into the bluish haze above the main island. Quint's hopes were raised. He saw a dot, climbing in great, soundless spirals over the airstrip, approaching now in a broad, high sweep out over the western sea. It took color, and he heard the thin drone of the wasp that he'd heard before. But as they watched, the plane seemed to falter, lurch, drop something. Quint stared. His hopes fell. A moment later a parachute billowed from the falling speck and he realized what had happened: the pilot had ejected. The plane coughed, bucked, shivered, at the mercy of the wind. Silently dipping its left wing—as if in a gesture of submission—it began its plunge. He knew then why Ah Sook had called him impatient: Miller was on board.

At first like a kite, round and round, down and down, it went, Quint marveling at its grace, recoiling at the agony it represented. Then, gripped by the vortex, totally surrendered, it corkscrewed in mad abandon. It must have missed the sea, because the last Quint saw of the plane or its passenger was a puff of smoke over a headland perhaps a mile away. From the boats came a smattering of applause.

End of Act One, Quint thought.

The crew nosed his boat expertly back into the tunnel. Minutes later Quint found himself crouching, handcuffed, on the bare raft—boat and light gone, Easy patrol huddled nearby. He described what he'd seen.

"That Miller," Sneed couldn't hide his awe. "Thirty years and not a word past his lips, drunk or sober. You think it really was him pulled the plug on us?"

"Oh yes," Cardew-Smythe's voice came wearily through the dark. "It was him."

"That's all well and good," Sir Frankie said decisively, "But what about now? I can't wait all day. I'm a busy man." He didn't seem to have grasped that this wasn't still some elaborate game.

"I'm sure Phoebe and the others'll come looking before long," Cardew-Smythe responded without a shred of conviction. He would willingly, Quint sensed, have plunged into the water in a death-inviting bid for freedom. But his family were his lifeline.

"In what?" Craddock spoke up tersely. "Even if they could, where would they look? No, you got us in here," he challenged Cardew-Smythe, "you bloody well get us out."

"Yeah," Peter joined in sardonically, "you're the officer."

"What's he gonna do to us then?" Briscoe asked, his voice rising out of control. "What's he gonna do? Just leave us here? If I knew I'd be all right."

"Leave us to rot," Sneed suggested. "Let the crocs do the dirty work. Clever bastard."

For an hour they shivered, speculating back and forth, as the silences lengthened. After one particularly oppressive pause, Craddock asked no one in particular, "So who gave the bullet to Corporal Jenkins? I've often wondered."

"Not me," Sneed said.

"Copped it fair and square in the back," Craddock continued. "I saw the wound. Close range, by the looks of it."

"Try pinning it on me," Sir Frankie growled belligerently. "Though, believe me, it's been done."

"I can guess who by," Craddock bated.

"Go to hell," said Jake.

"Who was behind you?" Craddock insisted. "Forby, wasn't it? Did Forby have it bad for our Gwendy? You wouldn't have thought old Forby'd do a thing like that."

"Had it pretty bad, did old Forby," Sneed affirmed.

Peter Forbes was strangely silent. He knows, Quint thought; because his old man told him.

Cardew-Smythe started to say something placatory, when there was a loud splash. The platform rocked.

"Peter!" Quint yelled.

But Peter shouted, "It's Briscoe."

Quint heard splashing, cursing, moaning, growing fainter.

"He's making a dash for it," an amazed voice declared.

"Stinki! Stinki!" Sneed's treble bounced from surface to surface, calling bewilderingly to itself. "Answer me, Stinki."

The answer came in an unexpected form. A roar and a rumble. An explosion. It winded them, tumbling them back against the rock wall, the raft rearing under them, wild water cascading everywhere.

CHAPTER THIRTY-TWO

The ten-seater Islander taxied in over the dry grass, the palm trees bowing obeisance. First off were two men in the starched blue uniform of the Malaysian police. They looked about, and, seeing Quint standing to one side by Vellu's brown Mercedes, walked over to him. "We are looking for a Mr. S. Padinki," one of them began, consulting a scrap of paper.

"What for?" Quint asked.

"To question him."

Four men staggered out of a nearby shed with a long wooden box. Quint pointed. The policemen hurried off. One soon returned. "Those fools know nothing."

"The man you're looking for is in the box."

"He is wanted for drug trafficking," the policeman continued, as if unwilling to be so conclusively cheated of his quarry. "We waited for him in Penang, but he gave us the slip."

"He's dead," Quint said.

The policeman looked again at the coffin, which had been set down by the plane. "Dead," he echoed.

"He died yesterday," Quint elaborated. "As you may have heard, the Joint Border Patrol freed a number of tourists who were stuck when a cave collapsed on one of the outlying islands. They used dynamite to blast their way in. Your Mr. Padinki perished in the blast."

"Most unfortunate." The policeman looked annoyed.

"I don't suppose," Quint looked at the policeman and saw that he was an officer, "you had any other reason for coming to Langkawi? A call, perhaps, to do with the murder of an American anthropologist?"

"Murder?" The policeman looked amazed. "On Langkawi?" He shook his head. "Very peace-loving island. Not even a police post." He strode off towards the plane.

"Typical bloody bureaucratic balls-up." Sir Frankie Jake came up. "Look at those clowns, will you." Six men were trying to jam the coffin into the plane; there was no way it was going to fit. Sir Frankie looked at his watch. "I haven't got all day. I'm a busy man. I'll have to intervene."

"I suggest," Quint said, "that you don't. It'll take less time in the end." He, too, had a connection to make.

Sir Frankie rounded on him. "That's what's wrong with you lot. Take your own sweet time. What I say is, never clear a damn thing with government until it's over. We're lucky we're not still sitting out there in that black hole waiting for some damn fool paperpusher in KL to give the go-ahead to some damn fool Thai general to come and get us out. Territorial integrity, my foot. If I ran my business that way . . . " He stalked off in search of his wife.

Vellu got out of the car. He had his eye on one of the incoming passengers, a large, shambling man with a butterfly net. "My new teacher," he announced to Quint, rubbing his hands together. "Always, always, there is never a dull moment. Maybe *he* is secret agent."

"What makes you think that, Vellu?"

"Why is he having butterfly net, I am asking myself, when butterfly season is at low ebb." He marched off to find out. "I am Vellu," Quint heard him say. The man followed meekly, just as a week before . . . Quint smiled.

"Give me that smile." It was Peter Forbes, with a long face.

"Give this to Leila, would you?" Quint pressed a folded white cloth into his hands. "Purdah. She may find it useful. I did."

Peter blushed. "I still haven't told her that I'm engaged."

"Ah, but you should, you know. It may be the one thing you have in common."

Peter looked flabbergasted.

"She confessed last night that she's to bring Craddock's harem up to four. His quid pro quo for putting her through college."

"She's his . . . He's not her . . . " A toothy smile spread on Peter's face. "Then he's not her old man? Rule OK," he said, making mock obeisance.

Over by the plane, the policemen, under Sir Frankie's direction, grappled gingerly with a bright blue plastic bag. A small boy in goggles walked by. "Hey, Mum, what's in that bag?"

"Mind your own business," said Phoebe Cardew-Smythe.

Advice, Quint reflected, he was glad *he* hadn't followed.

"Dear Miss McCall," Quint was writing in mid-air between Penang and Singapore, "I return to you your postcard. Someday we will meet again and I will tell you a story. Meanwhile, a word on your remarkable friend, Gail Sonnenberg.

"Her death, as you divined, was not accidental. If you believe in Fate, you could say it was written in the book thirty years ago, even before she was born. Dying, she passed two words on to a humble fisherman—who passsed them on to me. These words saved lives, though would I had seen their meaning sooner.

"I took it upon myself not to identify her body to the police at Penang so as to spare her parents unnecessary pain, but arranged for her ashes to be scattered over the islands of the people she loved. The *Orang Laut*, I am told, believe that the spirit does not die, but is released to begin a journey. I believe this to be true. On all journeys we may meet all sorts—crooks, cowards, bigots, fools. We know them if we know ourselves. The few, however—Gail among them—make it possible for the many to carry on.

"I'm not sure if this is good or bad, but I—for one—am grateful. Sincerely, Charles Quint."

From the seat behind Quint's came a child's penetrating voice: "Daddy, why did that man scream?"

"Which man, darling?"

"The one on the plane when we arrived."

"Why do you think?"

"Because he was scared." Pause. "Were you scared, Daddy?"

"Some of the time."

"Why didn't you scream?"

"I was too scared to scream," said Ian Cardew-Smythe.

Quint looked out of the window onto a seamless cloud-quilt of pink and orange, with shapes rising in it like shrouded jousting knights or soon-to-be-revealed state of the art tanks. He thought of war and the corruption of war; of war and racism, destroyers of reason and sanity.

"Hell," he said, and the woman in the next seat looked up. "I'm sorry. It just occurred to me: I have a dentist's appointment in Fort Wayne."

About the Author

J.N. Catanach grew up on the shores of a windswept loch high in the Scottish Cairngorms. He claims to have been intrigued by the mystery genre from a tender age when he discovered his sister's Agatha Christies. But the possibilities of the form finally came alive for him upon reading Doris Lessing's *The Grass is Singing* while in Africa where his travels as a journalist had taken him. An enthusiastic eavesdropper, he garnered the title, *White is the Color of Death,* at a traditional Chinese funeral in Singapore. Mr. Catanach lives in New York City.